Now the LORD God had planted a garden in the east, in Eden; and there he put the man he had formed. The LORD God made all kinds of trees grow out of the ground—trees that were pleasing to the eye and good for food. In the middle of the garden were the tree of life and the tree of the knowledge of good and evil.

A river watering the garden flowed from Eden; from there it was separated into four headwaters. The name of the first is the Pishon; it winds through the entire land of Havilah, where there is gold. (The gold of that land is good; aromatic resin and onyx are also there.) The name of the second river is the Gihon; it winds through the entire land of Cush. The name of the third river is the Tigris; it runs along the east side of Ashur. And the fourth river is the Euphrates.

—GENESIS 2:8–14 (NIV)

So the LORD God banished him from the Garden of Eden to work the ground from which he had been taken. After he drove the man out, he placed on the east side of the Garden of Eden cherubim and a flaming sword flashing back and forth to guard the way to the tree of life.

—GENESIS 3:23–24 (NIV)

MYSTERIES & WONDERS *of the* BIBLE

Unveiled: Tamar's Story
A Life Renewed: Shoshan's Story
Garden of Secrets: Adah's Story

MYSTERIES & WONDERS *of the* BIBLE

GARDEN OF SECRETS
ADAH'S STORY

Texie Susan Gregory

Mysteries & Wonders of the Bible is a trademark of Guideposts.

Published by Guideposts
100 Reserve Road, Suite E200, Danbury, CT 06810
Guideposts.org

Cover and interior design by Müllerhaus
Cover illustration by Brian Call represented by Illustration Online LLC.
Typeset by Aptara, Inc.

ISBN 978-1-961251-51-9 (hardcover)
ISBN 978-1-961251-52-6 (softcover)
ISBN 978-1-961251-50-2 (epub)

Printed and bound in the United States of America

MYSTERIES & WONDERS *of the* BIBLE

GARDEN OF SECRETS

ADAH'S STORY

To my beloved son, Robert Tyler Gregory.

May you hold fast to the source of all peace.

ACKNOWLEDGMENTS

Stranded on a desert island and allowed only two books, I'd choose the Bible and a thesaurus to keep me company. The Bible's words bring truth to life, and a thesaurus brings words to life—usually. Sadly, this time the thesaurus failed me.

There is not a word for *gratitude* that conveys enough depth or insight or sparkles. There are fluffy words, *appreciation*; or formal words, *recognition;* or time words, *everlasting.* Those are insufficient for what needs to be expressed.

To *grateful,* I add *honored* and *profoundly humbled* that others are willing to grace this work for our Lord with their time, expertise, prayers, and insight.

My husband, Tim, for listening to a hundred plotlines.

Stacie Ciesynski, Sheri Shannon, Rev. Betsy Sowers, Kay White—prayer team

Donna Holland, LuAnn Placeres, Texie Soltis, Rev. Victoria Warren—beta readers

Helen Gregory—sanity saver

Jane Haertel, Sabrina Diaz, Ellen Tarver, Rose Tussing—Guideposts editors

Bob Hostetler—agent

CAST OF CHARACTERS

Historical Characters:

Artaxerxes • king of Persia

Esther • king's stepmother

Ham, Japheth, Shem • sons of Noah

Nehemiah • cupbearer to Artaxerxes and governor of Jerusalem

Noah • builder of ark, survivor of flood

Major Fictional Characters:

Adah • young woman searching for peace

Emili • Nathan's widowed mother

Femi • Omari's son

Nathan • wagon driver

Omari • Mizraite man who buys Adah

Tavi • wife of Dror

Zahra • Mizraite servant in Aaron ben Hassenaah's home

Minor Fictional Characters:

Aaron ben Hassenaah • uncle of Adah's betrothed

Daven • abba of Nathan's friend

Donkor • Femi's twin brother

Dror • captain of Nehemiah's Persian guard

Eesho • governor of Tadmur

Inbar • Adah's employer

Jace • Adah's younger brother

Joezer • Nehemiah's servant

Jonah ben David • Adah's betrothed

Hiram • Adah's father

Noya • Tavi's sister

Samir • Mizraite jeweler in Tadmur

Zeb • Adah's older brother

Zephan • Emili's husband, Nathan's father

GLOSSARY OF TERMS

abba • father

howdah • a covered seat on the back of a camel

imma • mother

mezzeh • the midday meal

Mizraite • Egyptian

Polaris • the North Star

Urim and Thummim • jeweled elements on the ephod worn by the high priest

Locations:

Babylon • city on lower Euphrates

Beit She'an • a town in northern Israel

Damascus • an oasis city

Dira ze urta • city at crossing point over Euphrates

Euphrates • historically significant river

Jerusalem • city in Judah

Hebron • city of refuge in Judah

Ionia • Greece

Mizraim • Egypt

Mount Arbel • mountain near Sea of Galilee

Mount Qasioun • mountain overlooking Damascus

Sabkhat Muh • oasis beside Tadmur

Sea of Chinnereth • Sea of Galilee

Shenzhou • China

Susa • city in Persia

Tadmur • (Palmyra) town with oasis between Damascus and the Euphrates River

PROLOGUE

Noah, a man of the soil, proceeded to plant a vineyard. When he drank some of its wine, he became drunk and lay uncovered inside his tent. Ham, the father of Canaan, saw his father naked and told his two brothers outside. But Shem and Japheth took a garment and laid it across their shoulders; then they walked in backward and covered their father's naked body. Their faces were turned the other way so that they would not see their father naked.
~Genesis 9:20–23 (NIV)~

Noah crouched by the spitting fire. He shielded his grizzled face as he relived the shame that burned hotter than the flames. That long-ago memory yet ached—the near loss of his sons' respect from his lapse of judgment, his self-indulgence. Blessed be Elohim, the Creator, who'd used that reckless indulgence to reveal the worthiest of his three sons.

He prodded the burning logs apart with a stick, its edge shining silver, gilded in the flame's light. Bold stars spun into the dark, hissing, singeing the leather of his tunic before their lives were snuffed out—as his would soon be.

The heat dissipated, the chill edged closer. No matter. What would happen next demanded concealment, the covert mystery of night.

In the dimming light, he glanced at Japheth, sprawled on his back, snoring softly. A good man, this beloved son. He'd assisted Shem in covering his—Noah's—nakedness. He would do well in life even as the seduction of uncertainty lured him to venture ever farther into unknown lands. Thank the Almighty, Japheth's cherished wife would temper the bold impulses, keep him worshiping the Creator.

He shifted to study Ham, listening to his son's heavy, steady breath, although Ham—master of deception—could hold himself so still one was never sure if he was sleeping. Ham moved with uncanny stealth, and it often seemed he appeared from nowhere. It had been Ham who'd found his father drunk and run to tell his brothers. Poor Ham, forever seeking approval and acceptance, with neither the wisdom nor the kindness of his brothers.

Noah grimaced as he stood, his knees crackling in protest, his back slow to straighten. He hobbled to where Shem lay. This son— he'd been told—had hurried to cover his father's shame, even averting his eyes as had Japheth. Shem, more than the other two, sought the wisdom of the Almighty.

He nudged Shem with the ball of his foot. Shem bolted to his feet, drawing his weapons in one practiced motion. In the dimming firelight, Noah held a finger to his lips and motioned him to follow.

A distance from the others, Noah withdrew his dagger. He fumbled with the knot as he loosened the sheath from his belt. Drawing a thin line with the flint blade so only the top layer of the sheath parted, he slit it lengthwise. Fingers trembling, he extracted a scrap of rolled, flattened leather.

In the starless night, he knew Shem would not see the tears stinging his eyes nor that he held the scrap to his heart. Noah caressed the worn leather surface before raising it to his lips.

"Lord, will You not relent, allow us to return to the Garden, to Your paradise?"

There was no answer. There had never been an answer, no matter how fervently he'd pleaded through the years.

"Shem, my son, I entrust you with the world's most precious possession." He paused, willed his voice to remain steady. "This map marks the place of beginning."

He sensed Shem startle and knew his son's quick mind understood.

"The Garden, *Abba*?"

Noah nodded then remembered a small motion might not be visible. "Yes. Etched by a daughter of Eve on a clay tablet."

"Abba, so long ago. How...?"

"Someone drew it on leather. Through the years it has been recopied whenever the leather begins to brittle. The previous map is always destroyed. Others may claim possession of the map, but only ours shows the flaming swords, the true entrance."

Cradling the reminder of wholeness—the joy of walking with the Creator—Noah kissed it, once more inhaling its earthy scent. He fumbled for Shem's hand and curled his son's fingers around the treasure but did not release it. To do so acknowledged his end was near. Soon he'd walk with his fathers.

"Yours is the eleventh generation from Adam. Someday perhaps the Lord will order the flaming swords sheathed, reveal a way to return to paradise, allow us into His holy presence."

Embracing the sacred moment, Noah placed his hand on his son's shoulder, aware of their connection beyond familial ties, beyond memories of survival. For now, they stood not as parent and child but as two men bonded in ancient ritual.

With a deep sigh, Noah released the map. The responsibility, the entrusted duty, was no longer his. Shem must bear the burden of knowledge.

They returned to the campground without speaking. As Noah lowered himself to his bedroll, he scanned the fireside. Japheth had turned on his side, no longer snoring.

Ham was nowhere to be seen.

CHAPTER ONE

Many Generations Later, 435 BC
A small village east of Beit She'an

Adah measured out her words with flat truth—facts—no emotion, no inflection. "I have been sold—indentured. I am a slave."

If Jonah cringed or shifted away, she'd know and accept his truth. She searched her beloved's face for the slightest sign of revulsion or rejection. They'd never marry, but would her slavery repulse him?

His family abhorred the sale of relatives into slavery, and she was the third of her abba's daughters to be sold. No one, including her, would judge Jonah for walking away. In truth, he had no choice. She was unacceptable to his family.

Disregarding proper behavior, Jonah reached for her hand and brought it to his lips, the tenderness testing her will to remain dry-eyed and distant. She'd not bind him with tears or pleas.

"Adah, never doubt I will come for you. I am a hard worker, a fast worker." He flexed the bulges on his arms.

Adah blushed and wished she could run her fingers along those smooth muscles.

"As soon as I have earned enough to redeem you from servitude, I will claim you as my wife."

"Claim a slave as your wife?" She pulled away, voice rising as she dropped the pretense of indifference. "Abba sold me to them for six years."

"It will not be that long, I promise you."

"In six years, they can marry me to their son. Abba will never buy me back..." Her voice broke.

They stood in silence as the breeze freshened, ruffling the tall grasses and dappling them with shadows of acacia leaves. Nearby, birds called, dancing among the tree branches, flitting near and then darting away.

A rogue curl escaped from behind Jonah's ear. Adah imagined standing close enough to wrap it around her finger before securing it in place—a wife's privilege. She studied him, memorizing the slope of his neck, the curls of his beard, and the way emotions chased each other across his face, darkening his eyes, crinkling his forehead, pursing his lips.

His frown flickered before a smile softened his face. "They cannot marry you to their son if we are already betrothed."

Her dear man was a dreamer. "Jonah, you know your abba will never agree—"

"But, Adah, *we* have agreed."

We? Her nervous laughter did not seem to faze him. He held out both hands, smiling when she immediately placed hers on his open palms. "Adah, before the Almighty gave the law to Moses at Sinai, two people could choose to be together without a contract negotiated by their parents. Adah, step back in time with me. I choose you to be my wife."

An endearing uncertainty softened Jonah's usual brash confidence to stuttering. "W-will you choose me?"

"Jonah ben David, of course I choose you, but—"

"Stop, Adah. We have chosen, we have promised. Leave it there. We will take the next step of our betrothal as soon as possible. For now, it is our secret. Trust me. I will redeem you. We will face our parents. If they oppose us, my uncle, Aaron ben Hassenaah, in Jerusalem, might help us." He grinned, his wide smile cocky once again. "I have always been his favorite nephew. For now, we have done all we can do. Leave it there."

Adah loved the confidence and innocence in his eyes. If it came to be, she'd give thanks all her days. She swallowed past the lump in her throat.

All that was good and kind seemed to reside in Jonah. It was as if the Lord God had filled Jonah to the brim of his being with joy and gentleness. Adah blinked away a tear. This amazing man loved *her*. His parents might not approve of her family, but she would work hard to win their favor.

If she and Jonah did marry, she could claim his sisters as her own. This time, the tear fell. Years ago, when she was a small child, Abba had sold her two sisters. She still remembered the anguish of her *imma's* face and—though her sisters' features had blurred—she had never forgotten their wails as they were led away. It was not something she liked to think about.

Jonah tugged at her hand. "You seem sad."

"I was remembering my sisters and wondering if they are still alive."

"If they are, we will find them and I will build an enormous house and they can live with us. Your little brother too. We will live in a town large enough for a synagogue and praise the Almighty every day. We will go to Jerusalem for the holy days."

Adah laughed, seizing the joy of hope and dreams. "I will light the Shabbat candles, and we will always have guests."

"You must become an excellent cook while you are away."

His words sobered her. "Six years seems forever."

"Adah, I will come before then. There is no risk of you becoming betrothed to their son. It's impossible. Trust me." The lines around his eyes tightened. "I will make certain you are never under your abba's roof again. You have been nothing more than a slave to him, and I struggle to treat him with any respect, knowing he hires you out to do the lowest work in other houses."

Adah lowered her eyes in shame. Everyone knew her abba's disgraceful ways—his laziness, his cunning, his constant debt.

"Jonah, when we are married…" She blushed. "Can we move far away?"

A shadow darkened his face. "Do you mean to live among foreigners? Strangers?"

"Maybe not foreigners, but among our people who do not know my abba? And are they truly strangers if we all worship Adonai, the one true God?"

"Adah, this is what we must do. We must pray that Adonai guides us to a place where we can learn more about Him. We are His people, and I am certain He will answer us."

Adah nodded but did not speak. Although she knew Adonai was the one true God, she was not sure He knew or cared about her. Maybe He would guide Jonah and she could follow Jonah's direction.

CHAPTER TWO

Two Years Later, 433 BC
A small village near Beit She'an

Adah slammed her back flat against the mud wall. She slid down to crouch in the dirt and covered her face. If no blink or twitch exposed her refuge, the mistress might assume the gasp had been not of human origin but rather the wind or a brush of bird wings against an open door. Inbar's broken vows would remain hidden beneath the bed coverings—a secret known only to the transgressors...and Adah.

Secrets. Adah collected them as easily as sheep attracted briars and dirt. She did not search for secrets. She simply looked and learned more than she wanted to know—more than others wanted known.

Once, when Abba must have thought everyone was sleeping, she'd watched him kneel, wiggle a rock from the base of the wall, and remove a coin, though earlier that day he'd vowed to the tax collector they had none. Three years ago, her older brother, Zeb, had threatened to convince Abba she was the thief when she caught him stealing. They both knew Abba would believe Zeb instead of her. And for the last few years, by noon, Imma's voice slurred, and her breath smelled not of the sweetness of wine but bitter like the contents of the jug crammed beneath a sack of moldy olives.

Adah had watched the butcher weight the scales with his thumb. She'd overheard the scorn of those who murmured against the shepherd who snored through the night instead of guarding the flock. She'd heard the priest blaspheme and seen the "blind" beggar trap a bug flying near his nose.

And more than actions, she caught the change in a voice, felt the too long pause, saw the grimace behind the smile.

So many secrets swirled in her head that her lips stayed pinched to prevent the darkness from spilling out and angering others. If only she could shake her head, erase the unwanted knowledge, wash away the stains soiling her mind.

Inbar's heavy footsteps drew close. Adah tucked her head protectively between her knees. The scar by her ear proved her mistress's fingers wielded their long nails like knives.

Inbar loomed above, her shadow a respite from the sun, her voice a viper's hiss. "Speak of this and they will be the last words ever to leave your lips. Go. You are worthless trouble. Do not return."

Inbar pivoted, the hem of her hastily donned tunic flinging dirt up into Adah's eyes. When she'd blinked the specks from her eyes, Adah listened for the sound of a breath or a swallow. Experience had taught her not to move until she knew she was alone.

Inbar, she'd not miss. These last two years had been made bearable only by attending the synagogue and hearing the scrolls read. The rabbi mumbled, and usually she didn't understand what he said or what it meant, but it drew her, stirred a longing to know more.

She snuck into the house for her only possessions—a cloth drawstring bag containing a comb and a block of sand, clay, and ashes to clean her body. She snatched a chunk of bread for the two-day journey to her parents' home.

Some of her family would welcome her with open arms.

Some would not.

Adah stopped a short distance from the house she called home—a house ashamed to be seen. Mud walls slouched over the rough stone foundation like a beer drinker's belly over a rope belt. Thatch littered the dirt courtyard, evidence of birds scavenging the insect-infested roof. A scrawny olive tree by the crumbling entrance leaned sideways, too weary to stand upright or produce the fruit of its life purpose.

If Imma had not thrown out the tattered mat Adah had slept on, and if this was a rare day when she'd roused herself to cook, then food and a bed waited inside. Stalling, Adah switched the bag to her other hand. If she were welcome anywhere else, she'd go there instead of returning home.

If only she hadn't once again discovered what was meant to be concealed. Though she never spoke the secrets of others, they knew she knew.

The growl of her stomach propelled her a few steps forward. She'd portioned the bread to stretch it for two days, but the journey had taken longer than usual.

Besides, it was urgent she explain to Abba the truth of her dismissal before Inbar's husband arrived and demanded her sale price be returned. Whatever Abba heard first, he believed. Should he discover Inbar named her "worthless," he'd brand it on her arm. If they'd already reached him, he'd sell her to the lowest bidder and let that shame follow her for all time.

No, coins were too important to him. He'd sell her—Adah didn't doubt that—and to the highest bidder.

Unless he did not see her, did not realize she'd been cast out and returned home. If she stepped sideways into the shadows and let the blur of twilight and her dirt-colored tunic conceal her, she could go to Jonah, convince him the only way to be together was for the two of them to disappear. They'd go somewhere they could be safe and happy. If safe and happy existed, where would it be?

Jerusalem. She'd heard it no longer lay sprawled in ruins. Imagine seeing the place where so many of Imma's stories about Adonai took place. The flutter of joy stilled. She'd never see Jerusalem. She and Jonah would need to go so far away, her abba could not find them.

Mizraim, where they shaved off all their hair? The Ionian islands where they worshiped Zeus and Athena? Babylon, where someone returning to Judah might recognize Jonah's name and mention it in public?

Where else was there to go that might offer safety and peace? She tensed, remembering one of Abba's drunken rants. He'd leaned so close she saw the black hairs sprouting from his nostrils, felt the sour mist of his breath.

"I have a map. I persuaded your imma it is the one true map that leads to the Garden of Eden."

He'd guffawed and slapped his thigh. *"She believes me, the fool. It is a copy of a copy of a copy. Worthless."* He wiped his nose on his tattered sleeve. *"I promised my abba to keep it."* He belched, slurred his words. "*A man of honor I am, so I kept it—always keep my word. Never forgive. Never forget. A man you can trust.*"

His eyes narrowed into slits. He poked her chest with his dirt-crusted finger, and his voice sharpened. "*You will tell no one our secret, or I will find the biggest rock in Judah, tie it around your feet, throw you in the river, and laugh. I will not be ridiculed for harboring a sham of a map. I am a man of honor.*"

A sham—another secret she did not want to carry.

Abba stepped from the shadows. Her heart plummeted. Of course he knew she'd returned.

"Abba—"

"Took you long enough to slink home."

Resigned, she waited for him to continue.

"Inbar sent word she ordered you out of her house. Says she refuses to shelter a slave who lies and steals."

Adah did not argue. She would not be heard. Instead, she braced herself, knowing what came next. Abba never hit her. There was no need. His words carved out pieces of her soul. A bruise could be hidden. A broken bone would mend. Brutal words became invisible wounds.

Unexpectedly, he burst into laughter. "You are a shrewd one, Daughter, a schemer like me. Work a third of the promised time then walk away. I still hold all the coins they paid for you. I could not have planned it better myself."

Stunned, she endured his sweaty embrace.

"Adah, I misjudged. Thought you nothing but a thorn in my side—another witless girl like your sisters."

Releasing her, he paced away, then returned, grimacing. "Still, you have no dowry. No one wants you, and we cannot work this brilliant plan of yours again too soon."

His thick brows drew together until they became one. He contorted his neck into his shoulders until it disappeared then slapped his leg and chortled. "Clever, clever me. Heard of a caravan arriving in a day or two. You go with it. I will tell Inbar's husband you never returned home. They cannot demand repayment when I accuse them of hiding you." He jabbed his finger at her. "Trust me. You do not want me to hear you have been found."

The next morning, Adah knelt by her imma's pallet and shook the still form. "Imma? Imma, wake up."

She sat back on her heels. Imma was still sleeping? She must have drunk quite a bit. Would she leave before seeing Imma awake—before seeing her soft brown eyes or dimpled smile?

"Imma, please. I need you to help me."

Imma's eyes flickered before she rolled over, sleep softening the tear-carved furrows creasing her face. For a moment, Adah glimpsed the imma she'd once known, the one who hummed as she worked, who filled their house with laughter and the smells of rich stews, who each night told the stories of their people and Adonai—stories of a garden long hidden from human eyes, stories of a flood and harsh years in Mizraim and then the Promised Land and King David and Solomon's Temple on a hill in Jerusalem.

"Imma!" Adah shook her harder. "Wake up." She leaned closer. This was not Imma's usual stupor. She sniffed the partly open lips. The strong, sweet, almost fruity smell of impending death confirmed her fear. Adah lowered her head, a single tear squeezing through her tightly closed eyes to escape.

"She doesn't wake up very often anymore and never eats," eight-year old Jace said.

Heart sinking, she recognized the old-man look in his eyes. He'd seen too much to ever be a child. She reached for him and pulled him close. He accepted her embrace, patting her back as if she were the child and he the elder.

"Sissy, Abba sent me to find you. There's a man outside."

He said no more. Adah guessed he too had learned the danger of saying too much.

"Jace, when you can, find Jonah, tell him—"

Abba's bellow warned her to hurry.

Jace nodded. "Go, before Abba is angry."

She stood and kissed the top of his head. "Someday, I will come back for you."

Adah squinted as she emerged from the dimness of the house. Camels knelt outside the courtyard's crumbling walls, the sun bouncing off silver medallions and tiny mirrors hanging from their elaborate headdresses. The long, beaded fringe of their regalia proclaimed their owner's wealth and pride in his beasts.

"Rejoice, Daughter."

Adah stiffened when her father's pudgy hands grasped her arms in a pretense of affection. "You are betrothed to a fine man—an older man—willing to overlook your lack of dowry. Indeed, he offered riches exceeding your worth."

"Betrothed?" She shook her head. "No, Jonah and I are...we have promised—"

The words stuck in her mouth when Abba leveled a hard gaze at her, his eyes cold, threatening, warning her not to speak another word. "Nonsense." He shook his stubby finger in her face. "Your true betrothed, Omari, stands behind me. Today, you become his wife."

Aghast, she looked over his shoulder. A single glance at her "betrothed" assured her she could remain true to Jonah in body and mind. The man's oversized silks did nothing to hide his withered form or stooped shoulders. Food and drink stained his clothes and untrimmed beard. Gold rings flickered in the light as his fingers trembled violently, their long nails curved and dirty. This was not a man seeking a wife. This was a master buying a caretaker.

No. But her protest was silent. Did she mean nothing to Abba that he'd willingly bind her to this shrunken, worn man?

"Abba, I will leave here, disappear. Inbar will never know I returned. Please do not—"

He turned his back to her and nodded to the man. "My daughter says she is pleased and honored to accept your proposal."

Her betrothed studied her with deep-set, rheumy eyes. "A proposal, is it?" He raised his thin eyebrows. "Are you?" His Hebrew was thickly accented.

She averted her eyes, determined to flee. She was fast—very fast when she had reason to be, and the reason was hunched in front of her eyes. Neither Abba nor that old creature could catch her. She shifted her weight, gathered a deep breath, and grasped the side of her tunic to free her ankles and knees as she darted past them.

Two men—tall, lean—came around the corner of the house as if appearing from nowhere. They stood on either side of the older man. At a signal from one of them, servants emerged from the other corner of the house.

These men could not be outrun.

Trapped. Adah lowered her gaze and stepped back, and though she could not see into their heavy, lidded eyes, she sensed the heat, the intensity of their stares. Never had she felt this vulnerable—not when Inbar's husband had cornered her, not when her older brother threatened her, not when Abba vowed to drown her if she ever mentioned…the secret.

Adah kept her body still, her face expressionless. Inwardly, she hardened her resolve, sharpened her gaze, and set her jaw. One did not survive her family without knowing how to fight without words, guard against trespass, become invisible as needed.

"Collect your things, Daughter. It is time for you to leave."

She spun to face him, seeing her chance to escape during the night disappearing. "Today? Now? What of the wedding? We need a rabbi."

Abba's jaw jutted out. "If Rachel and Rebecca needed no rabbi, you need none. Cause me no more trouble, girl. You are married because I said so."

"You said I was betrothed, not married."

He stepped forward, lowered his voice. "Now I say you are married."

Sold, he meant.

He gestured to the open door. "Bid farewell to both your brothers and imma."

Adah walked stiffly into the house. Imma still slept. The shallowness of Imma's breath caught her attention, and she moved closer, noticing the bones outlined beneath the thin skin. Soon, little Jace would lose what was left of his imma.

She tied her cloth pouch around her waist and looked at the disarray that had once been a tidy home. Chipped bowls teetered on the greasy table. Fly-laden fruit stuck to a cracked bowl. A broom stood propped against the wall. Habit propelled her to grasp the splintered handle and smooth the dirt floor. A stone along the floor's edge shifted, and she pushed it to one side.

Abba's secret hoard lay exposed.

She stared at the coins spilling out of the opening. She'd not planned...had never considered... Seemingly of its own volition, her hand stretched toward a coin. Stopped. No, it was wrong to steal. Imma said Adonai's law stated it plainly. She stepped back.

So many coins stashed behind a rock, while Abba sold his children and Imma grieved them as if they were dead. Coins to buy food. Coins to replace their rags. Her life and those of her sisters— unnecessary sacrifices to his greed.

Anger smoldered, building until fire raced through her veins, until her body trembled, until everything reddened before her eyes. All of them betrayed by Abba, the one who should be keeping them safe. Breathing hard, heart pounding, her head throbbed, threatening to explode in helpless fury. How. Dare. He. Never again would she acknowledge that thief who fathered her with the endearment of "Abba." That person ceased to exit.

She glared at the coins as if they'd hidden themselves to spite her. Was it stealing if hers was the service? If she, the goods? Twice sold with not a single coin to hold in her hand as recompense for a life she'd never choose.

A glance through the warped door showed *his* back. Imma slept. The house silent, empty. Decision made, she gathered a few coins, then a handful, and slipped them into the bag at her waist.

She shoved the stone into place and leaned the broom against it. A hand touched her arm. Recoiling, she whirled, heart thumping.

"Jace!"

"I won't tell. Hurry. Imma wants you."

Adah crossed to the small room at the back of the house. Kneeling by the pallet, she smoothed away the limp gray locks that framed her imma's face. "I am here, Imma."

"Adahhhh." Imma caressed her name.

Adah's eyes welled, and tears splashed onto the pallet. For a moment she was safe again, loved by the one who knew her best.

Imma's gaze drifted to Jace. She nodded once. Jace left and returned with a small packet.

"Daughter…all I have to give. Remember the stories." Her eyes closed, then fluttered open. "Wait until…alone, until you need…"

Imma's breaths grew so far apart, Adah doubted she would draw another one. As she leaned over to kiss the worn forehead, Imma breathed one word more. "Truth."

"I will, Imma."

Imma's eyes glazed, and the slight lift and fall of her chest stilled.

"Imma's dead, isn't she?" Jace's voice sounded resigned.

Adah nodded. This time when she reached for her little brother, he melted into her embrace, his thin shoulders quivering.

"Come back for me, Adah."

CHAPTER THREE

A dah saw Omari had been settled in a *howdah*, its cover a protection from the sun to ease his journey. His twin sons, Donkor and Femi, rode side by side, leading the caravan. Adah's throat clogged from the dust kicked up by the baggage camels and servants' camels ahead of her. She did not look back at her father as they rode away.

With no reins—the camels had been tied together with ropes— she clung to the saddle's front stump and sat tall until hours of the rolling motions made her drowsy. If she fell off in the coming blackness of night, it would go unnoticed. Her camel turned and smiled with big droopy lips as if reading her mind.

A shout halted the caravan. Evidently accustomed to the routine, servants began setting up camp even before Omari's camel knelt and the elderly man was helped to dismount.

Adah peered over the camel's side, trying to reason the best way of descent, when the beast lurched forward, flipping her over its head onto the ground. The twin named Donkor spoke—his accent so heavy she struggled to understand him. He sneered and released the cinch belt from the camel's flank.

Adah did not move. Her head pounded from daylong exposure to the sun. Her thigh muscles throbbed from gripping the camel's wide body. Her arms and hands ached from her death grip on the saddle's stump, and her spine was a limp reed after hours of the camel's rocking gait. If she stayed face down in the dirt, maybe she'd be abandoned when the caravan traveled on.

Booted feet appeared in her line of vision. "You stay there, and your camel, Nefatari, wretched beast, will bite you."

She understood his words this time. But, thrumming with pain, she closed her eyes, uncaring. Death seemed a fine alternative to moving.

Strong hands hauled her upright and set her on her feet, but her abused muscles refused to cooperate. She swayed, unable to balance. The man, smelling of camel and sweaty perfume, tossed her over his shoulder and carried her into an elaborate tent. He threw her on a pile of soft, thick pillows.

At her groan, Donkor snickered. "Sleep, new imma. Enjoy your wedding night."

Adah clamped her lips together. Not another sound would he hear, no matter how she hurt. Too sore to move, she said nothing, and lying so still, soon slept.

Sputtery snores invaded her dreams. Rousing slowly, she stretched, wondering at the softness enveloping her and the difficulty in moving. Her muscles screamed in protest, and yesterday's events returned.

Imma had died with no one but a child to ease her last days. Her father was a miser playing poor. She'd married a man as old as Mizraim. Her stepchildren were grown and unwelcoming. Jonah was farther away with every sway of the camel.

The snores stopped. She eased her head to one side and looked into her husband's open mouth. Seeing his rotting teeth, she knew the source of the fetid air. He startled and resumed snoring.

Suppressing a groan, she rolled to the other side, gritted her teeth, and worked her way to sitting. Head spinning, she curled over and dropped back onto the fleecy pillows. The snoring stopped again.

"I am old."

Adah sprang away, aching muscles ignored.

"Not dead." Omari shifted until he was sitting upright. "I will not hurt you."

Adah swallowed a retort. Inbar's husband had promised the same thing. Indeed, he hadn't hurt her, but only because Inbar returned home early.

"I will honor you as my wife, not a slave, but treat you as a daughter."

She almost snorted. Being a daughter was worse than being a slave.

Omari looked away. "Ah, yes, of course."

His discomfort made her wonder if he had read more in her expression than she meant to reveal.

"Adah, I ask nothing of you other than kindness. I am ill—dying. My hands contest my will, trembling so that I struggle to eat. Writing has become almost impossible, nor can I hold others' parchments steady enough to read the words."

Omari's confession acknowledged what they both knew—she'd been bought, not married. Adah searched his wizened eyes and then braved speaking truth. "You made an unwise purchase. I am betrothed to another. I neither read nor write. I know cooking and baking and house care and growing herbs, but nothing of healing or easing pain. I am not what you want."

A slow smile spread across his face. "You are honest. I made an excellent choice. Will you stay?"

He offered to let her decide? His words felt like a gift, and Adah savored the rarity of having a choice.

Returning home guaranteed she'd be sold—again. Convincing Jonah to immediately disregard his parents' wishes and flee with her to an unknown place was a risk. Showing kindness to this man would be a way of thanking him until her beloved found and purchased her freedom.

Something—maybe hope—began to grow.

"I will stay."

He bowed his head, then looked up. "Thank you. I have a gift for you."

Omari winced as he crawled from his pallet, stood—joints crackling—and shuffled across the tent to a carved box. The key clattered until he held it with both hands to insert it into the lock. Adah heard the clunk of rings and scrape of his nails as he sorted through the box. With a little flourish of his trembling hands, he presented her with a jar.

"I have never seen anything like it."

"Obsidian and tooled gold."

"Thank you." She opened the jet-black container and peered up at him in confusion.

"Rub this into your hands, then your arms and shoulders, and lastly your legs. It will ease the tightness of your muscles." He chuckled. "This may be the most treasured gift you ever receive."

She dabbed a tiny smear onto her hands and rubbed it in, then looked up in relief.

"How wonderful."

When she was better able to move, Adah poured water into a small bowl and wiped away the food smeared in Omari's beard. He handed her a knife and pointed to his fingernails.

"My own hands have become my greatest adversaries. I would slice off a finger if I tried to trim the nails. If you can shorten these, it will be the most treasured gift *I* ever receive."

He held out a trembling hand.

"What is it like, Omari, being old?"

"Glorious. Tragic." His gaze followed a long nail as it dropped to the ground. "I have seen beauty and kindness, traveled to distant lands, learned more than I knew there was to be learned."

"And tragic?"

"Few share my memories. Those who loved me and laughed with me no longer grace my life. There will be more rejoicing in my arrival to the afterlife than mourners on this side." He examined his pared nails. "A jeweler in Tadmur, a merchant in Babylon. Few others will grieve for me. Some will rejoice, perhaps my sons."

Adah narrowed her eyes at Omari's twins. They made no secret of their dislike for her in spite of her care for their abba. Over the last week, neither Donkor nor Femi had commented on the changes, the clean silks Omari wore, and that neither food nor drink stained his beard. She did not need to be thanked, but each morning, Omari looked at them with expectation when he emerged from his tent. She saw his slight shrug and guessed he was disappointed they did not seem to notice his improved appearance.

Adah turned away and began limping to the end of the caravan. The balm Omari had given her helped, but she still ached from six days of sitting atop the camel's back.

"Adah?"

She paused and started back to where he stood with his sons. Omari studied her for a long time, then summoned his sons. "Adah is my wife. She will ride Babu in the howdah with me each day."

The twins said nothing, only bowed in acquiescence, but blackness deepened Donkor's dark eyes. Displeasure? Disapproval? Was the cracking of his knuckles after he helped her a reminder he could break small bones—like hers? As they journeyed south, she learned to clamber onto the camel's back without his help and move quickly away from his hand in dismounting.

Grateful to be near the front of the caravan instead of traveling behind nine camels' dust and unrestrained odors, Adah searched for something to say after "ouch" each time Omari's bony elbows hit her ribs as Babu lurched to its feet. A spark of gold on his finger caught her eye.

"That is a beautiful ring you wear. I have never seen anything like it." Not that she'd seen many, but it sounded as if she had, and it was different from those sold by the merchants who traded in Inbar's village.

Omari spread his fingers to better display the dark green oval. "It is more ancient than imaginable—rumored to be a possession of our ancestor, Ham. They are wrong though. It is known to have belonged to a pharaoh's wife of the eighteenth dynasty, over a thousand years ago, maybe more. In my family, traditionally this ring is an inheritance given to the most highly favored child, usually the firstborn but not always."

"You were the first child of a pharaoh?"

He smiled. "Not I. An ancestor from—unfortunately—forgotten memory. My people believe as long as our name is remembered, we remain alive in the afterlife. Your people would scorn that idea, believing it to be an offense to your God."

"We would? Why?"

Omari's hands trembled violently. "Child, your God and His rules are beyond comprehension. All people seek to know and please the gods and thus live beyond this life. Your people believe only in their God and that they alone know His secrets." A vein bulged across his reddening forehead. "It is a narrow, prideful belief. Hurtful and..." He rubbed his left arm.

Adah pinched her lips together. She didn't know any of Adonai's secrets, but He was her God and the God of her people.

She drew in a deep breath. It was time to talk of something else. People liked to speak of their children. That would be a safe question.

"Omari, do you have other children?"

As wind snuffs flame from a candle, light vanished from his eyes. Pallor replaced the flush of his face, and tears welled from his eyes. "A daughter. I am dead to her."

Only a short time she'd belonged to Omari, and already she'd said something to sadden him. How soon would he tire of her and gift her to one of his sons? She shuddered, thinking of the darkness in their eyes. Had her father thought of that when he sold her?

Babu swayed down a hill. She gripped the howdah's frame, still uneasy with the motion.

Omari's eyes lit with amusement. "Camels are new to you."

"They're so tall." She lifted the cover and peered over the edge. "Especially this one."

"Do not look down, and do not think about it. Instead, tell me the stories of your people." His voice sharpened, and he spoke firmly. "Adah, you are looking at the ground. Look at me."

Eyes wide, she twisted to stare into his face.

"Were you this frightened the first day?"

She shook her head. "I was too angry to be frightened."

"Angry with me?"

"No." She rolled her lips inward. *His* name would not soil her lips ever again.

"Ahh. I understand. We will not speak of it. Now, will you tell me the stories of your people?"

She frowned. He didn't like her God but wanted to know His stories?

"Which one?"

Palms up, he shrugged. "I do not know them. How can I say?"

Adah gripped the frame of the howdah, trying to balance as Babu's rolling gait increased. "Do you know the story of Noah and the Great Flood that covered all the earth?" She glanced nervously at the swaying cloth drapes. "My people are descended from Noah's son, Shem."

"And mine from Mizraim, son of Ham, also son of Noah. See, Adah, we are family." Omari chuckled. "My people too tell of the destruction by floodwaters—this is known throughout the world. Choose a different story."

She squinted, the morning sun peeping through a part in the howdah's cover. "The creation of the world and the Garden of Eden?"

Omari's shoulders drooped. "I know that one too. Pharoah Akhenaton created the Terrestrial Paradise on the banks of the Nile for his god, the Atun. The 'Isle of Flames' it was called." He stroked the delicate ring on his smallest finger. "Your people think a copy of the original map exists and paradise can be found and reentered."

"A map?" Her voice squeaked only a little.

"Rumors."

She cleared her throat. "Of course. I once heard the same rumor."

"People long to find the way to a place of perfection because they want to live in peace, to work their land without fear. I have often wondered if it was a real place or a story told to children to coax them to sleep." He batted at the air in dismissal. "Do you know other stories?"

"Our creation story says man did not make the Garden for our God. God made it for man."

A voice called out. She did not understand the words, but Omari's response was instantaneous. Hands trembling violently, he grasped at the covering on his side, yanked it back, and pointed. "Jerusalem."

It was not his home nor the place of his faith, but such yearning filled his voice—a soul desperate for hope—that she tore her thoughts from the place of Imma's stories and studied his face. The quiver of his chin, the moistening of his eyes, his audible swallow spoke of emotion beyond speech.

Perhaps the city affected everyone that way.

Looking out at the city, she gasped. "It is golden!"

Jerusalem—the place where Adonai dwelled—gleamed in the morning light. So this was the city of David—destroyed and rebuilt.

A stirring in her spirit drew her, filled her with a longing to be held within the walls' protective embrace, touch its stones, breathe its fragrance.

Adah knew her mouth was hanging open at the astonishing beauty.

As if from a distance, she heard Omari's voice, steady once again. "The highest point—see, Adah, on the hill? That is the Temple to your God."

Holy light gathered in and around the Temple's walls, glowing whiter than the wildflowers near her home. Lesser buildings spilled down the hills as if kneeling in awe. Overcome, she struggled between the desire to fill her eyes with its splendor or lower her head in deference.

"You find it beautiful?"

She nodded, still speechless.

"This is rather modest—rebuilt by a man named Ezra. I have heard the original was truly magnificent."

"Solomon's Temple."

"Oddly, this Temple was constructed before the walls." He frowned. "A man named Nehemiah rebuilt the walls with permission and supplies from the Babylonian king. Quite an unusual occurrence."

Shakily, Omari lowered his side of the drape, but Adah leaned forward and stuck her head through the front panel. She could not look at this place enough.

Someday she'd walk through those gates and climb the hill to see the Temple up close. Maybe when she and Jonah were married, he'd bring her here, and they could walk through the streets together.

Maybe they could live here. Maybe Jace would move here. So many wonderful possibilities. She clasped her hands together and squeezed them in joy.

When the camels sauntered past Jerusalem and she could no longer crane her head around the panel to see its beauty, she lowered the flap. "You have traveled this road before."

"Many times."

He closed his eyes and did not elaborate. Soon, a steady, soft clicking from his throat told her he was sleeping. When the clicking turned to snores, she opened the bag tied to her waist. Her fingers touched the cracked leather packet Imma had given her, but she was not alone, would not break her promise to her imma. Instead, she drew out a handful of the coins she'd taken. Silver and gold. Small, hard circles. This was her worth.

She shoved them back into the bag and jerked it closed.

Suddenly aware that Omari's snoring had stopped, she studied his features. His mouth hung ajar, and his lashless eyes did not flicker. Surely he'd not awakened, not seen the coins. As her husband, he could demand them from her.

She watched him breathe, waited for a sign he was not truly asleep. At last, in the stuffy enclosure, rocked by Babu's rolling gait, she rested her head against the howdah and let her eyelids drift down.

Dreams of Jonah's laugh-filled eyes and easy gait erupted into her father's harsh voice threatening to—

Jolted awake, she flung her arms wide, found a warm hand to grasp, and stared at the cloths surrounding her. The cloth walls shifted. Where—?

Long fingers snaked through the wall. Donkor's gaze shot to her hand clasping Omari's. His eyes narrowed. As Femi helped Omari dismount on Babu's other side, Donkor grabbed her wrist and wrenched her close, his spicy, sweet cardamom scent making her sneeze.

"You will never replace me. I am the sole heir. It has always been so." He flung her wrist from his grasp as if it were a despicable thing.

She glared at him and rubbed at his fingermarks. "Never touch me again."

His eyes were hard, dark slivers of obsidian. "You dare order...me?"

"I dare."

His hand rested on the ribbed hilt of his curved dagger—his eyes cold and cruel as its blade. "You are trouble."

"Donkor." Omari's sharp voice cut between them. "Do not touch my wife. Adah, attend me."

Donkor's lip curled in a sideways snarl before he bowed low and stalked away.

Adah's muscles had stiffened again. She reached for her bag. Not finding it, she bent double and ran her hands over the howdah's floor. There. She frowned at the loose opening.

How had the camel's gait shifted it to Omari's side and worked the knot free? A slight shake proved no coins had been removed. It was still heavy, and Omari didn't know about the map. She shrugged. After this, she'd brace it between her feet.

She crawled from the howdah, slid down Babu's thick fur, and hobbled to Omari's side. "We are stopping early?"

"I am tired. We will rest here several days then travel to Hebron—a short journey—then resume longer days. Jerusalem and Hebron are difficult cities for me to pass."

CHAPTER FOUR

One Week Later
Hebron

Adah shuddered. Tents, like black tears, trickled down the hills surrounding Hebron, bitter sadness emanating from the hovels, scarring the city's beauty. Without being told, she knew these did not shelter pilgrims to the patriarchs' tombs. These housed avengers, those who lurked about the gates waiting for a judgment or, better yet, for those accused of manslaughter—guilty or innocent—to set foot outside the city of refuge and forfeit sanctuary.

Imma had told her of the cities of refuge, where vengeance stalked hope like wolves circling sheep. Commoners and kings alike fled to their protection.

"To live confined for years within those walls. How do people bear it, Omari?"

"To live."

Alarmed, Adah studied the man beside her. Throughout the day his words had decreased, as if talking required too much effort. He'd eaten little yesterday and less today. Already skeletal thin, he could not miss many more meals and live.

Resting in the shade cast by Omari's great camel, she handed her husband a waterskin.

"Please, drink something."

Refusing it, hands shaking, he tugged the ring she'd admired from his finger and dropped it in her lap. "Hide."

"It's beautiful." She touched the delicate gold setting that curved around the dark green oval. A gold band secured the stone to its setting. She held it to the light, traced the minuscule markings on the flat underside. "Did you know there is something on the back? What do these signs mean? Is this writing?"

He nodded. "Mizraite. Secret."

"Tell me now?"

"Later." He shook his head. "Hide it, child, hurry."

"Please, Omari? It's so beautiful I would like to know everything about it."

"Adah, hide it."

Donkor and his silent shadow, Femi, bore down on them. Adah's hand closed over the ring. Had they seen the exchange?

Donkor sped forward, advancing until his sandals slung dirt on her tunic. Looming over her, he thrust his hand in her face and snapped his fingers.

"Not yours." Stone was not harder nor fire hotter than his voice.

Omari reached a protective arm across Adah. "Hers."

Donkor shoved him to one side.

"Donkor, no!"

Babu's groan thundered in Adah's ears. The beast lumbered to his feet, bellowing and stomping.

Screaming, Adah clambered to her knees and dragged Omari away from Babu's hooves. "Stop. Donkor, you have hurt him. He is bleeding. Stop!"

Shaking off Femi's restraint, Donkor grabbed for Adah's hand. She gripped the ring harder and twisted away. A flash of movement, a familiar face—Jonah? Here? How? Jace must have reached him.

In a whirl of motion, Donkor was jerked back and flung to the side. Jonah dropped to his knees in front of her. Before she could reach for him, Donkor staggered to his feet, drew his dagger, and charged forward.

"Jonah!"

He spun, his arm deflecting the blow and sending Donkor crashing to the ground where he lay unmoving, his head against a rock, a thin line of blood trickling from his mouth.

"Adah."

She dragged her gaze from where Femi knelt by Donkor's still form to Omari's stricken face.

"Go, child. Run."

"I am not going to leave you, Omari. You are hurt."

Jonah caught her as she reached for Omari. "He is right, Adah. Hurry."

"Omari…?"

"Go." He closed his eyes and slumped to one side, his hands stilled.

Jonah grasped her arm and tugged. Without a second thought, she grabbed her small bag and let him lift her to her feet. She staggered and fell. He pulled her up. Together they raced toward the city, swerving, veering left then right, toppling any who stood in their way.

Safety beckoned. The gates stood wide open, the surrounding walls stretching strong and tall. Their feet flew across the ground. Lungs burning, Adah pushed harder. Almost there. From behind her came a shout—Femi. His pounding feet closed the distance. She heard a thud, a grunt. Jonah faltered, then recovered his balance.

Muscles bulging, Jonah shoved her across the city's perimeter and staggered, crumpling to the ground. A dagger had slit his back.

Adah's legs buckled. She dropped to her knees, heart pounding, gasping for breath even as his slowed and ceased.

The stain spread across his back. Around her, chaos erupted. Voices—shrill, warm, harsh—bounced off her ears and blurred into a roar.

But disbelief silenced Adah. Moments ago, she'd been safe with Omari, cared for, content to wait until Jonah ransomed her. Now, two men lay dead—no, three—because of her.

Their deaths were her fault, her foolishness, her failure.

Inbar called her worthless. Her father named her witless, unwanted. Donkor called her trouble.

They'd known, seen her for who she was, spoken truth.

Trouble stalked her as if lured, and secrets clung like burrs.

Safety had vanished from the earth. Peace, for her, had never existed.

Two men covered Jonah's body. Tender hands cradled her elbow, insisted she stand, and guided her down a street and into a house. Told to sit, she sat. Given a cup of water, she drank. Asked her name, she could not form the word.

She was led to a pallet. She lay down, stared at the stems of feathered dill and lacy thyme hanging from the rafters until her hot, dry eyes closed and she slept, her fingers fisted around the ring.

Adah woke to gaping emptiness, the void so wide she could not grasp its edges and pull herself out. Her past and future were destroyed. The present was incomprehensible. Opening her hand, she saw the ring's imprint on her palm. Three lives for this? Splaying her fingers, she dropped the ring as if it were a fiery coal.

Tears scalded her skin as they trickled into the hairline at her temples.

Omari—the kind abba she'd longed for—slain for gifting her his ring. If she'd hidden it as soon as he'd given it to her…if she'd not teased him to share its secrets. She closed her eyes, attempting to block the memory of Omari's anguish. Closed them against the cruelty life dealt—that as he breathed his last, he witnessed his son's death. Closed them to block his stillness. She scrubbed her eyes to remove the image of those limp, gnarled hands.

Jonah. Images of the dagger protruding from his back choked her mind, filling all the edges, oozing to the corners until nothing else could be seen, only his strength and vitality turning to red dust. If she hadn't asked Jace to tell him…if Jonah had run when Donkor first fell…if he hadn't helped her when she fell…if he'd had one more tiny second, he'd be alive, talking as if they'd had a grand adventure, one to tell their grandchildren.

If.

Sobs ripped from her depths at the stupid, senseless desecration of Jonah's life. She groped for the ring and hurled it across the room. She spewed rage at her father's betrayal, at the humiliation of being sold, at the harsh wrongness of Imma's life. Screamed in fury until sound refused to cross her raw throat.

Spent, she quieted, panting, unable to whimper. A cup pressed against her lips. She swallowed honeyed liquid and lay limp, uncaring, as someone wiped her face and neck with a cool cloth. Through swollen eyes, she saw a woman—soft, round, gray-haired—looking at her tenderly.

"It is too much to bear alone. My name is Emili. I have walked in your path. I am praying for you. Sleep. Weep. Scream. Whatever you need, I will watch over you."

Adah turned her face to the wall, ashamed of revealing emotions better left unexposed. Vulnerability was not something she did well.

Adah woke. By the voices and rumbling carts and cooing doves, it was daytime, but her eyes refused to open, and weight like the stone her father threatened to use when he threw her in the river pressed her down on the pallet—weight so heavy she could not move.

"It is the burden of grief."

She turned her head toward the voice but could not open her eyes.

"I am Emili. When you can speak, please tell me your name."

Emili slid a hand behind Adah's head and lifted it. The rim of a cup touched her lips.

"While you slept, I removed the pouch from around your waist. It is here, by your hand." Emili hesitated. "And I placed the ring inside."

Adah frowned.

"Discard it later if you wish, not in the rage of raw grief." Emili's voice grew rough. "In my time of loss, wretched and in despair, I burned a letter. I would give anything to hold it again, to trace my finger over the words he'd written to me."

Adah welcomed the cool cloth placed across her eyes. When it had been refreshed several times, she pried her eyes open and squinted through graveled lids. She drew in a staggered breath and found she could whisper.

"Thank you. I am Adah. Has he...has my...?"

"Adah, I am sorry for your loss. Yes, he has been laid in a tomb. Was the young man your husband?"

She shook her head.

"Betrothed?"

Adah's chin trembled. She nodded and bit the inside of her mouth to still the trembling.

"You will find it is better to speak of loss and grief. Locked inside, it will fester, decay, seep its foulness into every part of life until you are poisoned. With me, it is safe to let go of your restraint. There is nothing you can say I have not thought, heard, or felt." Emili sighed before continuing. "Unfortunately, what I know about grief was learned the hard way and learned alone. I cannot prevent your suffering, but if I can spare you—and others—unnecessary heartache, then it brings good out of my own loss." Emili tsked. "Enough for now. Will you try to swallow some lentil soup? I simmered it all night, and it is mush."

Adah ate and slept. Ate and slept.

One morning, she found she could sit up. That afternoon she stood and walked across the room. The next day, Emili heated water for Adah to bathe herself and offered her a clean linen tunic.

"It has always been my favorite tunic, and it fit me ten years ago." She patted the folds of her soft belly. "But I think never again." Emili smiled softly. "I knew there was another reason I kept it. You."

Adah stroked the fine material. She'd never worn anything but rough wool. Unwelcome tears filled her eyes. "You have been so kind to me."

"I listen to our Lord, and He guides me." Emili drew her into a hug. "Would you like to hear my story, dear? Do you think you are ready? It might help to know you are not alone."

At Adah's nod, Emili patted the bench next to her and began, her voice steady as if she'd repeated it many times. Only her face betrayed the pain that lingered.

"Zephan and I had been married two years, and I had just learned I was with child—our first." She paused. "Our only. A man, newly come to our village, accused my husband of stealing. Our neighbors defended us, but words turned to blows, and blows to weapons. Zephan's accuser died. We packed what we could carry and fled to this city of refuge. We arrived safely, rented this house. I have been here twenty years."

"You said you understood my pain." Adah knew her tone was too sharp. "How, if you and Zephan arrived safely?"

Emili's eyes drooped. "The city meant safety to me. I was content, but Zephan had been a merchant, accustomed to traveling unrestrained. He saw the walls as a prison. He'd sneak out. He knew he risked death if the avenger's relative found him beyond the walls." Her voice caught.

Adah reached for Emili's hand.

"One day he was spied. He tried to reach the gates, but he was not fast enough. One more breath and maybe…"

"Oh, Emili. Were you there?"

She nodded once, slowly. "I was there, saw him stagger into the city much as your betrothed did. That patch of ground holds the blood of both our men—too many men. A few hours later, our son was born—Nathan—who'd never know my beloved, his abba."

They sat without speaking.

Emili's soft voice broke the silence. "For years, I carried both sorrow and anger—anger at Zephan for unnecessarily risking and losing his life, anger at myself for not trying harder to stop him, anger that Nathan would grow up without an abba, anger at Adonai for allowing his death."

Adah swiveled, her eyes widening. "Anger at Adonai?"

"If the prophet Jeremiah and our King David could be angry with the Lord, I could too. Until I admitted my anger to Him, it could not be released, and I could not have healing and peace or fully experience His love for me."

"And now you do?"

"And now I do." Emili withdrew her hand and pressed the tears from her eyes. "My sorrow remains. It always will. It is a normal part of life. After so many years, the loss is not as intense and sneaks up on me less often." She smiled. "The peace, now that is not a normal part of life. That is a gift from Adonai and worth all I entrusted to Him, worth all I surrendered to Him knowing He loves me."

"Emili, this sounds…foolish, but—trusting God? How? I know the stories of our people and believe He loves them—um, us—but I do not think He knows me, much less loves me." She forced a laugh as if it were no matter.

"He does."

"You don't understand. Jonah's death is my fault and so is Omari's and even Donkor's, though I do not care that he died. And if my own father does not want me, how can God?" She bit her lip, wishing she hadn't revealed so much.

Emili laughed softly. "You are one of His chosen people. He knows your name. Adonai told the prophet Isaiah that 'I, the Lord your God, holds your right hand' and 'Fear not, I am the one who helps you.' God is with you and waits to help you. Isaiah called Him Abba."

"I never thought...would never dare..." Adah shook her head and propped one elbow on the table, beyond tired. "I am sorry, Emili. I cannot seem to think, to understand..." She shrugged. "My thoughts are piled up like a week's worth of dishes needing to be scraped and scrubbed and sorted.

"Everything is confusing. A few days ago, Omari and I were sharing stories—we knew each other such a short time, only two weeks—and then he gave me the ring to hide, and suddenly Donkor and Jonah were fighting and Donkor fell against a stone. Then Femi, Donkor's twin, chased us. He is the one who killed Jonah, and now I am here...and before that, I was accused of stealing and then sold to the caravan, although Imma was dying, and my little brother is alone now. And I found my father's hoard...and before she died, Imma gave me the map." She peered at Emili. "Does that make sense?"

Emili shook her head, her eyes worn but serene. "I don't understand the story, but what I do understand is you are grieving and hurt."

"It doesn't seem like the Lord has helped me."

"You have been protected and guided in ways you don't yet understand."

Adah shrugged. "I understand nothing. So, what do I do now?"

"First, grieve as long as you must." Emili pushed a plate of food nearer to Adah. "Grieve your loss and injustice and your mistreatment at the hands of others. But, in your sorrow, talk to the Lord as you would to me or your imma. Ask for help. You know about Adonai. Now trust Him, let Him become the center of your life." Emili tapped her finger against her chin. "Adah, who needs to be told of Jonah's death?"

"His parents." Adah shook her head. "I cannot—will not—be the one to tell them. They believed me beneath his notice."

"Someone must tell them."

No. Emili could not ask this of her. She would run all the way to Mizraim before she faced his parents' shock and their scorn if she slipped and called him her betrothed. She twisted her fingers. She couldn't tell them if she wanted to. Femi probably waited outside the gates, ready to kill her too. Of course he did. She had the ring. She'd give it to him. If he killed her, who would care? She stood.

"No. You will not run. Sit down." Emili spoke as an imma to a child.

"How—?"

"I have walked this path myself and with others. We will find a way. Trust me."

Trust? She'd trusted her parents, who failed to protect her. She'd trusted Jonah. It had killed him. She'd begun to trust Omari, and he was dead. Trust was dangerous. What would it cost next?

"Adah, would your parents tell his family?"

She traced circles on the table. "No."

Even if they would, she didn't want them to know the story. Her father would haul her back and sell her again. She frowned, searching for a solution.

"My brother..." No, she'd not subject little Jace to that. Who could tell Jonah's parents? She spoke slowly, trying to remember the name Jonah had mentioned. "Jonah has an uncle in Jerusalem. Aaron ben...something. I will take word to him, let him tell Jonah's parents."

Emili raised one gray eyebrow. "An uncle. That is a start. How will you get to Jerusalem?"

"Walk." She snapped her answer, annoyed at the ridiculous question. Her head still ached. She'd wanted to retort, "Fly."

Understanding warmed Emili's voice. "Yes, of course you will walk. I meant with whom?"

"I am sorry, Emili."

"Grief has sharp edges, child." She stood and kissed the top of Adah's head. "My son travels to Jerusalem in a few weeks. I think if Jerusalem is where you want to be, you must go with him."

Emili placed a hand on Adah's shoulder and bowed her head. "Almighty Lord, blessed are You. We need Your help. Please guide us. Amen."

Adah blinked. Emili just popped in on God the Creator like He was a neighbor?

"Femi will expect you to slip out the gates at night. Most people assume that is when the avengers sleep, but it is when they are most alert, as large groups leave the city. He will look for someone wearing dark clothes, trying to blend into the shadows or merge with other people." She slapped the tabletop. "I have a plan."

Adah nodded, too tired to think or argue. Emili's loss and confusing serenity, alongside the anger and horror of Jonah's death, left her teetering on an indefinable edge. Another word, and the single slender reed she clung to would bend, plummeting her into an abyss. She stumbled across the room and curled into a ball on her pallet.

CHAPTER FIVE

Two Weeks Later

Adah woke to color flaring through the room. She rubbed the sleep from her eyes in wonder. Hues of red, yellows, unimaginable blues, and more greens than she'd known existed draped the chairs, hung from hooks on the wall, and covered the tables—a rainbow within reach.

She'd never seen such brilliant shades in one place except as the sun rose and set. She pinched herself, unsure if she was dreaming. No. Definitely awake.

Sitting up, Adah crossed her legs, reveling in the beauty of the display. Wouldn't Imma love to see this! And Jonah. She'd memorize exactly how it looked, then find the right words to describe it to them, and then—

She remembered. Jonah. Imma. Tears dimmed the colors. She covered her eyes, overwhelmed by the noise of reds vying with golds and green rivaling green. It was too close, too intense. Enough chaos churned inside her. She didn't need it surrounding her too.

She needed grays and browns and silence and stillness until she heard only her breath. She needed a place where she could sleep until the pain bellowed itself hoarse. She needed to be held together in one piece and for no one to touch her, because if they did, she'd crumble into dust and be swept away by the wind.

She wrapped her arms around herself. Swept away by the wind—that was what she wanted to happen. Nothing else. Ever.

Emili bustled through the door with a cloth bundle. After setting it on the table, she fanned her face. "I have another tunic for you and a cloak and sandals—all are gifts for you to keep, as well as the scarves you choose. Here in Hebron, we see so much tragedy, so many people resentful of being confined for years, that for someone innocent to escape is reason to celebrate. My friends were eager to help you."

Emili's voice sparkled with pleasure in the generosity of those she knew. She walked to a chair and sat heavily, her curved back speaking of strain. This almost stranger suffered while continuing to aid her.

Adah brushed the dampness from her eyes and the heartache from her voice. "I do not understand how this helps me escape."

"Femi will be watching for a poor young girl, not a heavily expectant woman with a wealthy husband who adores her and allows her to buy the most expensively dyed clothes or whatever she wishes. You will see. Stand up."

Adah grasped the chair's edges and pushed herself to stand. Emili tied a wide cloth around Adah's shoulders and back to create a sling. "Now, we fill this with your old tunic and this other one I have for you, cover it with a trimmed tunic—quite a luxury, you know—and look! You are due to give birth in a month." She stepped sideways, studied Adah, and then reached for the yellow scarf.

"This one. It shouts, 'Look at me.' Exactly what Femi will do. He will glance your way and continue to search the crowds, confident you'd never dare wear this bold color. It is completely opposite of what he will expect."

"I would never have thought of this. Emili, I do not know how to thank you." The dullness of her tone seemed unnoticed.

"Someday, it will be your turn to help another."

"And I will."

"When you arrive in Jerusalem at the uncle's house—have you remembered his name? No? It will come. When you arrive, you and Nathan must—"

A quick tap on the door, and it swung open.

Emili's eyes lit with love. "Nathan, we were just speaking of you. Adah, my son, Nathan. He and I have already discussed it, and he will see you safely there. Adah, once you have told the uncle, what will you do?"

Adah unwound the sling and folded the cloth and tunics. "I would like to stay in Jerusalem. I am a hard worker. Surely someone will hire me."

"No one will hire you." Nathan looked down his long, thin nose at Adah. "You are too old to train and look too puny to lift a loaf of bread. Not sure who would want you."

No one. He spoke truth.

"Nathan!" Emili thumped her fists on her hips. "Hush your mouth, Son. She just lost her betrothed. Show godly kindness."

Kindness—her Jonah, who had always spoken to her with kindness—would never speak again.

"Forgive me. I spoke truth without gentleness. May Adonai comfort you."

Adah turned her back so Nathan would not see her face crumple. They'd not even said hello and already she'd eagerly bade him farewell. It was sad Emili had such an unpleasant son.

Nathan cleared his throat. "Imma, plans have changed. I need to leave tomorrow. Wait, before you scold me, it is a better plan. A refugee who has just arrived with his family wants to send his two daughters to Jerusalem to live with an aunt and uncle until his case is resolved. The girls will travel with us as if they are our children. He has given me coins to hire a cart large enough for all of us. It will be a hard trip, but I think we can make it in one day. Imma, a family of four will pass even more easily than a husband and wife."

Emili clapped her hands. "See, Adah? The Almighty has provided for you. Go, Nathan. We have much to do before morning."

Cold with fear, Adah stood, turned, and raised her arms as Emili rolled the tunics into one large bundle and arranged the disguise. With every breath, she fought images of Femi racing toward her, screaming her name, and throwing a dagger. If the yellow scarf and the children's presence did not deceive him, she'd soon be dead. How horrible for the little girls to witness it. Perhaps she should choose a life in Hebron and just send word to Jonah's uncle.

She blinked back a tear and wiped her nose. "Is this what it is like to carry a child? I cannot see my feet, and I feel like a sway-backed cow."

"My dear, you are this way for one day, not nine months. You will be fine."

Adah cradled her "eight-month" belly, wishing her pregnancy was real and that Jonah's child nestled inside her body—life inside of life. An impossibility, but Jonah had been her refuge city—steady, welcoming, safe.

Israel might have six cities of refuge. She'd had one. Jonah. And he was gone.

No, she corrected herself. There had been others who'd been safe for her. Imma, before she gave up on life, and Omari and Emili, temporary havens so brief she barely recognized them as sanctuaries. They'd been different from anyone she'd ever known—gifts who touched her life.

Emili was humming. Adah watched her bustling around the small room, offering food, tsking to herself, popping a handful of almonds into her mouth. She wanted to shelter in the refuge of this dear woman, this house. Stay where Jonah breathed his last, where his bones lay, where his life soaked into the earth.

"When we leave Hebron, will the cart cross over Jonah's blood… where he died?"

The sudden question seemed to startle Emili. She stopped filling the basket with food and faced Adah.

"Yes."

Adah shook her head, and tears spilled down her cheeks. "I cannot do this. I cannot just ride over…" She covered her face with her hands. "It desecrates him. It is callous and disrespectful, as if his life didn't matter." She sobbed harder. "I did not think to tear my clothes or put ashes on my head. We did not even sit *shiva* for him. He has not been mourned."

"You were unwell, Adah. His family and close friends are the ones who will sit shiva, and when the year has passed, they will travel here to collect his bones and place them in their family tomb. All respect will be given him as an honored Hebrew man. This is why his family must know of his death."

"I cannot do this."

"You can. You will." Emili fisted her hands on her hips. "This is the way you show your love for Jonah, your gratitude for him sacrificing his life and saving yours. He did not hold back. He gave you his all. Grant his family the respect of telling one of them in person. Let them know so they can grieve for him in the way of our people." Her voice gentled. "Dear one, it is what he would have wanted, yes?"

"Yes." Adah let Emili wipe away the tears and embrace her.

"If you did not need to leave…"

Must I?

"If you ever want to return…"

To you, yes.

"I would welcome you, Adah, as the daughter I never had." Emili dashed a tear away and hugged her again. "I am a foolish old woman to ask it of you, child. Enough of this. I made a pouch for the loose coins and added a few things to your bag, things I thought you might need or enjoy." She wrapped the yellow scarf around Adah's head and cradled her face before stepping away.

Nathan pushed the door open. "Is she ready?"

Adah stiffened. "My name is Adah, not 'she.'"

When Emili followed him outside with a basket of food, Adah removed a few coins from the new pouch and hid them beneath a loaf of bread. Emili would find the gift too late to return it. It was the only way she could think to replace the poor woman's expenses on her behalf.

One more quick hug from Emili, and Adah clambered aboard the cart, where two little girls, teary-eyed, clung to each other. She almost smiled. Poor Nathan, with three weeping females. Served him right. She shifted on the bench and tried to balance her belly between her legs. How did women stand this awkwardness for so many months? With the enormous protruding bulge, it was easy to act uncomfortable. She was—even cushioned by padding on the wooden seat she shared with Nathan.

The cart lumbered through the narrow, winding streets. It was her first time outside of Emili's house. She gave little heed to her surroundings, noticing only the clutter of flat-roofed houses not so different from her indifferent village with its haphazard smattering of dwellings. Here, the sideways glances, shoulders curled inward, a hood pulled low over the forehead—these betrayed the city's crackling tension.

As they neared the city wall, the air thickened with dust and sound and the acrid sweat of antagonism. Too many people had thrown hate through these gates. Too much blood had spilled and been swept aside. She absorbed the uneasiness as her anxiety mounted.

Heart pounding, she swallowed convulsively. Her stomach knotted, and her jaw clenched. She would do this. She would escape this smothering place and flee to Jerusalem. For Jonah, she'd be strong—or at least pretend.

Adah saw Nathan glance at her from the corner of his eye. Emili must have warned him to watch her. The cart drew near the city's gateway. Had the stain of Jonah's blood been cleared away, or ground into the dirt? A warm hand closed over hers. Without thought, she gripped it as a lifeline.

Relentlessly, the cart rolled forward, forcing her to cross his death place. Unmarked. Unnoticed. *Forgive me, Jonah.*

They passed the line of trees circling Hebron. When Nathan began urging the mule northward, Adah realized what she'd done. She yanked her hand away and saw the tiny half-moons her nails had dug into his skin.

"I am sorry."

He shrugged. "It was a believable display between a husband and his wife. You are safe. Be at peace."

Safe? Did such a thing ever last? Peace. Had she ever dwelt in peace?

She didn't argue. Weary, she dipped her head. "Of course."

CHAPTER SIX

Jerusalem

Nathan steered the mule up the dark hill and through Jerusalem's gate. Adah held her breath, but as they entered, serenity greeted her, not grief.

He looked over his shoulder at the sleeping children. "I am glad tomorrow is not Sabbath or the city would be closed until it ended. By order of the governor, no merchants are allowed inside the walls. This gate is my favorite of the ten entrances. It is called the Gate of the Friend—it refers to Abraham, God's friend."

God's friend? Imagine that. She was hardly His acquaintance.

Nathan jumped from the cart and handed the reins to a boy. "We will leave the mules here and take the little girls to their family before it gets any later."

He lifted one sleeping child into his arms. Adah coaxed the older girl awake and, grasping her hand, followed him as he wove through the dark streets.

"You have been here before." She panted, her days of inactivity making the endless steps and uphill climb hard.

"Every few weeks. I guide families who leave Hebron for Jerusalem or rest here from their travels before journeying on to join a loved one in Hebron or to visit the Cave of Machpelah—you know, the tomb of Abraham, Isaac, Jacob, Sarah, Rebecca, and Leah."

Visiting a tomb was not something she'd thought of doing, but she wished she'd asked to go by Jonah's tomb. She could have said goodbye and thanked him.

Nathan stopped before a low door and knocked. Light appeared beneath the door's edge, and a bolt slid back. The sleeping child was transferred to her uncle's arms, the other girl welcomed with a warm hug. The children safely delivered to their relatives, he turned to her.

"Where to next? Imma said you have an uncle you are visiting?"

"My betrothed does...did. His uncle lives here. Aaron ben Hassenaah."

Nathan whistled. "High-and-mighty. One of those with money."

Adah tensed. Jonah hadn't mentioned his uncle was influential or wealthy. A powerful man could destroy her family if they blamed her for Nathan's death.

"You know where he lives?"

"His house is one of the few that has been almost completely repaired. It is a steep walk, and it is late, but he will welcome you as his nephew's betrothed."

She gulped. "He does not know of the betrothal." She smoothed her hand over her belly.

"Then, girl, you might want to deliver that infant right away."

She stepped into the shadows to unwind the sling. She folded the bundle into her bag.

Adah blanched, seeing the lights blazing from each opening of Aaron ben Hassenaah's dwelling. The whole of her village, if kneaded together like dough, would fit inside the courtyard guarded by men wearing swords. Past them, the house stood alone, unconnected to any other house, unlike the stacked houses that leaned together in the crowded lower city.

She shivered by Nathan's side as he explained that she needed to speak with the master at once. A loitering servant was sent for the head steward, who arrived suspicious and unhurried.

"My master cannot see you tonight. Return at a more opportune time." He scowled at the soldiers. "Do not disturb me with absurd demands."

"Informing your master of the death of his favorite nephew is not an absurd demand." Adah covered her mouth and retreated a step. She'd been thinking the words, not meaning to voice them.

In the torchlight, Adah saw his eyes travel the length of her body. She clutched the folds of her cloak.

"You are?"

"Jonah's betrothed."

The steward's eyes bulged. "You?" He faltered and took an unsteady step toward her. "Wait. Did you say Jonah is dead?"

Nathan stepped between them. "She has had a long day and grieves her betrothed. Can she speak with his uncle tonight or not?"

The steward's eyes narrowed. "And you are?"

"A friend."

"My master is with the governor in the upper room. He gave orders not to be disturbed."

Nathan raised his shoulders and hands in disbelief. "The governor is more important than a relative's death? Adah, give thanks you escaped this family."

Tears welled in her eyes.

The steward scratched beneath his beard on the right, then on the left. "I will show you to a room for the night, and you may meet with him in the morning, a better time to receive such news.

"I wonder…" Suspicion hardened the steward's features. "Why do you bring this information and not his brother or abba?"

Adah shook her head. "It is a long story. I can relive it only once."

Nathan touched her elbow. "If you like, I will return in the morning for your audience with his uncle."

"It is not necessary." She raised her chin. "I will be fine."

"Good. I will be here."

"She said she would be fine," snapped the steward.

"And I said I will be here. Shalom." Nathan turned on his heel and strode away.

The unexpected relief at Nathan's promise surprised her. She was capable of taking care of herself, but to know someone would be standing beside her—as if they cared about her—was like a warm hug.

———

Alone in a small room, Adah spread out the best tunic Emili had given her. She would wear it to meet Jonah's uncle. After dampening her hands in a bowl of clean water, she dribbled water on the linen and smoothed away its wrinkles before washing her face and arms.

She eyed the grapes and bread left on a table for her. Crossing the room demanded too much effort. She'd eat in the morning.

Adah stretched out, the raised bed almost like the squishy pillows she'd slept on in Omari's tent. But her muscles, still unaccustomed to anything but a thin mat, refused to relax. She turned, twisted, curled, straightened, and flipped back to the original position. When, finally, her body eased and she settled into the bed, her mind flared to life, refusing to stop its spinning and release her to sleep.

How much should she say to Aaron? Would he believe her? Blame her? Could she be arrested for causing Jonah's death if they were holding hands when he was stabbed? Would his family avenge him? Would they cause trouble for Jace? Imma was gone from this earth, but Jace? Who provided for Jace now that Imma was gone?

Sleep tiptoed in and out through the night so that she woke, tired, as the sun rose. She dressed in clean clothes and combed her hair in readiness for meeting with Aaron. Then she dug into her bag, curious about the treasures Emili had mentioned.

She unknotted the small pouch, emptied it onto the bed, and gasped at delicate gold earrings the size of her thumbnail. Beautiful. Never had she imagined owning such a thing.

Beside the earrings lay a tiny blue perfume bottle covered in gold filigree. She twisted off the lid and sniffed. This must be what the Garden of Eden would smell like. Tucked underneath the gifts was a roll of parchment. Unable to read its markings, she set it aside.

Omari's ring had been threaded onto a long gold chain, the delicate wires intricately braided. Adah slipped it over her neck. It was unnoticeable beneath her tunic.

Emili had not always been poor. She must have been from a very wealthy family, or Nathan's abba was a wealthy merchant. Not a word had suggested Emili was discontented with living in the small house on a street filled with the sounds and smells of people crowded together.

Adah examined the earrings, tracing her finger over the dainty etched flowers. She slid the long hooked backs through the piercings in her ears. She'd been so little when Imma used a bone needle to make the tiny holes. Father had laughed when Zeb jerked the string that prevented the hole from closing, tearing her earlobe. A few weeks later, Imma redid the hole, trimmed the string almost to her skin, and bade her wear her hair forward until the hole was formed.

Adah's throat tightened. Imma had used an herb or a plant— she wished she knew which one—to numb her skin so the needle wouldn't hurt. Imma hadn't scolded her brother—Father wouldn't allow it—but his least favorite foods had been served for two weeks, and those, a bit scorched.

Adah replaced Emili's pouch in her bag and rummaged through it until her fingers touched the leather packet Imma had given her. Alone for the first time since leaving home, she could finally look at it. She pulled out the folded leather and studied it as it lay in her lap.

It was the length of her hand, the leather a web of cracks and creases. She untied the strips that held it closed and turned back one fold of the wrapping. A comb tumbled into her lap—one she'd seen in Imma's hair—and the bone needle and a silver coin.

Adah's heart lurched. Imma had not known of the hoard, not known the unnecessary stranglehold on her life. A tear splashed on the leather. Adah wiped it away with her hem and undid the next two folds of the wrapping.

Except it was not a wrapping. It was a drawing. She spread it open on her lap, trying to uncurl the tight edges. Squiggles and curves, arrows and circular marks, covered the surface. She tilted the drawing's surface to one side and then the other, flipped it over and then sideways. Were the marks words or signs, or a splotch from a flattened spider?

What was…?

Before the question formed, she knew the answer. Reverently, she touched the cracked leather.

Oh, Imma—me, you trusted me with your treasure.

This was a map.

The map.

Fake, Father swore.

Truth, Imma whispered.

A fool's quest, scoffed Father.

Peace, insisted Imma.

Peace. Closing her eyes, she searched for a time she'd known peace. Times of laughter surfaced, days she'd had enough to eat, moments she'd pleased Imma—but peace? She squeezed her eyes tighter, trying to imagine such a thing.

Peace. No one angry or disappointed with her. Was it possible? Peace would be acceptance, maybe delight, or even joy in her— instead of being cast as a burden. She smiled at the thought. If those first two came true, could she discover what she sensed lay buried deep inside herself—be who she was meant to be instead of trying to be invisible?

Is that what the Garden held—the key to finding peace? Imma said the Lord was pleased with the first man and woman. They had been whole, had known peace and thrown it away when they doubted their Creator. They had been driven from completeness, from joy.

It stabbed her, this ache in her heart, this yearning to be more than she was now, to revel in acceptance, to love as deeply and wholeheartedly as she longed to be loved. If she could find the Garden, then maybe…

If this was a map, maybe the half circles on each side were suns. One sun had an arrow going up, while the other's pointed down. Was this a clue the lowering sun was toward the sea?

Adah rubbed her forehead, trying to recall the details of Imma's story—the two trees, the serpent, the flaming swords. If the map was true, and if the long *X* was two crossed swords, the Garden was in the direction of the rising sun, the east.

A knock sounded on the door. Flustered, she rewrapped the map and its contents and slid them deep inside her bag. She stood, smoothed her tunic, and opened the door.

The tallest woman she'd ever seen stood with her hand raised to knock again.

"You did not hear me knock?" The woman looked her over. "If Jonah was your betrothed, why are there no signs of mourning? Your clothes are untorn. Your hair clean." She looked closer. "Somewhat."

Adah frowned.

"Your friend is waiting, and my master is ready to hear your tale. I hope it is true."

"You hope his nephew is dead?"

The woman spluttered. Adah widened her eyes in innocence and blinked twice, tilting her head slightly as if confused. When the woman pivoted, she followed, frowning. Something about the woman stirred her memory—her carriage? The shape of her eyes? The glide of her step? She'd seen her before.

She touched Emili's earrings, remembering that dear woman's patience. She wished she'd kept her mouth closed instead of being insolent.

The woman stopped by a doorway and gestured for Adah to wait. A man, head resting in his hands, sat across from Nathan. Both men turned when Adah defied the tall woman and ventured forward.

The woman caught Adah's sleeve and jerked her backward.

"It is fine, Zahra. Thank you. Adah, shalom. Your friend Nathan has spared you and given me the grievous news that my beloved nephew has been gathered to his fathers." The man must be Jonah's uncle. He stood. "You have gone to much trouble to bring it to me and to his family." He took her hands. "Thank you."

The rhythm of his speech sounded like Jonah. His eyelashes curled on the ends like Jonah's did...had. He even smelled like Jonah.

Adah swallowed hard, but tears flooded her eyes and ran down to the corners of her lips.

"I am so sorry." She ducked her head, unable to look at him. Tears splashed onto the floor. "It is my fault he is dead. I would give anything, my own life, to—"

"Hush, Adah. Here." His uncle led her to his chair and gently pushed her to sit. "Will you please call me Aaron?"

She dipped her head, and he continued. "When you are ready, tell me your story, as much or as little as you choose."

Adah glanced at Nathan. He nodded. If caustic Nathan trusted him, it seemed she should too.

"I have known Jonah since his arms were skinny and his face was smooth. We would collect…" This was harder than she'd imagined. Her mind stuck on the first time she'd seen him. She'd been hiding from her father and had seen a boy gathering a pile of stones, mostly round and white like bird eggs, but a few shiny red ones had been added. He didn't ask her name, just began to explain he needed them to practice with his slingshot. For weeks, as often as she could slip away from home, she'd met him near the spring and helped him search for the right size. If he was not at the spring, she'd trek to his house and watch the antics of him and his sisters.

"When I was sold the first time…" Her thoughts drifted to that day. She touched her lips. The single kiss—too sacred to speak of, too sacred to share. "He insisted we could promise ourselves to each other, and we did."

Adah tried to order her thoughts. Had she spoken of Inbar's deceit? Should she tell of her fight to remain untouched for Jonah? She rubbed at the dull ache in her head.

"I tried to explain, but Abba"—she spat the venom-clad word then averted her gaze, unsure if it was pity or revulsion that raced across their faces—"denied Jonah and I were betrothed."

She stared at the floor. "But we *were* betrothed. Jonah said you would help us even if his parents turned away because they don't approve of my family. Jonah said he was your favorite. But then I was sold again…" Her voice trailed away as she debated how to continue the story. Aaron must understand Jonah gave his life for her even if his nephew's action angered him and he dismissed her from his house.

His uncle started to interrupt when she mentioned Donkor. Nathan held up a hand, and Aaron quieted. They must think her slow-witted with her struggle for words and her throat tightening until she struggled for breath.

When Adah finished, silence, disturbed only by the crackling fire in the brazier, settled over the room. She sensed Nathan watching her but could not summon the energy to meet his eyes and cope with whatever was reflected there. Probably scorn.

Aaron walked to the room's opening, keeping his back to them. When he turned, he spoke to Nathan. "You are aware there are informers in Hebron who will discover you assisted her and inform the avenger?"

"Yes."

"If he blames her for his brother's death, then your life, as well as hers, is in danger whether you return or remain here."

Adah's eyes widened. Nathan could die? Her death, no one would grieve, but Emili could lose her beloved son.

"I know. It is a risk I accepted."

Aaron eyed him. "Our governor is returning to Susa as he promised King Artaxerxes. He is in need of trustworthy men and drivers for the journey. It is a three-, possibly four-month trip north, north to Damascus, then along the Euphrates and east to Susa. You would return to Jerusalem with him in a year and be paid well."

"How well?"

Aaron barked a short laugh. "I will add to your wage double whatever he offers."

"Why?"

Aaron nodded toward Adah. "You rescued the beloved of my favorite nephew."

"Not for reward." Nathan folded his sinewy arms across his chest.

Aaron raised an eyebrow. "Then why?"

Red crept up Nathan's face, but his voice was clear and strong. "My imma asked me. For her I would do anything."

"More the reason to stay alive."

"I do not run from threats."

Aaron nodded. "No, you do not have that look about you, which is why I made the offer. You will help secure safety and service to a great man who has rebuilt our walls and, more importantly, helped restore our relationship with Adonai. I ask you for an unselfish act, not so you might escape danger in a reaction to fear."

"There is wisdom in your words." Nathan rubbed the nape of his neck and then nodded. "I accept your offer. Having traveled as far as Babylon, I know the risks. When does the governor wish to leave?"

"He will be here again tonight. Join us. Ask him any questions you have, but I would send word to your imma as soon as you leave here. Once Governor Nehemiah decides on a matter, he moves quickly. Remember, he had Jerusalem's walls repaired in fifty-two days."

"After so many years of them lying in rubble. Yes, I will send word immediately."

Adah's gaze darted between the two men, discussing an idea so reckless it frightened her. Mouth dry, she licked her lips. Dare she risk such a bold request? If they agreed, did she have the courage to leave them midtrip if the map led in a different direction? She chewed her lip. Could she decipher the map's markings?

"Adah."

She jumped at the proximity of Aaron's voice.

"I have not forgotten you. You are a woman of courage and integrity to bring this news to me. It is evident you deeply loved my Jonah. How can I thank you? Do you wish to return home?"

His eyes flickered when he said "home." She suspected he guessed more than she'd said.

"I welcome you here as a member of my family, or I will help you find work in Jerusalem. Anything within my scope of influence I will do for you."

Adah cleared her throat. "I want to live in this city. It calls to me." She blushed. That sounded absurd. Stone walls did not speak words.

Nathan looked at the ceiling and shook his head even as Aaron nodded. "I understand. Jerusalem has the presence of a person, a treasured friend."

"But first, I would like to go with Governor Nehemiah to Susa."

She faltered at their looks of consternation. "If you think he would let me. I would not be any trouble, and I can help with the work."

Nathan scowled down at her. "You have no idea what you are asking or how hard a long journey on the open road can be."

The scathing tone reminded her why she didn't like him. "And you do, city dweller?"

"More than you. I have traveled it."

"Adah." Aaron's tone felt like honey after Nathan's sting. "I would not consider it, and would even forbid it, if you were my daughter."

Nathan's smirk vanished when Aaron continued.

"Unfortunately, you are not my child, and I have no authority over you. If that is what you wish, I will help you, but it is not my choice. It is Nehemiah's decision. You must ask him tonight."

CHAPTER SEVEN

Adah sat on her bed and nibbled the nubs of her nails into non-existence. If she didn't convince Nehemiah to let her accompany the caravan to Susa, how would she get there? She knew the folly of a woman walking alone between cities in Judea—had frequently hidden when returning to her home from Inbar's village. Walking for months through foreign countries was too risky even for her—unless she disguised herself as a man.

She fingered her hair. Chopping it off wouldn't hide her curves. That would require so many layers of clothes, she'd waddle like a duck and lose the ability to run if necessary.

Hiding in a wagon might gain her a day or two before she was discovered and deposited in the nearest town. She grimaced. Nathan would know and enjoy gloating. She'd not give him the pleasure.

"Ouch!" The mindless gnawing had drawn blood and left her nails looking rat-chewed. She tucked both hands beneath her legs to stop from munching all the way to her wrists.

The gold. She'd pay someone to take her.

Right. If it was known she had gold, then once out of sight, she'd be robbed and left to die.

She flopped backward onto the bed. Her only chance was to persuade Nehemiah to let her accompany him. How? What did she have that he needed? Her handful of coins? Probably not. A servant? Maybe. Maybe not.

What reason could she give for wanting to go? The truth? She'd saunter up to him and say, "Shalom, Governor. My name is Adah, and I have the one true map to the long-lost Garden of Eden—yes, it is true—where I hope to find peace, so I insist on traveling with you because I think it is located in that direction, even though I have never held a map before and I do not know how to read it. What do you think? Are you all right with this plan?"

Yes, that should go smoothly. She folded her arms over her face and groaned.

Nothing worked out for her. She'd deserted Omari and lost Jonah. Nathan would be killed for helping her—a horrific way to repay Emili. Imma gave her a priceless treasure, and she could do nothing with it. Was she what everyone said she was?

No.

She sat up, fighting the despair threatening to choke her.

"Think, Adah, think. You see things others miss. Maybe you can help keep Nathan alive for Emili. Maybe you can prove Imma right and Father wrong about the map. Maybe you can do something to save a life instead of costing a life."

Emili had prayed when she needed guidance.

"O God…"

She stopped, unsure what to say next. Imma had prayed and lit Shabbat candles when they could afford them, but she couldn't remember other prayers. Father never prayed. He mentioned God's name a lot, but those had not been prayers. Her almost-a-village did not have enough men for a synagogue, and the priest at Inbar's synagogue mumbled.

She shrugged. Emili said to talk to Him like she talked to everyone—most everyone. Not Nathan. Too often, just talking to Nathan made her mad. Other times, he seemed so kind.

If God took offense, He could strike her with lightning, and none of this would matter.

"O God, forgive this interruption, but I need help, and since there's no one else to ask, I am talking to You. Emili said I could." Emili acted as if God knew her well. It might help to mention her name.

What next? Probably the truth, since it was a commandment. Imma had insisted they memorize all ten.

"I have a map to a place I need to find." That was truth—not all of it—but truth. "It is a long way from here, and if the governor does not let me go with him, I do not know what to do. Emili said I could ask You for help."

Desperation welled. She *had* to find the Garden. *Had* to find peace. Her words stopped as her heart squeezed out its own prayer. *God, help me.*

Strange how that silent reaching out seemed to hold more honesty than any words she'd spoken. Cautious, she waited. No lightning zipped through the sky, only the hint of a breeze—odd in a room with no windows and the door securely latched.

Adah fidgeted on the courtyard bench as she waited for a summons to meet with the great Nehemiah. How should she approach him?

Glancing left and right and seeing no one, she stood, smoothed her tunic, and practiced different entrances. First, she tried becoming invisible, lowering her head in respect, approaching with slow motions—the way she'd learned was safest and caused the least offense. No, she needed him to notice her.

There was another option—long strides, head up—a veneer of confidence she summoned when necessary. That didn't seem right either. Maybe something in between, a combination of assurance and humility. Somehow, she had to convince him.

Footsteps sounded behind her. Nathan strolled past her into the house. He didn't speak, but this area was sheltered and shadowed. Had he seen her shuffling, then striding back and forth?

"You have a decision to make?"

She whirled, seeking the voice's source. There. A man her father's age, seated on a bench shaded by an olive tree, his legs stretched out, ankles crossed. His features showed no ridicule, only curiosity. A hint of an accent warmed his words.

She approached slowly. He wore no dagger. If he was here, unchallenged in Aaron's courtyard, he must be known and of no threat.

"Are you a servant, sir?"

"As you say." His eyes twinkled. "I am hiding from my duties for just a moment or two. Will you keep my secret?"

She sat beside him and scooted back, the bench a little too high for her feet to rest on the ground. "I will. I have served most of my life." She sighed. "I understand the need for a safe hiding place."

Above them, a bird whistled, and a white splotch appeared on the bench between them.

The man grinned. "Is that his honest opinion of us as servants?"

Adah giggled and covered her mouth. "I am sorry. It has just been so long since I have had a reason to laugh about anything."

"You have been through recent difficulties?"

"Recent?" Tears pricked her eyes. "For as long as I can remember."

"How is this a part of the decision you must make?"

Adah exhaled a long, deep breath and slumped against the wall. "I have to go to Susa, or at least to Babylon, and a caravan is going there soon. There is a man—Nehemiah—have you heard of him? Of course you have. He is the governor here."

"Oh, that Nehemiah. I know him well."

She straightened and twisted to face him. "Tell me how to talk to him. Will he listen better to a humble plea or to a confident request? Should I be bold or prepared to grovel? How do I convince him to let me travel to Susa when he leaves? What do I say? Do I tell him I have family in Susa?"

"Do you?"

"No. Well, maybe. Doesn't everyone?" Shrugging, she followed the dance of a leaf floating downward.

He pursed his lips as if thinking. "I have noticed that with Nehemiah, truth is always best."

Adah groaned. "Then I am doomed. He would not believe me if I told him the truth. No one would." She swung her feet, the tips of her toes barely grazing the ground.

"Truth is often more extraordinary than a falsehood. Who have you tested with the truth?"

Adah shook her head. "No one. If what I have is real, it is priceless and would be stolen from me. If it is false, it is worthless, and I look the fool." She shrugged. "Either way, I need to know. I have to find it. I have to try."

"And 'it' is near Susa, and the only way to know if 'it' is true is to find it."

She nodded. "Thank you." Her throat tightened, rendering her voice a squeak. "For listening, for understanding."

The man stroked his beard. Such well-shaped fingernails for a servant. He must be a scribe with those ink stains.

"I am intrigued. How will you know you have found 'it'?"

"I will know because I will see it when I follow the map. It is a place."

"With a name?"

Adah's eyes narrowed. She pinched her lips closed. She'd told this man too much. She looked toward the house. "Aaron's guest will be here soon."

"Most people do not know when to stop confiding." He stood. "I applaud your wisdom."

Wisdom? Me?

He stood. "May I ask your name?"

She hesitated. It depended on who you asked. Thorn. Worthless. Trouble. "Adah."

"Adah, walk with me. Aromas from the kitchen assure me dinner is almost ready."

She wriggled off the bench. "What does your master call you?"

"Nehemiah."

"Oh, like the…" Her legs turned to water. "You are *the* Nehemiah."

He bowed. "Adonai's servant." He winked. "But do not tell that to the king of Persia. He assumes he is my master."

The meal might have been good. Adah ate but did not taste. The bread might have been warm or stale, the drink either sweet or bitter. She didn't notice. Or care.

Lost in self-deprecation, she circled through the maze of her humiliation, adding "inept" to the names she'd been called. Such a blunder was unlike her. She'd learned as a child to test before trusting, listen before speaking. She knew better than to share more information than absolutely necessary.

Eyes lowered, holding herself as still as possible, she hoped the others would forget she existed. If she edged back, bit by bit, soon she'd be close enough to the door to stand and run. Holding her breath, she slid backward.

"Adah, my dear, you have heard Nehemiah's answers to Nathan's long list of questions." Aaron paused. "Has that changed your mind about your request?"

Terrified, eyes riveted on Aaron, she wanted only to escape this room, disappear into the crowded lower city and from the life of everyone she knew. Panic and embarrassment knotted in her throat. She lowered her chin, near defeat.

Nathan rubbed a scar by his eye and stretched as if indifferent. "I hope so. It is a hard journey for a woman. If she is wise, she will remain here where it is easier."

That decided it for her. Nothing in her life had been easy. Why start now? Ignoring Nathan, she lifted her head and swiveled to face Nehemiah.

"Your greatness…"

Nathan snickered, and even Aaron appeared to be struggling to keep his face straight.

"Your greatness…"

"Just Nehemiah." He turned to the others. "Adah and I have already spoken. She explained her reasoning and the importance of her plan. I granted her request."

Three sets of eyes bulged. Three voices sounded as one. "You did?"

Nehemiah tapped his lips. "Adah, forgive me. When we discussed this, I was negligent and did not mention I can offer you only a ride on an open wagon and that we leave following the Days of Awe and Yom Kippur. Bring clothing for the desert heat as well as cold and snow. Can you be ready in time with all that is necessary for a long journey?"

Speechless, she nodded and blinked back tears. Was this really happening to her? *Thank You, Adonai.* The thought—or was it another prayer?—was unexpected. In a nice way. She said it again. *Thank You, Adonai.* It felt right.

Aaron and Nathan shared a long look. Nathan gave a subtle shake of his head, and Aaron reached over to pat her hand. "Adah, my should-be niece, if you allow me, as a tribute to Jonah's memory, I will see you are well provisioned for this trip. When you return, I would like you to reconsider joining my family as a daughter."

From the hallway, Adah heard a woman's angry hiss.

CHAPTER EIGHT

The next day, Zahra sauntered from Aaron's courtyard without a backward glance at the guards. Her long legs quickly covered the distance to the street that the message had named as a meeting place. Unsure who had summoned her, she'd hidden a curved dagger beneath her cloak. Nearing the street, she slowed and walked closer to the wall, protecting one side of herself from attack.

"Zahra."

The familiar voice came from behind. She whirled, letting joy shine from her eyes. But the delight was not returned.

"Femi?"

"We need to talk. Alone."

She retreated into iron-clad discipline. "Follow me."

She led him through an alley and up narrow steps to a wide, flat roof. Anyone who chanced to look up at the right angle might see them. No one could hear them.

She turned, heart racing. The blackness of Femi's eyes was startling against his skin's pallor.

"Are you ill? Where is Donkor?"

"Abba and Donkor are dead. The ring has been stolen."

Force of will kept her standing as he spat out the story.

"I have avenged their deaths. The girl, Adah, is here in Jerusalem, as well as the man who helped her escape my justice. They too will die."

"Adah? You are sure that is her name?" Zahra did not acknowledge his terse nod. "She is a guest in the house where I serve."

Femi's eyes gleamed hot. "Kill her. Befriend her. Lie to her. Do whatever you must, but take the ring."

"They leave in less than two weeks with Nehemiah." She nodded briskly to herself. "If I do not have it by then, I will travel with them for as long as it takes to repossess it."

"I will be close by you. I will not rest until it is again on my finger."

Or mine. Zahra—wisely—said nothing.

Two weeks later

Seated on the wagon, Adah pretended someone else—anyone other than Nathan—sat beside her. It was easy in the darkness with the sun yet an unfulfilled promise. Her only pleasure in being beside Nathan was his obvious annoyance at their assigned places. She doubted Nehemiah had mistaken them for friends. Maybe the caravan master had decided that she would ride with Nathan in this wagon.

A predawn breeze spun by, and she pinched her nose closed. Aaron said this was called the Fish Gate because merchants brought fish through it to sell at the market. Judging from the stench, fish were left to rot too.

Adah squirmed, wishing it would all begin—then hoped it would be delayed so she could jump off the wagon and stay where the food and language were familiar. Was this how Sarai felt when she and Abram began a journey to a place they'd never been? Imma said Adonai told them to leave and they'd trusted Him—there was that *trust* word again—gathered all their possessions and left to follow Him.

It was almost the same with her. Everything she owned was in the new nutmeg-brown bag at her feet. She touched it with her foot. Last night, assured she was alone, she'd rewrapped the map in the yellow silk scarf from Emili and placed it in the bottom of the deep bag.

Like Abram and Sarai, she didn't truly know where she was going other than north and east. The difference? The Lord hadn't told her to leave. He hadn't told her anything—they didn't really know each other that well—but she'd asked for help going, and it had happened. The Lord must not be opposed to it.

She knew Imma's stories about Him. She remembered Emili's words about trusting Him and had heard her talking to Him. It was a start but not much to go on. Understanding God might be harder than deciphering Imma's map.

The unseasonably cold morning air assured her fall was almost here. She snuggled into the thick mantle Aaron insisted she take for the journey and wiggled her toes in the soft new leather sandals. He'd purchased oil for her skin, a tightly woven scarf to keep the dust from her hair, and another tunic—so many possessions. And she was not really his family.

Angry voices from the front of the line brought Nathan to his feet. Without warning, he leaped from the wagon and disappeared into the dark. Alone, with the restless mules jiggling the wagon, Adah gripped the wooden seat. How dare he desert her? If the mules spooked and ran, she'd be thrown to the ground. She looked over the edge. It wasn't as high as Omari's camel, but it was too high to jump. Nevertheless, she stood.

"Sit down. Now."

Nathan's bark annoyed her and relieved her. The animals would not bolt, since he held the reins, but he'd spoken to her as if she were seven instead of seventeen.

"Why did you leave? What is wrong? Are we still going?"

His scowl was visible in the graying light. "Stop chattering, and I will tell you."

She crossed her arms and glared. Wonderful Emili had raised such an obnoxious son.

"The supply master became violently ill last night. A replacement was found, but no one informed Nehemiah or the wagon master. Having a stranger in charge of such a vital position did not go well with either of them. Or me."

Adah yawned. "Such a fuss. He is just driving a wagon. What difference does it make who drives?"

"When he loses or mishandles supplies, you will find out."

The mules lurched forward. Adah grabbed the edge of the wagon, excitement jolting her as much as the unexpected motion. There was no turning back. *God, go with me.* It was happening. She was going to Eden. She had the map. If she could find the Garden and peek inside—just one little glimpse—she'd learn its secrets.

She'd discover peace.

If she was worthy enough to enter the sacred space.

Adah eyed the road with longing and reconsidered what peace would mean. It was more than knowing no one could hurt her. It was not moving, not being jerked and jostled. Walking would be more comfortable than being flung back and forth while clinging to the hard wagon seat.

"Nathan, stop and let me walk."

"You will be in the way."

"I will stay to the side."

He darted a glance her way and shook his head. "Think, Adah. If I stop, everyone behind me stops. So, no."

"Will it be this way all four months?"

"No."

"Thank goodness."

"Worse."

Adah twisted away, pretending to look over the rolling hills. If Nathan spotted the dismay her face must show, she'd have to endure his ridicule—not that she needed or wanted his approval.

A sudden series of jolts—sharper than the ones before—clattered her teeth. The wagon lurched and tilted. Panicking, she flung her arms wide, scraping the knuckles of one hand against the rough wooden side and grabbing Nathan's arm with the other. Her side of the wagon dropped sharply, breaking her grip on Nathan and dumping her into the dirt.

Nathan lunged onto the back of the larger mule, grabbed its reins, and pulled to the left. The mules fought their harnesses, scattering small rocks and dragging the wagon sideways until it came to a stop, crammed between two boulders.

The frightened brays propelled Adah off the ground. Racing to where the mules were screaming their fear and straining to be free, their ears flat against their heads, she began to hum and then sing a low, rhythmic lullaby. Bit by bit, she moved closer until she could stroke the quivering necks and scratch the base of their ears.

"Keep singing, Adah."

Nathan undid the harness. "Twitch, Crook, come along. No one will hurt you. Come on, boys. That is right. One more step."

He coaxed the skittish mules from danger and tethered them to a tree. When he returned to the cart, he studied the damage and rubbed the back of his neck.

"A splintered sideboard is an easy fix, but this…" Squatting beside the wheel they'd lost, he frowned. "It is possible but difficult."

As other drivers approached, he pointed. "I checked this last night. It was secure."

One grizzled man bent over to peer closer. "Maybe got it too tight."

"Or not tight enough," another offered.

Nathan bristled. The scar by his eye whitened. "I know what I am doing."

"Settle yourself, boy. I am just guessing."

The grizzled driver ran his hand along the wheel. "Yes. Look here. Wood's rough-chipped, like someone hacked it without looking too close at what they were doing." He straightened. "Who is hunting you, boy? Who wants you dead?"

Adah stopped singing. Dead? No, they were safe now. Nathan had promised they'd be safe once they left Hebron.

Shaking, she wedged herself between the mules, their sturdy warmth a fortress shielding her from the world. Did Femi seek to kill Nathan for helping her or kill her to gain Omari's ring? It could be no one else. Her father and Inbar would not bother to find her, and the map was a secret.

She ran her finger against the short, stiff hair of the mule's muzzle. Well, the map was almost a secret. Imma knew—had known. Jace knew, but he was a child and far away. Emili could have dug through her bag, found it, and mentioned it to Nathan.

And she herself had told Nehemiah.

Closing her eyes, she let her memory flow back to the courtyard where they'd sat. No one else had been present unless they'd hidden in a corner's dark shadow or crouched on the balcony above the courtyard to overhear her words. A leaf had drifted down, but the breeze had sent it from on the roof.

She'd been nervous about meeting the formidable Nehemiah whose "yes" or "no" would be final. She'd become careless, used only her eyes and ears to recognize danger, ignored her other senses. She'd thoughtlessly trusted the "servant." Maybe she hadn't searched thoroughly, or grief over Jonah's death had dulled her mind.

The mule Twitch—from his frantic ear motions—stamped his hooves, demanding attention. Adah resumed singing, softer than before to avoid the attention of the drivers helping Nathan with a temporary wheel repair. When the others finally left, she sang as he hitched the mules to the cart and urged them up the incline and onto the trail.

"Adah, thank you for helping."

She gaped at him, his words unexpected. Gratitude from others? Unheard of. She did what she was told to do and what she saw was needed.

He slapped the reins to hasten the mules' pace. "I have never seen anyone calm a mule with singing."

Admiration was even more foreign. She turned away and mouthed his words over and over so they'd live in her mind

"We will catch up with the others in a bit. Meanwhile, there could be danger, since we are far behind. I need you to…"

I need you. She stopped listening, let the sparkle of those three words dance in her thoughts.

When they stopped to rest the animals through the heat of the day, she crawled into the shade beneath the wagon. Even lying motionless, her bones continued to vibrate with the jarring motion. If her body stilled, either she'd sleep or enjoy being completely still. Even her eyes were sore. They eased closed. She moaned and let her head drift to one side.

Someone tapped her shoulder.

"We have to keep moving. We are far behind the others and cannot go fast with the damaged wheel. I do not like it."

She forced her eyes open. The sun had begun its descent.

"Adah, admit it. This is too much for you."

Nathan, concerned? Over her?

"Ride with the other two women, or ask Nehemiah if you can turn back."

Turn back? She ached as if the wagon and Twitch and Crook had driven over her—as if all the wagons and mules had crossed over her—as if her bones no longer connected and she'd been sifted into fine dirt. She licked the dryness from her lips.

Crumble in defeat over sore muscles? Unlikely.

Hope had always been pried from her grasp. She'd learned to live with open hands, expecting to lose whatever she held dear, learning to cherish almost nothing—either tangible or imagined. Jonah? She closed her eyes against the pain. She should have known she'd lose him too. Absurd to have believed otherwise.

Not this time. Everything within her had latched on to this hope. It was worth the pain, worth the terror of the unknown, worth any risk. She could be broken and bleeding, but she'd persevere, dragging herself behind the wagon until he relented.

Turn back?

"No."

She crept from beneath the wagon. Dizzy, she clung to its side despite throbbing objections from every muscle. She'd survived harder things. This was just unexpected. Besides, Nathan needed her. He'd said so.

Swaying on trembling legs, she gathered her arguments and waited. He'd argue, insist she return, but she'd refuse.

CHAPTER NINE

As they rode through the night, long after the brilliant orange sunset faded to lavender, Adah wondered if she'd imagined the admiration on Nathan's face when she refused to return to Jerusalem.

She dismissed the idea when they caught up with the others and rolled into camp. A Persian guard hailed them and approached before the wagon came to a standstill. He nodded to Nathan and addressed Adah as she clambered from the wagon.

"Nehemiah requested you and the other women join him for the evening meal. Will you accompany me to his tent?"

"Now?"

"He is waiting."

Adah scolded herself for glancing at Nathan for approval.

She brushed dirt from her headdress and hid her grimy hands inside a fold of her clothes. Mouth full of dust and grit, she had to force her tongue to form the words. "I am tired and dirty from travel."

"We all are." The soldier grinned, his white teeth stark against the blackness of his curly beard. "And will be worse in another month."

She grimaced. She'd been poor all her life and a servant much of that time, but she'd been scrupulously clean. Seeing Nathan's smirk, she shrugged. "I am sure there are worse things, and the dirt will eventually be washed away."

The guard's agreeable nod bolstered her spirits. "When we are safe in my country, traveling along the Euphrates, you may bathe every day in the river. Until then, we must travel as quickly as possible."

Nathan interrupted. "Safe? You anticipate danger? Have other wagons been tampered with?"

The guard stiffened and turned his back to Nathan. "Nehemiah is waiting."

Adah followed him past more than a dozen wagons to the middle of the caravan, where a large red-and-white-striped tent had been erected, dwarfing the soldiers' tents surrounding it. Not far away, horses grazed, flicking their tales to scatter the flies.

The guard saluted his comrades at the entrance to the tent. One lifted the flap and bowed.

"You are expected. There is water for washing. Please, enter."

Two basins—one on the ground, one positioned on a waist-level pedestal—stood to the left of a curtained partition. Adah splashed water on her face and scrubbed her hands, removed her sandals to wash her feet, and shook more travel dust from her clothes before pushing aside the curtain. The smell of mule refused to wash away.

She stepped inside, into a world she'd never dreamed existed. The comforts of Omari's tent paled in comparison. Enveloped by the tent's cool interior, she paused to inhale a strong fragrance— overwhelming—but a welcome relief from Nathan's sweat and sitting near the mules' rear ends.

Taking a step forward, she tripped over the edge of a carpet so thick that any pebbles or underlying unevenness went unnoticed.

Intricate lamps cast shadows on fringed pillows lining the sides, the light glinting on golden dishes and vessels. Centered in the tent sat a table inlaid with a delicate white and black design. Adah drew into herself. Said nothing. Did nothing. Caution had served her well in the past. Until she'd had time to read faces, listen for discord, and search the shadowed corners, it was safer to be as still as a small, wild creature—unobserved if possible. Her lips parted, and her nostrils flared slightly. At times, an invisible danger could be smelled or tasted. At times—like now—the back of her neck prickled as if spiders were creeping along her hairline. A tremor ran down her back.

Nehemiah beckoned her forward. "The king's stepmother, Queen Esther, arranged my traveling accommodations. I would have been satisfied with a guard's tent." He gestured with a flourish of his hand. "When a gift is given by royalty, it is wise to accept and appreciate without protest. It pleases me to share this luxury with others."

Obediently, Adah stepped forward, studying Nehemiah's face for clues. Was he angry? Should she bow? Was she here to serve?

Nehemiah nodded toward a woman seated at the table. "Adah, meet Tavi, newly wed to the captain of the guard."

Clutching a wrinkled cloth with lace edging, the heavy-browed woman dabbed perspiration from her round face. Draped in a limp green dress with orange and pink embroidery and covered from chin to toe with drooping shawls and multiple scarves, the woman offered a wilted smile, a tentative welcome.

Adah looked closer. Was this the source of her unease? Tavi's eyes flitted to the entrance and then away. Tavi didn't want to be here. Was she unhappy about the journey to Susa, or did she have a headache? She didn't lean away from Nehemiah when he spoke. Maybe she wished to be alone with her new husband and shed layers of her too-warm clothes.

"…and this is the widow, Zahra, who joined us only two days ago. You met at Aaron's house."

Every alarm in Adah's body sounded, thundering up her spine, jolting into her fingers. Here was the danger.

The painfully thin woman offered no greeting, her expression cordial as a viper's. Dark olive skin stretched across a face too narrow for its bones, her eyes set deep above the cliff of her cheekbones. "Adah."

It was a judgment. A warning.

Always before, she'd liked her name.

"You are late. Again."

Adah's gaze darted between Nehemiah and Zahra. Averting her eyes or dipping her head would break focus on the danger and gave advantage to the adversary.

Nehemiah's faint smile did not reach his eyes. "Adah had quite a day and is not at fault for her lateness. The wagon she rode on lost a wheel. Had it not been for the driver's skill and her quick thinking in comforting the frightened beasts, we'd be waiting much longer or lamenting a loss."

The note of censure in his voice seemed lost on Zahra.

He glanced around the tent. "During the day, you may ride with whomever you wish. At night, you three will share a tent next to mine. It is safest and will be well-guarded."

Sleep with a serpent loose? Adah began to protest. Zahra was quicker.

"Sleep between a filthy peasant and a Persian who reeks of cheap perfume? No. How dare you ignore the Law of Moses? We are forbidden to share a room or a meal with a Gentile."

This time, though Nehemiah's voice remained mild, there was no hint of a smile, no opening for argument.

"First, it is neither a request nor a suggestion. It is as I say." A subtle shift in his shoulders revealed he'd not tolerate their resistance.

"Secondly, we are each Jews by birth or choice. Tavi, daughter of a priest, graciously adorns herself in Persian garb to please her Persian-born Jewish husband." His eyes narrowed as he regarded Zahra. "You, I recall, are Mizraim by birth, Jewish by choice."

Zahra crossed her arms, her face a mask of smoldering rage.

Nehemiah's piercing gaze targeted Zahra. "Do you still have concerns?"

"No. Forgive me. I am tired. I spoke without thinking." Tight words emerged from her clenched jaws.

But her neck held its tension, and no remorse flickered across her face. Zahra may have spoken without thinking, but she did not regret her words. Nehemiah's short nod said he knew it as well.

He cleared his throat. "The other rule all will follow is keeping the Sabbath holy. We will not travel that day. Those who wish may meet with me for teachings on the Almighty's law."

Adah's quick intake of breath did not go unnoticed. She squirmed when his dark eyes rested on her. "Sabbath is in four days. For now, I invite you to join me for a meal so that we may thank the Lord for His provision and break bread together."

Adah smiled her gratitude to the servant who placed the food before her. When he thought no one was watching, the servant broke off a huge piece of bread and shoved it in his mouth. He wiped his fingers on the sash below his paunch.

Seeing her watch the servant, Nehemiah tipped his head toward the man and shook his head with an amused smile. Adah admired him for not berating the man before the others.

Adah took tiny bites, chewing as quietly as possible. Did her swallow sound as loud to others as it did to her?

The meal complete, Nehemiah stood. "It is time to retire for the evening. Your belongings have been placed in your tents."

Adah gasped, and chills crawled over her skin. She'd walked away from everything she'd owned without a thought. The map, her coins, the earrings from Emili—all could have been stolen. She grasped Omari's ring through her tunic. It could be all she had left. She rose quickly and sped to the tent's entrance behind the other two women.

"Adah, remain with me for a moment."

Zahra looked over her shoulder with a sneer. "Already being a problem, Adah?"

"Zahra." Nehemiah's voice held a warning.

Beyond the silence of the tent, Adah heard voices murmuring, a clang of metal against metal, and the occasional whiffling from the horses. Inside, as the quietness smothered, her heart raced. Had she taken a misstep? Misunderstood her position here?

She readied herself for his reproval. Mouth dry, wondering how she'd offended. Nehemiah's voice broke into her fear.

"Adah, your eyes lit up when I spoke of teaching Adonai's law."

"I am sorry. Please forgive me. It is just that I do not know much—"

"Adah, it pleased me."

"It did?" Her voice wobbled, ending in a squeak, its feebleness annoying her.

"Indeed. Too often, our people do not crave this knowledge." He pinched the bridge of his nose. "There are many things beyond understanding, but this, most of all, confounds my comprehension. Adah, you have made my heart glad."

A bud of joy unfurled inside of her. The warmth of praise curled her lips upward.

"If you would like, I will teach you truths of the God of heaven each evening throughout the week, not just on Sabbath."

"Yes!" She blurted the word then caught herself. "If you have time and it is not too much trouble."

Nehemiah's eyes moistened. "To teach of Him is my greatest honor. We start tomorrow."

Outwardly, Adah walked sedately behind the guard to her sleeping tent. Inwardly, she danced and twirled. To be taught the truths of Adonai was a dream beyond a dream—one she hadn't known she craved until it was offered.

She'd memorized every word of Imma's stories, and during the two years in Inbar's service, had strained to hear and understand the rabbi's readings and teachings. But it was Emili who lived in peace. Emili promised the Lord knew her. The thought intrigued Adah, left her wanting to know if it was true.

If she could learn everything there was to know about the Lord and determine how to please Him, she'd convince Him to allow her to enter—just one step would suffice—the Garden of Eden and she'd learn the secret of peace.

"Thank You, God." There. She'd spoken to Him as Emili did.

Smiling, she slipped into the tent and gasped. Zahra's hand was in the bag Aaron had gifted her for the journey.

"What are you doing?"

Zahra slanted her eyes upward. "Unpacking my things."

"Those are my things."

"Oh. Our bags are so similar. My mistake." She shrugged. "Sorry."

Adah eyed the bags. Her bag was a rich brown, and though similar in shape and size, Zahra's was a pale gold.

Zahra smirked. "Better see if you are missing anything."

Adah snatched her bag from Zahra's grasp. She'd empty it, check the contents, and wrest her belongings from the snake-eyed woman before she could claim ignorance. She stopped. If Zahra had taken anything, she'd be hiding it. This was a trick to discover what the bag held.

She ducked her head and masked her face. When she looked up, she spoke with deference honed over years of being a submissive daughter and servant. No one could tell the words came through gritted teeth. "How could I mistrust you, Zahra? My betrothed's uncle trusted you in his home, and Nehemiah is allowing you to journey with him."

Adah exhaled a long sigh. "I cannot fool you. You know I am nothing but a poor peasant. How could I have anything of value?"

She yawned. "We are all tired. It was an honest mistake. Please forgive my harsh tone."

The corner of Zahra's eye twitched. Adah smiled inwardly with satisfaction. Now she knew better how to read this woman as well as how to confuse her with an unexpected response.

Adah glanced at Tavi, who lay on her pallet. Tavi met her gaze and nodded infinitesimally before giving a smile and a slow wink. Without a word, she rolled away from the other two women and pulled up a blanket. Could she and Tavi become friends?

Adah placed her pack beneath her head ostentatiously as a pillow. Always a stomach sleeper, she wrapped her arms through the bag's straps, making sure the opening faced down. Accessing the bag while she lay on it would require a stealth few possessed—and she was a light sleeper.

Zahra stretched out her long frame, her feet dangling over the pallet's end. No matter. Seldom was a bed's length sufficient for her. She arched her back and smiled languidly. Today was only the beginning of the journey, and already she had rattled Adah.

Remembering Femi's admonishment to kill Adah or befriend Adah, she snorted. Befriend her? Not a chance. Kill her? Maybe later. Annoy her, unnerve her, break her—oh, yes—the pleasure would be hers.

That mule-scented peasant, Adah, had caused the death of two who had been dear to her. And Adah had the ring—the only inheritance worth a fight. Femi was as delusional as Donkor had been if he believed she'd hand it over. It was hers—promised to her from childhood. It held the memory of being loved and cherished.

Adah must have hidden it securely—either in that bag she clutched or on her person. Zahra rolled to face Adah's pallet and bore her hatred into Adah's body. Adah moved restlessly. Zahra smiled.

CHAPTER TEN

The next morning, Adah woke to the bustle of the camp as it prepared to begin the day's journey in the dark. She knew from her own trips the advantage of traveling in the predawn coolness— before the bugs emerged, before the heat drained her energy, before she was seen and followed.

Stiff from yesterday's fall and jolting ride, she tucked her chin to her chest and rotated her head from side to side, feeling the pull down her spine. She stretched her arms, and the kinks in her shoulders began to loosen. She wiggled her toes, grateful at least one part of her body didn't hurt. Four months of this? She groaned then remembered today's promise and wrapped her arms around herself in a hug. Tonight, Nehemiah would begin teaching her how to please the Lord and enter the Garden.

She folded her pallet, slung her bag over her shoulder, and, after sharing a smile with Tavi, began the trek to the back of the line. Having arrived last, Nathan's wagon was farthest away.

He scowled at her approach. "You, again? I thought you would ride with the other women. Hoped so too."

She batted her eyes. "And miss annoying you? Not a chance."

They pulled the mules into line, climbed aboard the wagon, and set off as the morning's somber gray lightened. Streaks of light shot through a scattering of clouds, turning the sky a pale pink.

"Know what that means?" Nathan gestured to the sunrise.

"Daytime?"

"It means that no matter how many Babylonians or Assyrians come against us, no matter how often we are enslaved or exiled, we are still Adonai's people, and He will bless us and restore us as a nation. No matter how many times we as a people fail and are judged, He will keep His promises to us."

Adah stared at him. "All that from a sunrise?"

Nathan clicked to Twitch and Crook. "All that. My imma taught me it is important to look for the Lord's hand in everything."

"Even in the dust?"

"Reminds me He's everywhere, like this never-ending dust."

She swiped her tongue over her dust-filmed teeth. "That is an unfortunate comparison. What about flies?"

He chuckled. "God is persistent and inescapable." Nathan steered the mules to one side as a group of travelers came alongside them from behind. One turned, glanced back at them, and then sped forward.

"Adah, turn your head or lower your chin when others are on the road."

Heart thumping, she squinted, trying to see through the caravan's dust clouds to the group ahead. "We are being followed?"

"We are being careful. We are only one day from Jerusalem and close to Jericho. It is better if you are not noticed."

She could be careful. She could make herself almost invisible. People were always forgetting she was there, watching and listening.

Watching Nathan switch the reins from one callused hand to the other and wipe a bead of sweat from his forehead, she decided he'd never be invisible. There was something different about him—something solid. She bit her lower lip, searching for the right words. It couldn't be physical. He wasn't a powerfully thick-muscled man like Jonah had been.

Had been.

She sucked in a breath as the grief of those two innocuous words swept over her, drenching her in the memory of all those who "had been." Words wielded such power. Even she, who "had been" a beloved and betrothed woman, was no more. She counted each precious one lost to death or her father's greed, conjuring the image of their smile or the sound of their laughter. So many in her seventeen years lived only in her memory. Bowing her head, she mourned each loss.

Sly grief—layering sorrow upon hurt and what-if upon regret—inexorably diminishing, controlling, defining her as—

No. She raised her chin.

Resolutely, she rolled back her curved shoulders. She would find the Garden and live in serenity instead of sorrow. Sorrow may be unavoidable for now, but it would not define her like it had Imma.

"Not me!"

She'd spoken out loud, considering the look Nathan shot her.

"Not me. I—I do not want to be seen." She searched for something to say. "Nathan, your imma told you the stories of our people, yes?"

"Yes."

"What did she tell you of the Garden of Eden?"

Seeing his sideways glance, she hurried to explain. "Of course I know about it, but my imma was sick so often she might have left something out. For instance, once, I heard there was a map—"

"Drawn by Eve's daughter and showing flaming swords? Yes, I have heard of a map, but Adah, even if that is true, it has been lost for centuries—probably during the Great Flood."

"What if it was not lost?"

"It is still useless. The flood changed the face of the land. Maybe a few rocks didn't move, or a mountain range or even a river, but tracing the map to Eden would be almost impossible."

"Almost, but not completely."

Nathan leveled his gaze on her. "Adah, what is this about?" His eyes narrowed. "Is this why you want to go to Susa? Do you think you have the original map?"

"Nathan! What an idea! It is a four-month journey. We have to talk about something. I am playing the what-if game. Didn't you ever play that? No? What did you do as a child?"

"I went to synagogue. Learned to read and write. Worked as an apprentice to a wagon builder and helped Imma. Why are you intent on going to Susa?"

"You can read?" The man was persistent. She'd been too obvious with her questions.

"Adah, diverting me does not work."

She stared into the distance, sighed, and started to speak. Then she dabbed her eyes, pretending to wipe away a tear.

"Nathan, I have something dearer to me than any old map. But I cannot read it."

"I will read it for you."

"It is written to me. I do not really know if I can trust you. You might laugh or lie."

His lips tightened.

Adah braced for the scathing denial that would cause him to forget everything else she'd said. Nathan looked straight ahead, silent. Puzzled, she waited for his reaction. She'd never known anyone who would not take offense at such an accusation.

The sun rose to mid-sky before he spoke.

"How can I help you, Adah?"

His question baffled her. There'd been no sarcasm, no rancor—grace instead of offense.

She twisted on the wagon seat and scrutinized him. His hands held the reins lightly. His shoulders remained relaxed, and no lines marred his forehead or strained his neck. He glanced at her, his eyes clear and calm.

Peace ran deep in this man. Where had he found it? She didn't know peace, but, oddly, she recognized it in him. She wanted to blurt out the truth about her map and ask if he'd already found the Garden of Eden, that place of peace and safety. He spoke as if he'd been there, as if he lived there, protected from bitterness and the need to avenge.

But he didn't live there. He was here, beside her in this rattling old wagon, and he possessed what she wanted. Pressing her fingers to her temples, she tried to understand, to grasp what eluded her. His imma had been the same way, as if life's ugliness may have scarred her but could not destroy her.

Adah crossed her arms. Well, she was strong too. Life had not crushed her, though Nathan's and Emili's seemed a different sort of strength. She tapped her fingers against her arm. They knew something she didn't know. How to understand God? The secrets of Eden?

He had offered to help. Maybe she could describe the map's symbols and ask him what they meant.

Delighted with her plan, she could not suppress a wiggle of joy. When they stopped in the hottest part of the day to rest, she would pull out the map and memorize the markings. There might be secret signs she needed to watch for along the way.

Nathan flicked the reins as one of the mules slowed. "Come on, Crook. That is right. Keep going. The faster you walk, the faster you will be past it."

"Twitch's name, I understand, but Crook?"

"Crooked ear. Crook."

"Why is he balking?"

Nathan pointed to a crumble of stones that might once have been walls. "Over there is Jericho. Babylonians decimated it more than a hundred years ago. Animals still sense the death and destruction. It makes them uneasy."

Despite the sunlight blanketing the rubble, Adah shuddered at its ancient desolation, its unredeemed darkness. Here, no life eked out an existence. No birds claimed residence, and not even the wind acknowledged Jericho's presence.

Dead Jericho—so different from Jerusalem, teeming with life. Her uncertainty—so different from Nathan's peace. Adah wiped perspiration from her forehead, wishing she could as easily wipe away the comparison.

Adah scanned the wagons parked in front of them. Nothing moved except the shimmer of heat. Nathan lay near the mules with his back to her. Under the wagon's shade, she rummaged through her pack until her fingertips touched silk. Emili's smile flashed through her mind. The dear woman had looked so pleased when she chose the colorful scarf for Adah's disguise.

After removing the packet, she brushed bits of gravel and debris from the dirt, covered the tiny clearing with the silk, and unfolded the map, careful to place Imma's things to one side where they'd not be misplaced. Of little worth to others but precious to her.

She smoothed the map open. Sweat beaded on her upper lip. Using her headdress, she wiped it away. This crinkled leather needed no more spots or splotches. She rubbed a finger over a cluster of dots near the top, discovering they were not dots but holes. Insects had bored their tiny tunnels through the leather, each a perfect circle. Gently tracing each mark, even the blob of a squished spider, she pored over the shapes and scribbles then closed her eyes to mentally recreate them.

Confident she'd memorized each section, she dabbed dampness from her forehead again and closed her eyes to picture the map in its entirety. A kink in her neck protested the odd angle she'd lain in while studying the map. She lowered her head to her arms, and the pain eased. Images of the map blurred, but her eyes refused to open, refused…

"Adah." A hand shook her shoulder. "Wake up."

Startled, she pushed upward, her head colliding with the underside of the wagon. The map! Instinctively, she curled herself protectively around it.

"I am awake. Go away."

After a long pause, the crunch of gravel confirmed that Nathan had left. Hastily, she slid her imma's gifts onto the map and folded it, wrapped it in the silk, and shoved it to the bottom of her bag. She crawled out into the sunshine and squinted at Nathan. How much had he seen? She gnawed her lower lip. Was it better to assume he'd noticed the map, or not?

He ignored her gaze, adjusting the harness on each mule, scratching their muzzles and talking to them in low tones. Adah crammed her bag as far under the seat as possible. If the bag was out of sight, maybe he would forget whatever he saw. Maybe he had not seen the map. Maybe. She rolled her eyes at the absurdity of her thoughts.

He knew something. She read it in the extra space he kept between them on the wagon bench, the rigidity of his arms and his head angled away from her. Sometimes she wished she could live in ignorance and not see people's signals. Today, she wanted to speak truth to Nathan but not answer his questions.

Somehow, it did not sound right when she thought it through. *Yes, Nathan, the insults were to distract you because you understood too much. I have the true map to Eden, so your guess about my reason for traveling to Susa was correct. However, I do not trust you or anyone, actually, so you will never see the map.*

"Nathan?" Unsure what to say next, she stopped.

"Yes?"

"Um. The mules like you."

The look he gave her was unsettling. The ride to the night camp was quiet.

CHAPTER ELEVEN

Adah wrapped both arms around her bag as she left Nathan and trudged past the other wagons to the sleeping tent. She washed in the water provided and ate bread and cheese before hurrying over to wait outside Nehemiah's tent.

Officers bustled in and out. Servants, guards, drivers—a steady stream of people needing to speak with him or report to him. Such an important man would never remember his promise to her—an ignorant peasant girl who had begged her way into being allowed on the journey.

As she turned to leave, Nehemiah emerged from his tent and looked at her questioningly.

"You have changed your mind, Adah? Are you too tired from the day's travels?"

She scuffed her toe in the dirt, uneasy but unable to look away from his regard. "No. I—I was afraid you had forgotten or would be too busy."

His steely gaze pierced her uncertainty. "I gave my word to you."

Her tension ebbed. Neither anger nor annoyance weighted his voice. So far, this man was safe. She bobbed her head. "I will not question you again."

Together they walked to a large campfire. "Others may decide to join us." He gestured to a low bench. "This time, your feet will touch the ground."

She grinned at his reference to their first meeting and settled herself to listen.

"Adah, to know the God of heaven, you must do three things."

Only three? Easy. She'd know all about Him before the week was over.

"First, understand He is pleased when you talk to Him. Then you must listen to Him. This talking and listening is called prayer. You cannot do all the talking. Remember to listen. Then you must learn to obey."

She wrinkled her brow.

"Let me show you." He closed his eyes and lowered his head.

Adah sensed his focus shift, and stillness encircled him. She watched from half-closed eyes, uncertain what she should do.

"Blessed are You, Lord our God, Ruler of the Universe. O Lord, let Your ear be attentive to the prayer of this Your servant who delights in revering Your name."

He looked up.

"Those exact words, Nehemiah?"

"It is not the words that are most important. It is your attitude. The prayer comes from realizing the privilege of speaking to the Almighty, the Creator of all, the God of the heavens. He is worthy of your praise, and you are humbly asking Him to hear you."

"And then He says...what?"

The lines around Nehemiah's eyes crinkled, but it felt like a warm hug—not shaming as if he was laughing at her. "Adah, this time of teaching you is going to be the part of the day I most enjoy."

At the end of their lesson, she smiled all the way to the entrance of her sleeping tent. Zahra was not there, but Tavi greeted her with a nod and patted the side of the pallet—an invitation to sit and talk. Adah left the bag on her pallet and sat cross-legged beside her.

"Tavi, Nehemiah said you are newly wed. How terrible to be separated from your husband so early in your marriage."

"My abba—the priest who married us—advised me to wait, but I did not listen once it was known a caravan would travel to Susa so soon." Tavi's cheeks rounded with pink stain. "I mean, my husband, Dror, did not want to delay—rather, he could not because of his position as captain of Nehemiah's guard." Her mouth drooped. "Actually, my sister is ill. I wanted her to be part of the wedding."

Adah frowned, trying to pinpoint what bothered her about the muddled explanation. Maybe she'd missed something. She was tired from the long day with Nathan.

Tavi stretched her neck forward, her eyes bright and curious. "Tell me about you. Where are you from? Why do you travel alone? Are you going to your betrothed?"

Uneasy with being questioned, Adah pulled back. Tavi gave no sign of noticing the subtle recoil.

"He died."

Died. The word echoed through her mind. *Died.* It was the first time she'd spoken that hard, harsh truth. An image flashed through her mind of a dagger protruding from Jonah's back.

She closed her eyes and pushed her fingertips against each eyelid, attempting to press away the memory. Lowering her hands, she saw Tavi's wide eyes, her plump ringed fingers covering her mouth.

"Adah, I am so sorry. I did not know that part."

That part? "Of course not. Few do." Adah counted her fingers and the colors of Tavi's scarves to turn her mind from the horror and erase Jonah's pale face.

"Do you want to tell me about it? I will listen. Are you going to Susa to be with your family so they can comfort you in your grief?"

"No. My imma is dead. They are both dead." *Or dead to me.* "I am trying to fulfill a dream for my imma."

"A dream? In Susa?"

"Forgive me, Tavi. My head hurts, and I am so tired. It is a recent loss, and I—I cannot talk about it right now." *Or ever.*

The next morning, Adah clutched the bag against her chest—a shield—as she dragged her feet to Nathan's wagon. Tavi might have offered a ride in her covered wagon if Adah had shown more interest in sharing bits of her life. Adah kicked a pebble from her path. She had said too much, opened herself up to more questions.

A headache—though true last night—would only work so many times before it was seen as a lie. She'd learned to be suspicious when her father regularly vowed he'd lost coins or was owed payment or had paid more than he'd expected. He, the thief, cried robbery. Was she becoming like him?

Head down, she reached the last wagon and stepped on the wheel to climb in. She darted a look at Nathan to judge his mood. Except the balding man laughing down at her was not Nathan.

"You missed your ride." He pointed back the way she'd come. "Go back six."

She pivoted and saw Nathan standing on his wagon, looking back at her. "I thought…"

"It is safer. Your mule's lead was cut last night. We are going to see if it is you or the last wagon someone's after—thieves trying to pick off one wagon at a time."

He spat over the opposite side of the wagon. "Probably you. Go on, now. Hurry. He is waiting. We all are."

Adah hurried forward. Nathan jumped on board, and though he avoided her eyes, he offered a hand to pull her up.

"Ready? Jericho is downhill from Jerusalem. Secure your things well."

She nestled the bag between her feet. "Nathan, are Twitch and Crook hurt? That man said there has been more damage."

"No, but with this descent, they would have been dead by mid-morning if the frayed rein had been overlooked."

"Do you think it is directed at us?"

"I suspect so. Adah, maybe you should tell me the whole story. I know Jonah rescued you from someone and then he was killed, but why did you need rescuing? Imma said you were too upset to explain much, and she did not want to press you when you mentioned a ring and coins and a map."

Map. The word lay coiled, pulsing with life. And the threat of death.

She closed her eyes against memories of the starlit sky, of leaning against Babu's solid warmth, of the camp's muffled sounds before the night erupted into chaos. Outraged screams, flailing hooves, blood, and her heart pumping so fast she thought it would burst as they raced to the city of refuge—and Jonah's death.

She swallowed to clear her throat. "Omari gave me a ring. His son, Donkor, Femi's twin brother, tried to take it from me, but Jonah interceded and they fought. When Donkor fell against a rock and his head began bleeding, Omari told us to run. We ran, and Femi threw the dagger."

"Just like that?"

She heard the skepticism but managed one tight nod.

They rode in silence. From his sideways glances, Adah knew he was studying her, granting her time to recover from the memories she had shared. How could someone be so annoying and also be so kind?

Exhaling slowly, she considered the map—what to say, whether to show him, or lie and say it was just a scribbling her little brother had drawn. It looked like scribbling to her except for the insect holes. Maybe Jace had poked the leather with their imma's bone needle. If Nathan knew of the map and realized what she wanted to do, would he help her or try to convince her it was not real?

"Nathan—"

"Adah—"

Their gazes met as they spoke simultaneously. Bubbles of laughter eased the tension.

She tried again. "Nathan—"

The laughter disappeared. He held up a hand to quiet her. Facing straight ahead, he spoke as if he'd recited his words. "Me first.

I already know about the map and that it is a secret. Obviously, you are going to the land between the rivers, so I have an idea of what you are searching for. Whatever else you decide to tell me remains between us, but do not lie to me again." The steel in his voice reminded her of Nehemiah's eyes.

Adah sat silently, mulling his words, her thoughts shunting back and forth with the wagon's jarring motion. She'd be bruised inside and out by the time this journey ended and probably a madwoman as well.

She worried her lower lip. What to do about the map was the real problem. Hide it, or ask for help?

Indecision curled her shoulders forward. Whatever certainty she'd once held about the integrity of people had been lost in the folds of time. Truth was overlayed with deception. Hope, creased with grief. Trust, trod unnoticed into the mud.

She no longer knew herself. She, the keeper of secrets, had revealed her own—three times now—to Emili and Nehemiah and Nathan. She, who'd scrubbed the filthiest of clothes and hauled dung for fuel, was a student of Jerusalem's governor. Her tunics equaled Zahra's. Her stomach no longer growled through the night.

It was disconcerting. If shadowed corners and the skills she'd honed to survive—the silence, the watching, the listening—no longer defined her, what did?

Choice!

She'd chosen to be different. She'd claimed the courage to walk into the unknown, to speak as an equal to others, to search for what she wanted.

She belonged only to herself. The decision to follow the map was hers alone.

She angled herself to study Nathan, seeking out a sign of deception or greed or darkness. He turned his head and looked her in the eyes. There was curiosity, nothing else. His strong brown hands held the reins lightly, and she remembered him talking quietly to the mules and giving their muzzles long, gentle scratches.

"Nathan, I am afraid. I want to trust you, but I hardly know you, and I usually do not like you." She covered her mouth. "That was not what I meant to say."

He flashed a grin. "I appreciate your honesty and think the same about you." He swatted a fly. "Adah, do not tell me anything you are uncomfortable with me knowing. We are strangers, and this map is important to you." He raised both eyebrows and flattened his lips. "No matter what I think of it."

"What does that mean?"

"This map you have. How old do you think it is?"

She shrugged. "Old."

"Leather wears out—brittles—in about a hundred years. Either your map is not very old, or it has been replaced every hundred years or so for thousands of years. Thousands! Do you think it is still accurate?"

"Yes." She snapped the word. The map had to be accurate, even with the spider splotch and the insect holes.

"Assuming you are right, do you know how to read a map?"

"I could learn to read."

"You could. But it will not help. Writing had not been developed back then. Whatever markings are on the map are not words."

Her stomach plummeted.

"One more question, Adah. Where does the map end?"

She flicked a stray hair away. "That does not matter. I am going where it all began."

"Adah—"

He stopped and turned his head away, but his shoulders were shaking, and she realized he was laughing at her. She really didn't like him at all, and she'd never show him her map. How had she ever considered it?

"Adah." It sounded like he was trying to suppress another burst of laughter. "Where will you start following the map to reach the beginning?"

"At the... Oh."

She ignored his cough-disguised laugh in order to picture the left side of the map, the first hint—a rock or an enormous wave beginning to curl over a river. She searched the rock walls on each side of her. There was no river in sight.

Had they passed it? Was it months away? If she dozed during the day, or they traveled while it was too dark to see, she'd miss it, lose information. She could be traveling forever and not find it. How many roads were there in Judah? When should she begin searching?

It was hopeless. She shrank into herself. How foolish she must seem to Nathan and also Nehemiah, who'd likely guessed "the place" she'd mentioned. Heat ran up her neck and into her face. Her father was probably right. That worn, cracked leather was nothing but a fraud.

"Adah. Look at me." Nathan spoke softly, his voice barely audible over the wagon's wheels.

She braced herself for more derision and shied when he touched her arm. "Do not touch me."

"Please. Look at me."

She obeyed and didn't. She stared at the narrow lines between his eyes—a trick she'd learned whenever her abba demanded her attention so she'd not see the threat or disgust in his eyes and he'd not see the fear and anger in hers.

"Adah. I was unkind. Forgive me?"

She looked straight ahead, body stiff, hands folded in her lap.

"You can look away, but listen to me." He ran a hand across his face. "I shared this once before and thought to never speak of it again, but I think you need to hear it. When I was a child, all my friends had an abba. Everyone except me. I would pretend a friend's abba was mine too and watch the way he squeezed his son's shoulder or taught him to clean a fish. The other men were good to me, included me in games and long talks, but at night I went home alone. The abbas and sons went home together, ate together, kept the Sabbath together. Every night, I would fall asleep dreaming I was the beloved son—my shoulder patted, my hand guided to scale a catch."

She understood—more than she wished, more than he would ever know. So many times, she had stood in the shadows beyond Jonah's house and envied his sisters giggling with their abba, sharing stories or running to him for comfort over a scraped elbow or imagined bruise.

"Why are you telling me this, Nathan?" She kept her voice distant, cold.

"Because I know what it is to hold tightly to the impossible, to have a dream dismissed."

"Your wish stayed impossible."

"True, but it was mine to have and mine to release. It did not deserve mockery, nor did yours deserve my ridicule."

She felt her heart soften a little at the remorse in his voice.

"Can I ask something, Adah?"

Such as, what is wrong with you or why are you holding onto the impossible? She shrugged one shoulder. He could ask whatever he wanted to. It didn't mean she'd answer.

"What makes the map so important to you? This is a hard trip, and you endure it for the sake of that map. Why?"

She blinked at the unexpected question and lowered her eyes, pretending to study her fingers. Of course the map was important because of its giver and because Imma had chosen her to keep the family treasure. She had never admitted—even to herself—the satisfaction in knowing it would anger her father when he discovered it was missing.

But precious though the gift was, she knew it was not the reason she began the search. It was leaning her head against Imma's knee and listening to her stories about Adonai and their people. It was Imma's conviction that the worn leather map revealed the path to peace and safety, a way to return to the Garden of Eden, to exquisite beauty and abundance beyond imagination. Eden was the place where she would never be hungry again, never again be discarded or shamed. The map held reasons to sacrifice everything. It held hope and made belief possible.

In losing Jonah, she had lost her hope as well as her refuge, her future. Peace, she'd never had, so she hadn't lost that. She had opened the map when she was frightened and alone and struggling to find a direction, a purpose, a truth—something to hold on to that was hers alone and could never be taken from her. The map had been her answer. That cracked piece of folded leather held her heart's desire—the promise of safety and worth and healing.

Adah burrowed deeper, probing until all the hurt and fear she'd hidden or denied lay naked, writhing in raw agony. Gasping for breath, she recoiled and scraped darkness back over the wounds. Someday she'd face them, but not here, not now.

"Adah? The map? Why is it so important to you?"

She'd forgotten Nathan was sitting beside her, waiting for an answer.

"Because I want to believe in the impossible."

"That Eden can be found? Is that what you mean?"

Adah shook her head. "It is more than that. I want to know safety and peace and God's truth." *And that I matter.*

CHAPTER TWELVE

That evening, Adah rounded the corner and halted at the sight of a small crowd milling outside Nehemiah's tent. Zahra stood as tall as the guards, who admitted one person at a time. Waiting beside her was a man, his shoulders severely hunched, and dressed completely in black from his turban to his sandals. Evidently, Zahra and the elderly man were next. Zahra glanced to each side before ducking to enter the tent. For the last week, she'd avoided the woman except for the tense moments each night. Not wanting Zahra to see her but eager for her lesson about God, Adah backed away. Looking around, she considered the possibilities of where to hide until Zahra left.

A dark corner? No, depending on how long Zahra's meeting lasted, shadows would change under the shifting sun. Near the animals? Someone would lead the mules away, and she'd have no explanation for standing between them. She settled on kneeling behind the bundles of sacks and baggage piled haphazardly against a wagon. In case someone questioned her, having lost something was a good reason for crouching low to the ground.

She tugged her headdress across her chin and nose and forward to almost cover her eyes. She tucked her hands beneath her knees and her hem over her feet. No skin showed except through a slit for her eyes. She was sticky, hot, and miserable and needed to sneeze.

She didn't need to hide for long. Zahra and the old man emerged from Nehemiah's tent and, without a glance in her direction, walked past her, leaving a waft of cardamom in their wake. Zahra smiled at her companion—a triumphant smirk Adah knew would follow her into sleep and lurk in her dreams.

The tingling of her cramped legs convinced Adah it was safe to stand and approach the line to enter Nehemiah's tent. She was almost next when his servant hurried out.

"Adah, there you are. Our Nehemiah offers his great regret that tonight he cannot meet with you." He adjusted the sash under his paunch. "He seemed quite sad about it."

"Is he ill? Why are all these people waiting to see him? What has happened?"

The servant raised an eyebrow in disbelief. "You have not heard? A damaged wagon, frayed reins, and two wagon masters gone. May the good Lord help us. We should be praying for mercy as our Nehemiah does. The driver of the supply wagon disappeared and has just been found dead. The first driver—in Jerusalem—was taken violently ill, but this one is dead. That is much worse."

Raising both hands above his shoulders he swayed to and fro. "Woe! Woe!"

"Dead?"

"Murdered? Smitten by the Almighty for blasphemy? Who knows? Guards are questioning everyone who might have information as well as searching for a new driver."

He peered at her. "Our Nehemiah does not like chaos, only order and routine. Routine and order." A quick breath, and he continued. "The Persians refuse to ride behind a mule—they think it is demeaning.

But there is no one else to drive, so our Nehemiah has been forced to hire an unknown driver—a friend of your friend, Zahra."

Adah's stomach flipped. Not her friend.

"I am confused. We are not near a town, are we? The new driver was part of the caravan?"

"That is the amazing part. He was traveling to Jerusalem and stopped to speak with his cousin Zahra—or friend—or friend's friend. So many details I forget these days. He arrived just when the driver's death was discovered. I understand she had known him long ago and vouched for his skills. He did not say much. Excuse me, I am being summoned. Rest well."

Rest well? After seeing Zahra's chilling smile, and knowing her cousin or friend was to drive the supply wagon? Nathan said it was the most important wagon in the caravan.

That evening, Adah laced her arms through her satchel's straps and held it close throughout the night, throughout a brittle sleep broken by images of Zahra's smirk. She woke to Zahra's soft humming. Unnerved, she clutched her satchel closer.

Nathan frowned. "You look grumpy and act grumpy. What is wrong? Still angry with me about yesterday? I said I was sorry."

She stared at him blankly. Why would she be angry with him about Zahra and the new driver? "Yesterday?"

"Asking you about the map."

"No. Well, yes, maybe. But no, I am... Nathan, did you hear about the supply wagon driver? The dead one?"

Grim-faced, he nodded. "It is strange—two replaced in just over a week. Nehemiah was upset about the first one. He must be raging. Our leader has a bit of a temper, I have heard. They hired a new driver. I wonder how long he will last. Are you worried?"

"No. Yes."

"Adah! Make up your mind before you speak."

She humphed. Glaring demanded too much effort. "Someone Zahra knows was hired."

"So?"

"She hates me."

"And?"

She summoned the strength to glare.

"Adah, you are being ridiculous. Think. Even if she does hate you, that has nothing to do with who drives a wagon."

She gazed at the side of the path as they rode past. Pale dust covered the smattering of flowers straggling alongside the well-worn road. "Something is wrong, Nathan. I cannot explain it, and I cannot tell you what it is, but there is something not right." She clenched her fists. "Maybe it has nothing to do with Zahra or the driver. Maybe it came in a dream or I overheard someone answer without answering—"

"Answer without answering?"

"It is when someone ignores the question or refuses to comment or distracts the other person instead of giving an answer."

Nathan nodded. "Go on."

Living with her father, avoiding Zeb, her older brother, and serving Inbar's family had sharpened the skills the Lord gave her. She'd learned to use the information she gathered to protect herself—until she'd begun to trust Omari and lowered her guard. She bit the inside of her lip. What was she thinking, to trust Nathan?

She studied him out of the side of her eyes. He wasn't laughing and seemed to be listening intently.

"Adah."

She braced herself. He'd argue. He'd snicker. He'd tell her she was imagining things like a child invents stories. He'd share what she'd said until everyone laughed at her.

Nathan smiled. "You remind me of my imma. She looks and listens too."

Nathan wasn't so bad after all, and when he smiled, she wanted to smile back at him.

"I am not sure about the new driver, but I agree. Something is not right, unless a big rat gnawed the wheel connector and Twitch chewed a leather strap under his belly."

The hair on his arms glinted red in the sun. His scent was warm and fresh—so different from Jonah's earthiness or the sweet spice the Mizraites had worn.

"This Zahra who hates you—have I seen her?"

"She escorted me to Aaron to tell him of Jonah's death. She is taller than a lot of men and wears heavy eye makeup. Nehemiah said she is Jewish by choice."

"Why does she hate you?"

Adah grimaced. "I do not know. She knocked. I opened the door, and she stood there hating me."

"Do you often have that effect on others?"

He laughed. She didn't.

"My father, brother, Inbar, Femi, and Donkor. Mostly everyone—a few exceptions."

Nathan sobered. "Why?"

"I notice little things—a set jaw, a change in a voice, narrowed eyes. People reveal what they are feeling if you watch and listen."

"But not Zahra."

"Yet."

Nathan rubbed the back of his neck. "I have a question for you, Adah."

"What do you do with what you see and hear—the things you notice?"

She relaxed. That was easy to answer. "Survive."

"That is all?"

"What else could I do? People's secrets are safe with me. I do not use what I know to hurt anyone, just to protect myself."

Nathan's silence bothered her. He clicked to the mules, checked the sun's position, and said nothing else.

The man knew she was waiting for him to say more. She delayed until the suspense was more annoying than the man. "Nathan?"

"My imma once told me that Adonai's gifts—like being very observant or good at explaining or knowing which herbs heal—are given to be shared, used to help others."

Adah shook her head, baffled. "How? Sometimes I cannot explain even to myself exactly what I saw someone do."

"Think on it—how you can share your gift."

CHAPTER THIRTEEN

That night, Adah entered the tent and suppressed a groan at the sight of Tavi. The plan to wash her face and hands then hurry to meet Nehemiah might be delayed.

Tavi was sitting with her head propped on her knees. "Adah, sit and talk to me."

"Can we talk later? I am going to meet Nehemiah and learn about God."

"Can I go with you?" Tavi sounded like she'd been crying.

"Of course, Tavi. He will be delighted to have another person to teach, and we can walk together."

Tavi sniffled. "What do you talk about?"

"Talking to God and listening to Him."

"Praying? My abba does that." Tears welled in Tavi's eyes. "He has been praying a lot lately. My sister…"

"You said she was sick."

Tavi nodded. "So sick. We have tried everything we know to try and consulted so many physicians and the other priests, but she only worsens. That is really why I am traveling—to bring home the cure."

"The cure? You know what it is?"

Tavi's gaze bounced to the ceiling and then the floor. "I have heard there is a cure for almost everything somewhere near Babylon." She shrugged and stood. "Ready?"

Adah saw the evasion but ignored it. Nehemiah was waiting. He stood when they approached. "Tavi, Adah, welcome."

Seated, he spoke first to Tavi. "I am teaching Adah about prayer."

Tavi nodded. "My abba and imma pray often. When they wake each morning and at meals and before we go to sleep and…really, it seems they pray all day, every day." Primly, she folded her hands in her lap. "Of course, I do too."

Nehemiah's eyebrow rose the tiniest bit. "Do you, now?"

Adah listened in disbelief. If everyone talked to God all day, He must become very tired of listening. She tried to imagine talking to Him all day.

"Tonight, we will learn about heart prayers. These are not the ones we have memorized, the ones many people know. These are prayers that overflow from our sorrow or our joy. Often, they have no words."

Adah held out her hand. "Wait, please, Nehemiah. Last time, you said to talk to God, and now you say words are not necessary. How do you talk without words? It is impossible. Talk to someone I cannot see without saying words?"

"The God of heaven sees your heart. You may speak aloud or whisper or think your prayers, you can say all the right prayers, but He sees past your words to truth. He knows the wounds you carry that no one else perceives, the ones so deeply hidden—perhaps even denied—that when you and I encounter them in others or in ourselves, they emerge as scorn or fear or even foolishness."

Adah stared at the flickering fire. "Then what we see in others may not be truth."

"It is more like a symbol on a map leading to truth."

Her gaze swung to his face. He smiled benignly and turned to Tavi.

"Tavi, you know of heart prayers. Prayers beyond what we say each day?"

"For my sister, Noya," she whispered. "I have pleaded with God to heal her."

"When you pray, Tavi, begin with praise."

She looked shocked. "Absolutely not. I will not give praise for my sister's illness."

"Offer praise for His greatness. Then ask Him to hear you and confess your shortcomings, your failures to obey Him."

Tavi shook her head. "*My* failures should not prevent Him from healing *her*. I am doing everything I can, even taking this terrible—" She rolled her lips into one defiant line.

Adah looked back and forth between Tavi and Nehemiah, wondering at his calm acceptance as Tavi lashed out. Her eyes widened with understanding. Tavi's reaction came from one of those wounds Nehemiah spoke of, one that couldn't be seen by human eyes.

"This terrible journey." Nehemiah nodded. "I understand, Tavi. It is a difficult and demanding time. You are frightened and worried about your sister and willing to do whatever it takes to help her."

Adah blinked. Nehemiah deciphered people as she did. He heard people and responded with kindness so they felt understood. Remembering Nathan's words, chills ran up her arm. *"My imma said God's gifts are given to be shared, used to help others... Think on it—how you can share your gift.*" Is this what Nathan had meant? Help others by understanding? Do more than protect herself?

Tears flooded Tavi's face. "She cannot die. She is my dearest friend."

"I will add my prayers to yours that the God of the heavens will heal her." Nehemiah clasped his hands. "Tavi, since you are praying for her, you must repent of any sin in your life." He held up a hand as she began to protest. "I did not make these rules. This is what the Almighty has taught our forefathers. Humble yourself as you ask for mercy. Go now, child. You need to eat and sleep. Adah and I must speak alone."

Tavi nodded and plodded away. Uneasy with his insistence they speak alone, Adah watched her leave.

"Walk with me, Adah. Our words are not meant to be overheard."

"I am sorry I was late. One of the mules was limping, and Nathan had me sing to it so he could inspect his hoof."

"A kindness, Adah. Do not apologize for helping others."

"I should have asked before bringing Tavi—"

"Adah." He stopped walking and faced her. "We have moved apart from the others so you can speak freely with me and not be overheard, not so that I can scold you."

"Oh." An upbeat of relief and then a surge of tension. "Speak about what?"

In the moon's full light, his face was clear. "The map."

The map.

Arguments, denials, evasions swarmed through her mind. She remained silent, her face shuttered.

Nehemiah shook his head. "This is not a battle between us, Adah. In our first meeting, you spoke of a map—if authentic—that was a great treasure and led to a place in the direction we are traveling. It is not necessary to be a priest to discern where the map leads."

A lifetime of caution cast a shadow over the trust she'd felt toward Nehemiah. Let him probe. She'd not confirm. Let him assume. She'd not deny. Lips sealed, she refused to disclose a scrap of information.

What did he want? His authority was absolute. He could demand she relinquish the map, but she'd never willingly submit it to him. She'd burn it first. To think she'd felt safe, trusted him.

Nehemiah turned and walked away.

Stunned, she waited to see if he'd turn back. Was this a ploy to lure her into trusting him?

He kept walking.

It was cold standing alone in the dark. Cold inside. Cold outside.

Alone—so often as a child. Always alone as a servant. Now, alone as a woman.

It hollowed her, the pain echoing in her empty self. Weary from the loneliness, she trudged to her tent and hid beneath the blanket.

She was good at hiding—concealing herself in shadows, masking her emotions, avoiding any who might betray her. The hiding did not hollow her. It dug trenches and crammed barricades around her life. Defenses in places that did not need protection. Hollowness where trust might venture.

Trust with Nehemiah. Not once had he given her a single reason to doubt him. Every time she'd pulled back from sharing information, he'd respected her hesitation.

Adah opened her bag and fumbled through its contents until she felt the silk-wrapped packet. Setting aside the bright fabric and

Imma's treasures, she tucked the leather map into her sleeve and crept out of the tent.

Somehow she'd known—or hoped—he'd be waiting by the dying fire. He was alone without even a guard or a servant nearby. He looked up as she approached, and she searched for a sign of triumph. There was none.

Wordlessly, she handed her treasure to him. He studied her face and, seeming content with what he saw, unfolded the map.

He held it close to his face in the dim light. Startled. Hands trembling, he closed his eyes then opened them and pored over the map again.

"Is it the real one?" she asked, despite knowing the answer from his reaction.

He drew in a deep breath, held it, and then slowly exhaled—the great Nehemiah rendered speechless.

"Imma said it was. Father said not."

"Do you understand what you've been given, Adah?" His intensity surprised her. "This piece of our people's story created by a daughter of Eve, survived the Great Flood before being entrusted to Shem thousands of years ago."

"Noah's son?"

"The same. What do you know of the map?"

"It is old. Redrawn when the leather cracks." She pointed. "It has two spider splotches and holes. Either an insect made them or my brother, Jace, poked it with a needle. Tell me, how do you know it's the real one? My father insisted this is a false copy—a sham—and Omari said the map was a rumor."

"I believe it is real." Nehemiah pointed to the blazing swords. "I have seen many purported maps to the Garden, although of course there may be others I have not seen. None have this marking. This gives the true picture of what Adam and Eve saw as they were forced from the Garden of Eden. Neither would have forgotten or neglected this part of the story." Moonlight glinted on a tear running down his face. "What a terrifying, desolate time—driven from the presence of their Creator. Lord, have mercy."

A weight settled on her. She'd neither respected nor liked Inbar, but being driven from the woman's home had been unnerving. Imagine being driven from the perfection of paradise.

He flipped the leather over to look at the back then turned it right side up again. "Tradition holds that this drawing—though on hundreds of different pieces of leather, maybe even at one time etched on stone—has been handed down from generation to generation, sometimes given to the firstborn, sometimes to the child most trusted."

Oh, Imma. Adah blinked back a tear. The trust was the true gift.

Nehemiah reverently closed the map and held it out for her to take. "I would like to study it further, even decipher where Eden is, but for now, Adah, conceal this where it will not easily be found."

"You hide it."

"It is not mine to protect, child. It has been entrusted to you."

She folded her hands around it and stood to leave.

"And Adah…" He touched her hand lightly. "The legacy must remain among our people. Memorize it so you can recreate the drawing if the leather is…lost."

Zahra did not move a muscle. Though guilt was a waste of time, she'd not intended to eavesdrop. How fortunate she had stayed and listened. The gods—no, the God—favored her.

Even when Adah's and Nehemiah's footsteps could no longer be detected, she remained unmoving, thinking. A sharp breeze whipped sand in her face, stinging her eyes, and yet she stood, sphinx-still, ignoring the discomfort, intent on dredging up memories buried in a childhood she had mostly forgotten.

A map to the Garden of Eden—paradise, she'd heard Abba call it. And what was paradise other than perfection, peace, eternal life—her desires, her people's desires, the desires of both her Jewish imma and her Mizraite abba.

A story her abba once told tickled the edges of her mind. An ancestor of too long ago to care about had been denied his inheritance of a treasure or a map—perhaps a map that led to a treasure? Yes, that sounded right. Bitter, he'd left his brothers and abba and settled along the Nile. Could it be the same map?

If she could obtain the map and the ring, she could persuade Femi that the map led to a land of treasure, that it was the greater prize. She had manipulated him since he was a child, convincing him to do as she wished. This would be no different and the ring would be hers.

More than the gold was the ring's significance to her. Losing it would be another piece of life ripped from the little she had left. Her abba gone, her husband dead, another child relinquished, this time to death—she swallowed past the hard lump lodged in her throat.

She scowled, so angry it hurt to breathe. How was it possible that death-causing, mule-scented, brash peasant-person possessed the ring as well as a map to paradise? Adah had stolen Donkor's life and Omari's life and pushed Femi to near madness. To lose both her abba and her brother, maybe even Femi, so soon after losing her husband and their child was unthinkable. She forced herself to remain upright, to keep from buckling under the rawness of her grief.

Gritting her teeth, her jaw tightened, throbbing with dagger-sharp pain until she surrendered to its demand and massaged away the ache. If Femi had not insisted on the retelling of Donkor's death and the accuracy of his dagger throw at the city gate, she'd have been here sooner, heard more, conceived a plan.

In the predawn coolness, Zahra finally returned to her tent, controlled enough to not strangle Adah as she lay asleep. Yet.

CHAPTER FOURTEEN

Adah, time to go. Scratch their muzzles later. We have been on the road for barely a week, and they are already spoiled."

She gave Twitch one last pat, shooed a fly from Crook's eye, and crawled aboard. Her bag rested between her feet.

"Crook cannot flick the flies away with his crooked ear. He needed help, Nathan."

"Twitch does enough for both of them." He pointed ahead. "Passing the Sea of Chinnereth today. Freshwater. Guess we will be stopping early tonight."

Adah wiggled in delight. Clean body, clean hair, clean clothes. She'd walk into the water and soak until her skin crinkled into a raisin.

He grinned. "You seem happy today."

"I talked to Nehemiah last night and showed him the map." She locked her hands together to keep from waving them in glee.

"Really?" He cocked his chin toward her. "Did you like his response?"

"Maybe. Maybe not." She could hide the grin but not the gloat. "It is the real one. He said so."

Nathan's face darkened. "I wish it were not."

"Of course not. You are like my older brother—never happy for anyone else, upset whenever you're wrong."

"I am upset because I believe you are in danger. Think, Adah. Both the damaged wagon and the frayed rein were on your side of the wagon. You, not I, could have been seriously injured."

"No one other than you and Nehemiah know about the map... and your imma, and my imma, who is dead, and my father, who thinks it is false. Who would hurt me?"

But he was right. She'd known something was wrong, sensed a danger she'd not seen or heard, felt the uneasiness that prickled her neck, but when she turned, she saw nothing. She'd hoped her senses were off kilter from Jonah's senseless death or even knowing Imma no longer lived.

Nathan's voice interrupted her thoughts. "Adah, I want to show you something. We are almost there. Ready? Look to your right...now."

Concerns forgotten, Adah gasped. "It is beautiful. That is it? The Sea of Chinnereth? I have never seen anything so blue—well, the sky—but there is so much water."

"Sit down."

"It goes on forever!"

Nathan laughed. "Not exactly. In a little bit, you will be able to see almost all the way around it. There, just past this curve, look. See to the west, the mountain. That wide strip below Mount Arbel is the Plain of Gennesaret—I have heard anything will grow there—and to the north the..."

Adah stopped listening. Forgot the sea. She shook her head to clear her vision, blinked, and rubbed her eyes. She could not be seeing what she was seeing. It must be a dream. She had studied the map so intently that after talking with Nehemiah last night—and going to bed so late—her eyes had conjured the image.

Towering above the surrounding land stood a cliff—proud though battle weary, as if much of its strength had been chiseled away. Its lacerated top was ridged so deeply she wondered at the force that had shaped it. Huge rocks skirted the sharp drop to its base as if clinging to their source and refusing to crumble into mere dirt.

Dizzy, she closed her eyes and covered her open mouth. Slowly she opened first one eye and then the other. The drawing on the map was identical to the cliff.

Without taking her gaze from the cliff—if she looked away, it might disappear—she reached over and shook Nathan's arm. Wordlessly, she pointed.

"Adah? Are you sick? You do not look good."

She pointed again when her mouth refused to open and form sounds.

"Adah?"

"M-m-map," she choked out.

Nathan swiveled to face her. "That crag is on your map? You are sure?"

Nodding, she reached for her bag and dug to its bottom. With her hands trembling as violently as Omari's had, the silk resisted being unwound. The needle and coin escaped her fingers and dropped into her lap as she unfolded the leather.

Nathan switched both reins to one hand and took it from her. "I cannot see with it shaking so hard."

His low whistle was all the affirmation she needed. Together they stared at the map, up at the rock cliff, and back at the map.

She twisted to face him. "Nathan, when we camp tonight, I want to walk to the base of the cliff. Will you come with me?"

"I can go with you after Crook and Twitch are fed. Why?"

"What if the appearance of the crag and the map is a coincidence? Maybe there is something we can see if we are closer."

Was that admiration in his eyes? Adah busied herself refolding the map.

Adah felt her feet were barely touching the ground as she sped to the mountain's base. "Nathan, hurry."

"No, you slow down. We do not know who or what might be in those caves." He hurried forward and grabbed her elbow. "Stop, Adah. Someone is in there. I hear hammering."

Adah's mouth went dry. If Nathan had not stopped her, she'd have charged inside. Slowly, so he would not notice, she edged closer to him. "What should we do?"

"Leave. Now."

Before they could retreat, a man carrying tools in one hand and a torch in the other stepped from the mouth of the cave. He stared at them without speaking, seeming neither angry nor surprised at their presence.

Nathan held out his hand in a placating manner. "We did not mean to disturb you. We are leaving."

"Did you come to see the mark? I have just completed it."

Adah could not stop herself. "A mark?" She tugged at Nathan's arm. "I want to see it."

He hesitated so long she thought he would deny her request, but at last he stepped forward. "Yes, thank you."

Winding through the cave, the man held his torch high and led them to a narrow indentation in the wall. He paused, stepped aside, and pointed his torch toward the wall.

Neither Adah nor Nathan made a sound as they stared, open-mouthed, at the flaming swords chiseled into the rock.

The man stepped forward and ran his fingers through the stone flames. "Like my fathers before me, I do good work. The edges are beveled. The cut is deep. Come, it is time to leave. It will be dark soon, and my dinner is waiting for me."

Nathan and Adah followed him out as the sun began to fade.

"You chiseled the flames?" Adah searched his eyes for truth.

The man snorted. "The flames existed long before my father or his father's father were born." He shrugged. "They have been here from before memory."

Nathan frowned. "But you said…"

"Each generation of my family is tasked with ensuring the mark remains. The lines of the flame are never changed, never varied."

Intrigued, Adah leaned forward. "Who tasked your family with this?"

"I never asked. It is what we do."

———

Adah moved as if in a stupor as they returned to the camp.

"Adah, let me see the map again."

She pulled it from her bag and handed it to him.

"You know what this means, Adah?" He traced his finger over the sketch.

Her heart beat wildly. "That we are on the right path, and it is real."

"More. Adam and Eve, or at least their children, came by here. They could have traveled right along this road." His voice held the wonder she wanted to express.

Chills prickled her arms, and her eyes rounded. "We have become the link, holding hands with both the beginning and the present."

Fresh from a soak in the beautiful water, Adah hovered close to the fire where Nehemiah conferred with his officers and drivers. Chilled, though blood flamed through her veins, she tapped her fingers against her arms. She squirmed, sitting, standing, and sitting again.

Clasped in her hand was a rock chosen because it looked—if she stretched her imagination—like the mountain beside her. As she waited for Nehemiah, she rolled it between her palms, measured it against her fingers, and tossed it from one hand to the other.

Did everyone in the entire camp need to talk to Nehemiah tonight of all nights? A loud groan escaped her when the captain of the guard, Dror, settled in beside him and stretched out his legs as if planning a long discussion.

Nehemiah looked up in Adah's direction, his eyes twinkling. He tilted his head to the mountain looming above them and smiled.

He knew! He'd seen the map and recognized the mountain. She grinned back at him and relaxed. So much joy bubbled up she wrapped her arms around herself to contain it. Twirling in circles and laughing deliriously might have her labeled as a madwoman.

Zahra scrutinized the interaction between Nehemiah and Adah. Her eyes narrowed. What new secret knowledge did they share to bring Adah such obnoxious joy after a miserable day of travel? The girl radiated delight. With two fingers, Zahra rubbed the ache from her temples as she considered the possibilities.

An upcoming event? Nothing happened within a caravan that remained unknown. A clandestine affair? Absurd. Not even she could imagine those two together.

Additional information about the map? Of course!

She grimaced. She'd not slept last night, but that was no excuse. Her abba would have been annoyed with her slow, methodical thinking. He'd never understood she needed to look at every option before moving forward and, once she decided, she would not budge. It had cost her everything except her memories.

Zahra pulled her thoughts back to the present. Nehemiah and Adah shared two things. The desire to know more about the gods—God—and belief in the map. Since God had not appeared in the sky, something had happened today with the map—something they'd both seen—or recognized.

Befriending Adah might be the most efficient way to regain the ring and obtain the map to bribe Femi. The ring had been promised to her when her abba still loved her. She had to have it, hold it in her hand, and remember being treasured. Then maybe her heart would be quiet and still. She'd find the strength to be grateful to those who'd accepted her first child despite its unwed mother and the peace to accept the deaths of her husband and their child.

Endless regret and the need for sleep overwhelmed her. Leaving Adah and Nehemiah with their foolish grins, she returned to her tent. There, unguarded on Adah's pallet, was the bag. Watching the entrance, Zahra fumbled through its contents until she found a parchment. With one swift movement, she slipped it out and into her sash.

Tavi entered and, seeing Zahra by Adah's bed, frowned.

"Adah's bag toppled onto the floor. She should be more careful."

"She never goes anywhere without it."

Zahra shrugged. "She probably knew you would be back soon. She trusts you." *For now.*

CHAPTER FIFTEEN

One Month Later

Nehemiah bowed his head in prayer—a long one. When he lifted his head and searched Adah's face with those eyes that missed nothing, she squirmed.

"Adah, you have been patient with the trials of this journey. You are a quick learner and a joy to teach, and I have shared many of the Lord's truths and laws with you."

She'd misread him. Relaxing, she beamed at his praise.

"Have they changed you?"

Changed her? Stomach clenching, she eyed him uncertainly. "Changed how?" she hedged.

"I see your woundedness. Have you come to the place of forgiveness for the wrongs done to you?"

Adah stared into the fire. "Forgiveness?" The word curdled in her mouth like soured milk. "Inbar threw me out because I knew her lies. She and her husband are less than nothing to me." She flicked the air as if shooing away a gnat. "Imma retreated to a stupor rather than protecting her children or fighting for her own life. My father sold me to Omari." A smirk twisted her lips. "He misjudged Omari's heart and unintentionally did me a kindness. When Nathan and I left Hebron and drove over the dirt that drank Jonah's blood, Omari's family ceased to exist. Femi could be tossed over a cliff for all I cared."

"And now?"

"I hate them." Said with no passion, merely a casual observation—the fire is hot, the moon is pale—it hardened her words into implacable facts. "I will find Eden. I will prove Imma spoke truth. I will—"

"No." Nehemiah spoke with authority. "You will not "

"I have the map." Confused at his shift to disbelief, she did not hide the hurt, the anger of his unexpected denial. Her voice shrilled, defiant and accusing. "You said it was the real one."

"It will be impossible for you to discover or enter Eden."

She scowled. "I do not run from hardship. I will find Eden."

"You cannot find the Garden with hate in your heart."

Her felt her eyes narrow to slits. "A place does not disappear, does not rise up and dance around to the other side of a mountain because of how someone feels."

The sad confidence on Nehemiah's face bewildered her as if she'd failed a test or dropped in his estimation of her.

"You are right. A place does not move. Adah, tell me of Eden. What will it be like? What do you expect?"

His agreement flustered her, more because the expression in his eyes did not change.

Suspicious, she looked away, gathering her thoughts. "Beautiful, with flowers and fruit and streams sprinkled with jewels sparkling in the sun and trees for shade. I think colors have sounds and sounds have colors, and we will know what the animals say."

"How will you feel? What will you think about?"

"Safe—what home is supposed to be like. And right. Everything right with no distrust or hurt or anger. Peaceful." Her lips curved. "Loved. I will think of Jonah and Imma and Jace, Omari, the sisters I lost, and Emili." She felt herself blush. *And maybe Nathan.*

"What of your abba, your elder brother, and Inbar and Donkor and Femi? What of Zahra?"

Images of the Garden's beauty vanished. Her joy dimmed. "Them? Never."

"Because?"

"They are evil. They have no place, no right to be in the Garden of Eden—nor even in my thoughts. It is a good place, where everything is perfect."

"Including you?"

Adah looked away and then back at Nehemiah. "No, I am not perfect, and maybe I cannot go inside the Garden, but I can think about it and find it. I will find it."

He regarded her steadily. "If I hire a guide who is determined to thwart me, will I arrive at my chosen destination?"

"No."

"Adah, who is guiding you? Are you trusting the God of heaven, or letting hate lead you? Hate will take you to places you do not want to go."

His calm concern took the sting from his words. She watched the flames curve and entwine in their endless search for freedom only to slump, unable to escape their bondage.

Hate led her, but confessing it aloud was too hard. "Trusting Him is becoming more familiar. Your teachings help."

"Do you remember the story of Joseph and his beautiful coat, how his brothers abandoned him and sold him into slavery?"

"Like Father did me and my sisters. Of course I remember."

"Joseph trusted God to show him how to release hate and forgive."

Forgive being sold? Forgive living hungry? Forgive the slurs and belittlement? She leaned forward in disbelief. Surely she'd misunderstood. Maybe the others she could forgive. But Father? "You expect me to forgive even my father?"

Nehemiah held both palms up. "Adah, I expect nothing. This is your journey in many ways. You may forgive or not. You may trust God or not. Both begin with obedience. All are your decisions." He spoke with unshakeable surety. "Choose carefully. Our expulsion from the Garden of Eden began with a decision to trust our own understanding, to question God's wisdom and disobey."

They sat in silence as sparks flew upward from the hissing fire. Nehemiah stretched and stood. "We have an early morning, Adah." He signaled a guard. "He will see you to your tent. Shalom."

The guard lifted his torch, letting its illumination define his path. Adah trailed behind him, stepping where he stepped to avoid snakes and animal droppings. When she found Eden—and she would, no matter what Nehemiah thought—she'd walk without fear.

Sleep refused to gift her with its usual blessed escape. She tossed first one way and then another as Nehemiah's teachings collided with her anger. She arched her neck, clenched her fists, and silently screamed in frustration until her heart raced and her breath came short and shallow.

Love thy neighbor as thyself.

Impossible.

If she'd known God would start talking, she'd have screamed longer to block His voice.

Love thy neighbor.

She flung her elbow across her eyes.

Love.

If He wanted to have a conversation, they'd have a conversation.

"Why?" she whispered. "Father stole from us."

And you from him.

"He lied."

As you did to Nathan.

"Zahra hates me."

As you do Femi.

She clenched her teeth. "With good reason. He probably wants me dead!"

And you hate him.

"Who wouldn't?" She turned her back. Maybe God would get her message.

He didn't.

Love Me with your choices.

"It is different."

How?

"I have honor."

Her father's voice echoed. *"I am a man of honor."* His words flew into her face like a bird of prey, talons stretched out, mighty wings curving, thrusting death forward, golden eyes locked on hers.

Her blood—no, *his* blood—ran cold through her veins. She carried his name, Adah bar Hiram. The shape of her face mirrored his. She stared at her body and despised it for being of his.

Her thoughts, were they of him? His hate, his deception, his degradation of anyone who defied him? Was she—him? *Years and years ago, your abba too..."* With sudden certainty, she knew what her imma had started to say. *"... your abba, too, understood people like you do."*

Heart thudding, she cringed at their sameness. Recoiled as from a venomous serpent.

"I am different from him, from all of them."

Are you?

She lay motionless, digging through years of hurt and revenge, searching for a time she could point to in rebuttal, a time she'd been without fault in deed and attitude from beginning to end.

She did not have the honor she claimed. She dismissed those who displeased her. Of hate, she could not plead innocence.

Her eyes burned dry and gritty as she stared into the blackness of night, the blackness of her thoughts. The promise of dawn with its sleepy stillness and cool breezes had begun to ease into being before Adah responded.

"No. I am not different. I am just like them." She sat up. "But I refuse to remain like them."

The scent of morning's sweetness wafted through the tightly closed tent. She rubbed the grit from her eyes, exhausted and relieved, as if a battle had been waged and she, declared victor.

Zahra stretched and yawned. "You snored all night."

Another hidden talent—to snore while wide awake and arguing with God.

"I am so sorry, Zahra."

The consternation on Zahra's face was almost worth a night's lost sleep.

The next evening, Adah approached the fire circle cautiously. Nehemiah waited for her, his face serene.

She eyed him ruefully. "God kept me up all night."

He chuckled. "Sometimes He does that." He cocked an eyebrow. "So, the Lord spoke to you."

"I never thought it would be like a conversation. Is it always?"

"Often. Other times it is a profound sense of being led by His hand. Or it can be the counsel of a godly person. Some profess to have heard an audible voice."

Adah sat down so abruptly she almost missed the bench. "I can hardly believe God—*the* God—spoke to me." She twisted to face Nehemiah. "To me, Adah, a nobody."

"You are one of His chosen people. You can never be a nobody. He is our Abba."

She sat silently, thinking. For years, she'd believed God had tossed her in a pit and abandoned her like Joseph's brothers abandoned him.

"I am not Joseph." The words spilled out.

"You could be like him. Joseph trusted the God of the heavens no matter what happened."

"And if I do not?"

"Not trusting hurts both you and Him and often others too."

Adah bit her lower lip and measured each word with careful deliberation. "If I hurt God…" She cringed at the thought. "Then…I am no better"—her lip curled in distaste—"than those who hurt me."

Nehemiah gave a slow nod. "You have remarkable insight, child."

"But I do not know what to do with it."

"Yes, you do. Forgive them."

She raised clenched fists. "It is so hard."

"It is waking to the Lord's leading, a part of healing, a chance at true freedom. It is the gift of being exiled from the Garden—the choice to return to obedience. Adah, think. What you search for has been lost in plain sight for thousands of years."

"Lost in plain sight?"

Nehemiah rubbed his hand across his face. "No. Forgive me. I am going too fast, skipping lessons you must learn before you can understand." His eyes smiled at her. "You grasp the deep things of the Almighty so quickly that I forget this is all new to you. Sleep well. Soon, you will face more difficult matters."

CHAPTER SIXTEEN

The next morning, Adah swung her bag into the wagon and climbed aboard. "Nathan, have you ever hurt God? Nehemiah said we hurt Him when we do not trust and obey."

"Shalom and good morning to you as well." His hands tightened on the reins. "Yes. I have. It is forgiven. Gone."

"You are not going to tell me?"

"No."

She lifted her hands and dropped them in frustration. "I do not understand how God can be hurt."

"Has Jace ever not trusted you when you were helping him?" Nathan cocked an eyebrow when she nodded. "Did his lack of trust hurt you?"

"Of course. I have cared for him since he was born. I am his big sister."

"You love Jace. God loves you. What is not to understand?"

Adah studied the barren mountains that lined their path. On the other side, as the oasis of Damascus grew closer, they'd passed a village and then another with outlying orchards and vineyards. It was evident water was near. Was God's love that obvious, that easy to grasp?

If Imma had known the Lord loved her, her life could have been so different. Adah's stomach tightened. None of them had understood, neither her sisters nor parents. If they'd known would they have—dare she think this—accepted their worth and felt safe enough to love each other? Tears stung her eyes. If only someone had told them.

———

Adah yawned. The wagon's rumbling motion prevented any chance of sleeping. Even if she could have dozed, it was important she stay awake and search for the next landmark.

She pulled the map from her bag. "I can hardly wait to see Eden. Will it be filled with butterflies and birds and bees that don't sting? Nathan, when will we see another marker?"

"Maybe never."

"Stop saying that."

"Stop asking."

"I want to know what you think."

"My thoughts are not important."

"They are to me." Adah bit her lip and closed her eyes. What was wrong with her? She fluttered her hands to distract from the admission and disperse the heat flooding her face. "I mean, you know what to look for."

"I am not questioning the map. The question is the road. More than one road goes past Mount Arbel."

That was true, and yet her inner surety dismissed Nathan's concerns. She was sure they were on the exact path Adam and Eve had first forged. She could offer no explanation of her certainty any more than she could explain how skin tightened over the planes of a face when a person lied, or how she smelled fear.

This assurance, the sense of being led, was this of God? Claiming she sensed God guiding her journey was too daring. She'd honor the line between bold and audacious. Besides, God might not want it known He was directing her steps, no more sure of her than she was of Him. Coexisting with Him was working. Complete trust remained risky.

"What is next, Adah?"

"More trust."

"What?"

"Mm. Dust. More dust. Dust everywhere. So dusty. Oh, you are asking what is the next marker?"

She ignored the confusion on his face. Let him think the journey had addled her mind. "I am not sure. You saw how the leather has been folded or rolled so much that it is hard to tell what is a crease and what is a marker. I think the next one—unless it is where the leather bent—looks like long, thin bread on a flat dish, like it did not have yeast to rise higher."

Nathan pointed. "Like that?"

"*Yes!*" She covered her mouth, smothering a squeal.

"It is called Mount Qasioun. I did not realize it would be the one on the map. Sit down. Are you going to jump up every time we pass a marker?"

"You knew? How did you know this?"

"Another driver mentioned we would see it today in Damascus."

"Nathan, we have to stop and see if there is a symbol like the one at Mount Arbel."

"This time it must be enough for you to know that thousands of years of tradition says Cain killed Abel near here."

Adah clasped her hands over her racing heart. She could almost see Cain's silhouette, fists clenched in anger, standing beside Abel in the fields that stretched below the mountain, his stealth as he chose a rock to crush the skull of his little brother, the birds' hush, the sun's darkening, the wind rising in protest.

Had the earth's warnings alerted Abel to Cain's mounting storm of fury? Did he turn and see his brother's arm raised in anger? Had Abel run, or fought, or stood in broken disbelief? The stone Cain used—how many passed by that first weapon and suspected nothing?

She ached for the people broken and stained with human hatred. Did a person ever completely heal from such ugliness?

Nathan swatted a swarm of gnats. "I think Cain was a man of pride. Remember? He made the first offering to God, but God preferred Abel's gift. Why? I do not know." He shrugged. "He was angry with God, so he killed his brother. We all have Cain inside us—we resent God but lash out at someone else. It is sad, but often an innocent pays the price for our anger."

An innocent like Imma or Jace or...her? The map would never be safe, but who wanted the ring? For someone, it was worth killing her. She shuddered. A round piece of metal was not worth the price of death—especially hers. If Omari had not insisted Adah have it, she'd give it away. Who could possibly covet the ring? Zahra? Tavi? A guard?

That night, Adah scrutinized Tavi as they sat across from each other in the tent. Either the woman's family had more wealth than most in Jerusalem, or her husband was well-paid by Persia's king. Judging from the number of bracelets and necklaces she wore, adorning herself in elaborate strands of jewels was important to her. Would one small ring interest Tavi?

Adah debated, waiting for an indication of interest or confrontation.

Shalom, Tavi, we do not know each other well, but I have an important question to ask you. Be honest, please. Are you trying to kill me for this ring of Omari's? Because if you are, I will give it to you, and I can stay alive, return home, and rescue my little brother from our evil father. What do you think?

"Adah, I have a question to ask you. Do you mind?" Tavi frowned. "What? Why are you looking at me like that?"

Adah choked, sputtered. "Sorry, Tavi. I was thinking of something else." She grimaced, hoping they were not referring to the same thing. "Toothache." She cupped her jaw. "Ouch."

"Maybe you eat too many almonds." Tavi brushed away Adah's comment. "My abba—he's a priest, you know—told me that, in the Garden of Eden, there's a tree called the Tree of Life and that whoever eats of the fruit will live forever. Did your abba tell you the same story?"

"No. He was not much for telling stories." *Lies, yes. Stories, no.*

Tavi toyed with her stack of bracelets as if they were new, admiring first one and then another. "Do you think the tree still exists or could…um…cure illness? Can Eden be found? My abba said there was once a map, and then last night, I heard someone in the caravan was seen with a map. I wonder who has it."

Adah noted the tight shoulders, the attempted indifference, the carefully averted eyes. Omari's ring might hold no interest for Tavi, but if she knew the map was within reach, would she kill to obtain it?

Alarm knifed through her, and familiar defenses clicked into place. Adah feigned interest in the bracelets.

"You have heard of the map?" Tavi's eyes flicked up for a second.

"Campfire rumors, yes."

Tavi tilted her head and slanted her eyes at Adah. "Do you think it is real?"

Adah shrugged. "That would be incredible. Tell me about this bracelet. It is beautiful." Lips slightly parted, putting on a relaxed, slightly bored face, she ignored Tavi's long look.

At last, Tavi resumed her chatter. Adah listened. Tavi knew more than she admitted about the map. Maybe she was not to be trusted. Eventually the woman would betray herself, revealing more than she wanted known.

Escaping at last, Adah walked to where the mules were hobbled, chewing her thumbnail. Crook displayed his teeth in greeting. She caught his head and rubbed his muzzle and chin.

"What do you think, Crook? Who wants the ring? Who wants the map? At least Zahra is honest in her dislike of me. But I suspect Tavi is hiding something. Who can I trust to help me see clearly? I wish you could speak. You, I would trust."

Asking for help felt unnatural—just wrong. She could reason things out. She'd always had to, so she always had. Besides, telling Nathan of her suspicions risked ridicule. Telling Nehemiah risked another lesson on trusting God.

"Trust is not my favorite word, Crooky."

Who wanted what? Mentally, she picked up each piece of that puzzle—ring, map, Tavi, Zahra. Head spinning, she fit them together first one way and then another. But no picture emerged. Nothing connected. Nothing made sense.

Even more confusing was the delight of talking with Nathan while still missing Jonah. And the way her heart jumped when Nathan smiled. And how her feet seemed to speed up when she saw him waiting for her each morning. Even when he laughed at her, she wanted to be near him. What was wrong with her?

She scratched Crook's bristly ears and turned her thoughts back to the ring and map. Nehemiah spoke of God as his Abba and their people's Abba. She'd always wanted an abba. He'd not wanted her.

Dare she risk approaching Him as Abba? Her stomach turned over. If He too denied her, then maybe she was all she'd been called— worthless, trouble, unwanted. Yes, He'd spoken to her, but that was before she presumed to call Him Abba.

Maybe she'd wait on that. Just talk to Him like He was God.

"It seems safer, right, Crook?"

Safer, but even that risked the unfathomable silence, the sense Someone heard you but chose His own time and place to answer. Still, there was no one else to turn to.

"Excuse me, God. I am still learning about You, but I know You are the Creator and Your world is beautiful, except there is too much dirt." She shooed a fly from Crook's eyes. "And too many bugs."

She groaned. She'd just criticized God.

"I have probably done a lot of wrong things, but I have not bro- ken the Ten Commandments except for taking my father's coins, and don't You think I deserved to have those? I need to talk to You." She took a deep breath and spoke before she could change her mind. "As if you are my Abba and you like me. It is about the map and the ring. Someone wants them. Maybe two someones. I am not sure who wants what, but the map and ring were entrusted to me—to protect—and I think to lead me to peace and safety."

Her throat tightened. She pressed her head against the mule's solid neck. "Abba, I do not know what to do, but I am so tired of running and being unwanted. Please want me. Please?"

Words ceased formation. Pleas flowed from her heart—and were heard.

So, this was an abba's love. For a moment, she basked in the warmth surrounding her, letting it fill her mind and heal secret hurts—until memories slithered in and coiled into doubt. The past had taught her that love could be lost or withdrawn or fade. Even God's?

CHAPTER SEVENTEEN

Four Days Later

Tavi uncoiled her bracelets and spread them across the pallet. "Abba gave me this one when I was an infant, and this is from my cousin's neighbor's grandparents. This one, I have always liked, but it is a little small. It reminds me of…"

Tavi droned on about the box she kept this bracelet in or the pouch or the embroidery on the pouch. Adah stifled a yawn and pinched herself to stay awake and catch Tavi in a lie.

"Now that one, with stones on the gold band. That is obsidian." She handed it to Adah to admire.

Adah took it between two fingers as if it was delicate and of great worth. In truth, it reminded her of Femi's eyes. She dropped it as soon as Tavi glanced away.

"Adah, you wear no jewelry." Tavi turned back as the bracelet clunked with the others. "How can you make yourself beautiful without it?"

Adah laughed. "The mules do not care how I look."

"What of Nathan?"

"He would never notice."

"Maybe. Maybe not. I have seen how he looks at you. But do you have rings or bracelets for when you must make a good impression? I wore all of mine and some of my sister's when I met Dror."

If Dror was like her brothers, she doubted he'd cared about Tavi's bracelets. Her father noticed jewelry only to gauge the wearer's wealth and determine how much to steal.

"Adah, do you own anything to make yourself appealing?"

The splinter tip of Tavi's hidden wound protruded through her words. Only jewels made her beautiful.

Flustered, needing a moment to think, Adah snatched the closest bracelet. "Oh my! This one is unusual."

"That is a gift from my husband's family in Persia. Do you think they will like me?" She traced her finger lightly over the circle's delicate scrolling. She held up a matched set of bracelets. "These two are from my sister." Tavi's voice wobbled.

Adah turned from eyeing the bracelets to see black kohl trickle over Tavi's cheeks.

"You are very worried about her."

"I told you! She is sick."

"Sick is not dead." Adah spoke without thinking, her mind snared by Tavi's earlier admission of needing jewels to be beautiful. Tavi must want the ring.

Tavi's eyes filled.

"I am so sorry, Tavi. That was thoughtless. Please forgive me."

"You do not understand. You must never have had a sister."

Adah did not refute her.

"I am sorry your sister is sick. It must be so hard on you."

"I should never have…" Tavi rubbed her hand over her mouth.

"Never have…what?"

"I should never have mentioned it." Tavi shook her head and smeared her cheeks with the heel of her hand.

"You love her very much."

"I did not think it would…"

"Did not think what would…what?"

"Stop repeating me," Tavi snapped. "Leave me alone."

Adah swung her feet off the pallet and stood.

"Where are you going? I thought we were friends."

Adah stared at the distraught woman. *What am I supposed to do now, God?* Startled, she sat down. Was that a prayer? She canted her head, listening. Nothing. No answer.

Tavi sniffled. "Thank you, Adah. My sister was so beautiful she needed no jewels, and now she is wasting into nothing, and I…"

"…and then she talked and talked. Was that a prayer, Nehemiah?"

"A prayer and an answer. God used your response to praying to keep you there and meet Tavi's need."

Adah rubbed her eyes. "She finally talked herself to sleep. I wondered if you would be gone by the time I escaped."

"God kept me here to meet your need."

They shared a smile.

Adah looked over her shoulder, reached inside her sleeve, and slid out the map. "I do not know what to look for next."

Together they unrolled the cracked leather. Adah traced the route they'd covered.

"I think these lines up here might be a river—a rocky beach I would guess, judging from these little circles that must be rocks. Maybe these zigzags could be mountains, but what if this spider smear is hiding something important—pointing in a different direction?"

Nehemiah brought the map closer to his eyes. He coughed and covered his mouth to hide a grin that burst into a chuckle. At last, he raised his face to guffaw at the starry night. Adah had never heard such a deep, reverberating sound. He should laugh more often, and if an outline of a dead spider was funny, she didn't understand why he didn't find more things amusing. She flattened a bug against her ankle. Maybe she should show him so he'd laugh again.

"Adah, you are the delight of each day."

Nice to hear. She smiled uncertainly.

"Dear girl, your spider splotch"—he grinned again—"is an oasis, Sabkhat Muh, beside the city of Tadmur."

She peered at the map. "Oh." It looked like a flat spider to her. She shrugged. "It is supposed to be there?"

"Yes. These zigzags are the mountains on each side of us. We will stop in Tadmur, replenish supplies, rest the animals."

"And sit in the shade and soak this dust off in the water."

"I would advise against that soak. The water is salty."

She puckered her lips. "A city-oasis with salt water?"

"People drink the rain water that collects in cisterns and wadis."

Adah yawned. "How much longer?"

"To Tadmur? A week since one of the drivers is ill. However, tomorrow is the Sabbath, and we will not travel."

She nodded, stepped away, and squealed as her foot landed on something soft and wiggly.

Nehemiah caught her before she fell. "It is a lizard, Adah."

She returned to the tent, sliding one foot forward at a time until her toes and sandals were thick with dirt. In the Garden of Eden, there'd better not be any lizards.

———

Adah raised her head when Nehemiah finally completed his prayer. If that was the type of prayer God liked, she'd never please Him. She nudged Tavi awake—how did the girl sleep while standing?—and saw Zahra use her toe to smudge the markings she'd traced in the dirt during the Sabbath prayer.

Nehemiah rubbed his foot over the uneven ground in front of him. "Look around. A stony desert encircles us. Stones are everywhere we step and as far as we can see.

"Abba Moses calls God a rock who is perfect, whose ways are just. King David calls God his rock, his fortress. We pass through mountain ranges, see towering rocks, and rest in their shelter. The prophet Isaiah says God's love for us is more steadfast than the mountains.

"But today, we walk among stones that bruise our feet, cause us to fall, and slow our travels. Stumbling stones. We kick them from our path, shove them aside when we stretch out to sleep. What use are they other than a nuisance?"

Adah fingered the two memory stones in her waist sash. The first one, she'd chosen at Mount Arbel, the second, at Mount Qasioun.

When they reached the oasis tomorrow, maybe she'd add a dead spider to her collection.

Grinning, she ignored Tavi's reproving frown. If Tavi could sleep during Sabbath worship, she could smile. She giggled, thinking of Nehemiah's face when she'd referred to the oasis as a spider. Tavi shushed her. Adah laughed a bit louder. She'd spent her entire life being told what to do, and she refused to be shushed ever again.

"Goliath was slain with a small stone, smoothed by wind and water. Twelve gemstones dressed the ephod of our high priest. Were they beautiful when first mined? Absolutely not. And consider the *Urim* and *Thummim*. What are they? Stones.

"As we cross this stony desert, remember our God uses the humble, broken pieces of rock as the stones of great beauty. Both are valuable to Him as are people who may seem to be only insignificant stones."

Nehemiah motioned for them to stand for the final prayer. Adah stood with the others but her leg had numbed, and she stumbled against Zahra.

She righted herself, surprised Zahra didn't jerk away or sneer or push her into the dirt. "I am sorry, Zahra."

"Are you dizzy, Adah? No? Think nothing of it. We all need help sometime."

After the prayer, Zahra moved away. Adah stared after her, mouth ajar. Maybe she was dizzy. Or dreaming. Or Zahra had a twin.

Could people be like stones? Appearing one way and then, showing a different side? Stumbling-block people turned into jewels?

She wandered to where Crook stood watch over the napping Twitch and held her hand flat to show the mule she had no food to share. Crook stepped closer, shoving her nose against Adah's shoulder.

"It will not happen again. I promise next time there will be food." Crook shoved her backward.

Adah retreated until she bumped against a warm solid object. She gasped and whirled. "Nathan!"

He nudged her away from him. "Annoying the mules?"

"Yes. I neglected to bring bribes." Looking sideways at him each day, she'd forgotten what he looked like face-to-face, or maybe she'd never noticed how his eyes laughed, or realized the ever-escaping curl fell exactly in the middle of his forehead.

"Thought so." He pulled a sweet from his belt and held out his hand. "You looked distracted when you left worship."

A smile tickled her lips. He'd watched her? Knew when she left the gathering? Followed to see if she was upset?

"Is something wrong, Adah? You were talking to Zahra…"

One word could hold enough power to alter a life—sold; or a belief—chosen; or a lovely feeling—Zahra.

The air lost its sparkle. The small stone wedged between her foot and sandal felt sharper.

"Zahra was nice."

"'Nice' says nothing. Be specific."

"I did not add her to my memory collection, but neither did I stub my toe."

Nathan eyed her. Wrinkled his forehead. "Women!"

Adah grinned. It made sense to her.

CHAPTER EIGHTEEN

One Week Later
Oasis of Tadmur

A day away, yet Zahra could almost smell the tang of Tadmur, hear the rumbling echoes of danger from the days when it had been a den of thieves, imagine the outlandish garments of merchants from distant lands.

Twice she'd traveled through here when Abba let her journey with him to Persia. Each time, she'd begged to linger, intrigued with the city's bustling pace, the people with strange eyes and ways, the merchants enticing buyers with exotic goods, extolling their wares in languages she did not understand. She inhaled deeply, remembering the warm, sweet spices from India and the amber tea and white porcelain from Shenzhou.

Last time, Abba bought her silks from Shenzhou and a red vase with white cranes. Last time, Abba still loved her.

When the caravan made camp for the evening, she stopped by Femi's wagon and spoke softly in their native language.

"Femi, remember the temple in Tadmur we visited? Meet me there tonight when the others sleep."

He'd heard her. He faced straight ahead with no acknowledgment, but she knew he bristled at the command. A sister did not easily frighten at a little brother's sullenness. When she explained her plan to retrieve the ring, he'd change his attitude.

———

Shivering in the cool morning air, Adah admired Zahra's stoicism and avoided looking at Tavi's fidgets. The three of them waited outside Nehemiah's tent in answer to his summons. Did the others know why he'd called them together?

His servant lifted the tent flap. "Our Nehemiah will be with you in just a moment—or moments. Not too long now. Most unexpected, his last visitor. King's business. Never a moment's rest for our Nehemiah, no indeed."

Adah heard Nehemiah call for them. Dark circles sagged beneath his eyes but he smiled, seeming delighted to see them.

"We have received a coveted invitation. You, the only women to grace the evening, Tavi's husband as captain of the guard, and I have been invited to share a meal today with the governor of Damascus. I have accepted for you, as it was more of an expectation than a true request."

Zahra crossed her arms. "No."

Nehemiah bowed his head in acceptance. "Very well, I will advise Governor Eesho of your choice. He will honor your preference and make arrangements for your immediate return to Jerusalem." His eyebrows and shoulders raised in perfect synchronization. "He perceives himself as the gatekeeper to the northern desert. To proceed without his approval is…inadvisable."

Zahra's eyes narrowed and her face contorted, but she nodded her acceptance.

Adah and Tavi exchanged a glance. Would they hear of Zahra's displeasure when they returned to the tent?

"Dress in your best garments. We will arrive at his home together for the *mezzeh*, the midday meal."

Zahra pivoted and left without a glance at the others. The tent's flap hung open, a small rip evidence of her rapid exit

Tavi's lip curled. She summarized the governor's house in one succinct word. "Ugly."

Adah agreed despite Tavi's rudeness. It was not decrepit like her home in Judah, but the appeal was the same. None. They had followed Nehemiah through a narrow maze of cobblestone and rock-lined streets and stood outside an entrance that would decapitate Zahra if she didn't bend over and tuck her chin to her flat chest before entering. It would be a miserable dinner, in a drab house with unfriendly Zahra and untrustworthy Tavi.

"This is it?" Tavi's scorn was unmistakable. "The all-powerful governor of Tadmur lives in...this?"

Nehemiah tried and failed to conceal his amusement at Tavi's disdainful comments. His eyes crinkled with mischief when he saw Adah's face, but she did not mirror his smile.

"Ready?" Nehemiah lifted a large iron knocker and let it fall against its plate. A servant opened the door and bowed low as Nehemiah led them inward through a dim, dismal corridor. At its end, he stepped aside and, with an elegant flourish, invited them forward.

At their collective gasp, Adah understood Nehemiah's mischievous smile. Sun slanted through an open courtyard, illuminating a corner furnished with couches. Thick rugs overlaid colored marble. Towering trees arched over the immaculate courtyard, casting silhouettes over the enormous pots of flowers. In the center of the space stood a long table with a profusion of flower arrangements, the elegant chairs surrounding it padded with leather, their backs inlaid with silver.

Zahra sidled closer. "There must be thirty dishes on that table. Who can eat so much?"

Adah covered her mouth and whispered, "I do not even know what most of them are. Chicken, rice, dates, bread, hummus, and vegetables. The others"—she shrugged—"I do not know. Oh, and stuffed grape leaves. My imma made those."

"I know a few." Zahra grinned. "Everything is good if you dip it in the tahini, that white sauce in the yellow dish. It is a ground sesame seed paste—so good. Tabouleh, my favorite—cracked wheat with a lot of parsley and garlic and lemon. Baba ghanoush—mashed eggplant. I have no idea what the others are. Watch what Nehemiah eats. That should be safe."

Was the inside of the house or Zahra's grin more astonishing— as if they were friends sharing an adventure? Adah drew herself in, uncomfortable in the strangeness of both.

"Peace be upon you." Eesho placed one hand over his heart and bowed to each of the women. "You are welcome here. Be at ease."

He grabbed Nehemiah's face and kissed him twice on each cheek. "Ahh, Nehemiah, my friend. It warms my heart to see you again. You are well, yes? And you have brought these three lovely flowers to brighten the drabness of my poor home, the dullness of my life."

Adah listened, mesmerized, as Eesho spoke without slowing, saying nothing with each flowery deprecation. He was shamed by the meager meal he served, beset with incompetent cooks, apologetic for the shabbiness of his home.

As the meal ended and a servant bent low to whisper in Eesho's ear, Zahra elbowed Adah. "I have never seen such elegance. Have you?"

Adah gave a slight shake of her head. If Imma could see this, and Jace—did they know so much food existed?

"To earn your forgiveness and distract you from the inadequacy of my hospitality, I have employed a storyteller to entertain you. Nehemiah, if I may call on our long friendship and seek your esteemed wisdom in a situation that robs me of sleep and appetite, will you sit with me and hear my woes? May I beg you to allow your commander to attend us?"

Adah's eyes darted back and forth, tracking the flurry of movement as Nehemiah and Tavi's husband stood to follow Eesho. The ill-fitting garments of strange food and customs and Zahra's friendliness chafed, leaving her restless. Listening to stories was of no interest. She wanted only an escape.

A servant glided a low stool into place for the entertainer. The storyteller—a well-paid one, judging from the soft rolls his silk tunic accentuated—bowed low and began. In spite of herself, Adah was drawn in, lulled by the rhythm of his voice. He wove stories into stories until Tavi clapped her hands and the harsh vertical lines between Zahra's eyes softened.

"It has been my honor and privilege to share these stories from many lands and many kingdoms. Now I finish with the familiar but most intriguing story of your people's beginnings. Step back with me to the first breath of time, before heartache, before death. It is told that in the beginning God created, and all life breathed at His command and all creation knew indescribable peace and joy."

Adah's hands tingled. *In the beginning God created.* Imma said those words told great truth and to hold them closely, that if she ever became confused, to go back to the beginning. She shook her head and wrested her attention back to the storyteller's captivating voice.

"God placed the man and woman in the Garden with the other creatures He'd made—lions and birds, and foxes and camels." He clasped his hands over his heart, his voice lilting with awe. "Imagine vines heavy with luscious fruit, beautiful in color and form, brimming with earth's sweetest nectar. Envisage plants of stunning green and vivid purple, the gold of the sun and the red of a sunset. Trees, their branches hung low with bounty. Perfection. Perhaps too perfect." His shoulders slumped, and his hands lowered to his lap. "In the center of the Garden, God placed two trees different from all the others. One, the Tree of the Knowledge of Good and Evil. The other, the Tree of Life. Whoever ate from the Tree of Life would live forever, as if he were God."

"I know all this," Tavi blurted. "I have heard it all my life. But is it true, or do you name it a tale?"

A frown flickered across the storyteller's features. "I am a story weaver. All I say is true."

Zahra leaned close to Adah. "Or not. Mizraim has a different story of creation."

Adah squirmed away from Zahra's moist breath in her ear.

Tavi angled closer. "Are you certain it is true?"

"Legend holds that all who find the Tree of Life and eat of its fruit are healed. They become one with God."

Tavi edged forward, challenge in her eyes. "If it is real, then where is the Garden?"

The storyteller raised his eyes and hands to the cloudless sky. "No one knows. Not even I know."

"I heard there is a map."

Adah riveted her attention on the man.

He stared at each of them, his slow nod unnerving. Did he pause when he sought her eyes? Heart thumping, she too leaned closer.

"There was once a map. After the Great Flood, Noah entrusted it to his son, Shem, father of the Israelites. It has been passed through the ages to his descendants. Ah, but there is a mystery no one has solved. Who has this treasure, if it still exists?"

Her *whoof* of relief earned a long look from Zahra. Adah smiled weakly. "Good story."

Adah held her stomach and groaned. She'd never eaten as much as she had today at Eesho's house. She fanned herself in the stuffy tent. Plus, it was too hot to sleep, although Tavi, as usual, had no problem, her soft purr the strangest snore Adah had ever heard.

Sitting up, Adah piled her hair on her head. If her neck cooled, maybe she could sleep. But when she lay back down, the temporary respite disappeared. After a few moments, she slid off the pallet and slipped out of the tent. Relief flooded her as cool air dried the dampness on her face and throat. She lifted her arms and turned in a slow circle. Alone. Gloriously alone.

Campfires scattered their light across the ground. A sliver of moon peeked between night-grayed clouds. In the dim light, no one could see her. Better yet, she saw no one, heard nothing other than the stamping of hooves, an owl's call, her own breathing.

From their tent, Tavi cried out. Another nightmare, poor girl. Adah cringed at Tavi's shuddering sob, thankful when she quieted.

Adah wandered to the edge of the campfires. A few steps beyond would do no harm. She could see the light, would not become lost, and for a few moments, could pretend she had the world to herself.

The temple she'd seen before dark was not far. A walk there and back before donning the burden of people—their sounds and odors and endless motions—and she'd sleep well.

When she reached the temple's steps, she sat and looked up at the stars. Funny, they were silent, but—like people—couldn't stop moving. Yawning, she wished she could sleep here with only the sigh of evening's breath in the dark's silence.

Voices brought her to her feet.

Familiar voices. Zahra. And Femi? Here? Together?

Furtively, Adah melded into the dark shadow of a pillar.

Zahra waited, giving Femi time to process her ideas.

Femi peered through the darkness at her face. "The map is to a land of treasure? Zahra, it is a good plan. Our abba would be proud of you."

Warmth flickered in spite of her attempt to dismiss his compliment. A small piece of her heart still stretched across the broken pledges and ragged words, yearning for a bridge to Abba's approval. Approval she'd never receive in this world. Because of Adah, her abba was dead.

The warmth bent, inciting bitterness. Abba had promised her the ring. She was to decipher and claim the words for eternal life inscribed on its back. How dare he discard her and replace her with Adah as his daughter? Chosen Adah as most favored? Entrusted Adah with the family secret? Offered Adah the chance for eternal life?

Zahra stepped closer. A waft of Femi's cardamom-scented hair oil assaulted her senses. She waved away its offense.

"By all the gods in Mizraim, on that night, cover your hair or she will know it is you. Do not speak. Do not hurt her. Understand?"

"Yes." He leaned closer, the heat of his hatred searing her. "Listen to me, my sister, one day, I will kill her."

"That is unnecessary, even excessive, but do what pleases you. First, I must have the ring and the map."

"The ring, which you will give me as your older brother—your only brother now."

Zahra flicked his words away. "The map is priceless, far more valuable than that tiny ring. I agree to surrender the map to you and keep only the ring because it reminds me Abba once loved me."

"You do not deserve it. You walked away. He wept for you every time we passed Jerusalem." Femi looked down his hooked nose and sneered. "I did not weep."

"He refused to accept my child."

"You shamed us—unwed, with child."

"He forced me to relinquish her." Her voice broke. "I will never see my baby, never know her name, never hear her laugh."

He waved away her words. "It was only a girl."

"It is as if she died."

He thrust his head forward, spitting his words into her face. "You said our abba was dead to you."

Zahra dodged truth with practiced agility. "He is dead to both of us now. It is because of Adah."

Adah stood paralyzed as Zahra's words penetrated, as she grappled with what she did not want to know, as their hatred of her became palpable. Her heart raced, urging her to flee. Her knees locked, refusing to obey. She stared, dry-eyed, into the dark. She was going to throw up.

If they saw her, realized she'd heard, they'd kill her now. She tried, and failed, to move—a pillar of salt like Lot's wife. Nehemiah had told her the story last night. He said her fate was the cost of not trusting, of not obeying.

God?

I am a shield around you.

She hadn't realized she'd been holding her breath.

The trembling began. Her knees—which before had refused to bend—gave way. She sank to the ground, wrapped her arms around her legs, and dropped her head onto her knees.

"Hush, Zahra. I heard a sound."

"A wolf. A viper. It could be anything. A jackal, a bear, a fox."

"Or a person.

"Where are you going?"

"To look around."

Adah hunched her shoulders, shrinking inward to be as small as possible.

"I want to go back. Walk with me."

"My big sister is scared of the dark?"

Zahra snapped a one-word reply. Femi laughed. Their voices faded.

They were gone. She was safe—not safe, but alive. *Thank You, God.*

I am the Lord your God, your Savior.

Gratitude swelled until she could not hold back a whispered "Thank You."

Limbs as heavy as the knowledge she carried, Adah pushed herself to stand, to stumble forward, to drag herself back to the camp.

Outside the tent, she stopped. If Zahra had returned, she'd see Adah entering, maybe suspect Adah had been the sound she and Femi heard. She nibbled her lip. She wasn't ready to face Zahra or dodge questions.

Adah braced herself, aware of what she'd feel next. As fear subsided, fury would sweep through her. Fury that Zahra and Femi dared accuse her of Omari's death. Fury that she had not guessed Zahra's relationship with Omari—there was a look about Zahra. She should have known. Fury she'd cowered. Fury that she had not marched up to Zahra and defended herself.

Her shoulders slumped. Now she knew who wanted the map and the ring. She touched the tiny bulge between her breasts.

"Adah."

She bolted forward as a scream squeaked loose, and spun to face the voice.

Her hand slipped from her mouth. When her heart no longer pounded in her throat, she whispered his name. "Nathan."

Lightly, he touched her shoulder. "Come."

A word. A touch. Not alone. *Thank You, God.*

They moved to the nearest campfire, sat close, forgoing traditional formality.

"I followed you." He spoke quietly.

She did not berate him for his concern. "They are both Omari's children, and they are planning to kill me." The quaver in her voice annoyed her. "You heard them? You know?"

"I know. More, now." The thin line of his lips warned of his displeasure. "Adah, if you want me to help you, do not withhold information."

"I do not need help." The lie tasted bitter.

He didn't argue. The lack of conviction in her tone named her liar to both of them.

"I do not want help." Closer to truth.

"Adah, I want to help you. Let me."

"I cannot sleep in there with her beside me."

"I will be right outside. I will let nothing harm you. I promise."

The warmth infusing her was not from the campfire. *Safe,* she realized. *He makes me feel safe.*

CHAPTER NINETEEN

Nathan was waiting for her the next morning. "Adah, may I see the map?"

She handed it to him. He pointed to the spider splotch, looked at the sun's position, and traced his finger to one side of the oasis's outline.

"I think it is here. Walk with me? I heard a rumor that I want to investigate. Besides, after last night, I don't think it is safe to leave you here alone."

She nodded and slid the map inside the bag. Nathan slung her bag across his shoulder, ignoring her protests. "It is a long walk, Adah. It is on the other side of that farthest date palm orchard. Can you walk that far?"

"Twice that far!"

"Good, because we have to walk back too."

Adah giggled then covered her mouth. They walked in silence until Adah began to cough and wave her hand in front of her face. She pinched her nose. "Nathan, what is that terrible odor? It smells like rotten eggs and it worsens with every step we take."

"Brimstone. You have a good nose."

Adah gagged. "I want to go home."

"Trust me?"

She hesitated then nodded. Yes, she did trust him.

When her nose became too tender to pinch, she took her bag from Nathan's shoulder and pulled out a scarf to wrap over her nose and mouth. "Where are we going?"

"We are here. Afqa Spring, the source of water for Tadmur. Take off your sandals, or your feet are going to get wet."

Adah wrinkled her sore nose. If she stepped in that water her feet would smell like brimstone.

Holding her sandals, she dipped a toe in the water. The water was warm and heavy and soft. Nathan grasped her arm as they waded past a wide cave and toward a smaller one.

"I think this is the one I heard about."

"Nathan, those red streaks." She pointed to the streaks on the wall. "They look like once they could have been the flaming swords. How did you know another mark was here?"

"I was not sure. I heard there were cave paintings at the spring, and since the oasis is on the map, it seemed like maybe this is where another sign would be found."

"I think we are still on the right path. Can you imagine what Adam and Eve thought of this odor after being in the Garden of Eden? Eden must have smelled glorious—like flowers and warm honey and fresh breezes and perfectly ripe fruit."

"And my imma's freshly baked bread."

Adah laughed. "Exactly like that."

Nathan smiled. "Come, we need to return to camp. I plan to go by way of the market. Adah, do not do what my imma does where I turn my head and you have disappeared—wandered off admiring some shiny trinket and I have to spend an hour searching for you."

"You have my bag. I am keeping it—and *you*—in sight."

"Fine."

"Fine."

When they reached the market, Adah twisted her neck trying to see and memorize everything so she could tell Jace about it. Spices of every shape brimmed from woven baskets. Trinkets and jewels, cloth in shades of unimaginable color, hats and clothes and curly-toed shoes hung beneath limp awnings. Guttural voices mingled with singsong tones, scents beckoned and clashed with odors that repelled. Shadows and dusky corners and alleys opened just wide enough for a man to lurk.

A child called for his imma, two lovers stood blind to those who streamed around them, and a man, tall and lean, scanned the teeming crowd with his ebony eyes.

Adah gasped, grabbed Nathan's arm, and pulled. Ducking her head, she darted behind a jeweler's blanketed stall.

"Femi is here."

Nathan pried Adah's grip loose. "So am I. And God is with us."

Zahra yanked her brother into a side alley and glowered into his sullen face. "She sees you and she is warned, you fool."

"She did not see me."

"Are you certain? I saw you."

He shrugged, his complacency irritating her.

"Do you want me to recover the map and ring, or do you want them lost forever? She can run. Join another of the caravans that leave here every day. Adah is not afraid of much and certainly not afraid to go off on her own. Her presence on this miserable trip should tell you that."

He looked at her in surprise. "You like traveling."

"Not with her and Nehemiah's rules."

"If you had obeyed Abba's rules, we would not be here."

Zahra spun on her heel and stalked away. Raking her nails across his face would ensure that everyone saw what they needed to hide—Femi as a young man instead of the older, hunched driver who could not speak.

"Adah, you seem far away tonight."

Adah's gaze flew to Nehemiah's eyes. "I am sorry."

"I have asked you a question several times. Are you thinking of something else, or are you too tired to learn tonight?"

"Both."

He raised an eyebrow. "Tell me."

"I prayed again today. It was not planned. It just popped out."

Nehemiah's eyes twinkled. His lips parted in a wide smile. "The best kind of prayer. Reaching out to the One who is always listening, always with you."

"That is what Nathan—he was with me—said. 'God is with us.'"

CHAPTER TWENTY

Two Weeks Later
Tadmur

Tavi poked her head through the tent's opening. "Adah, you're not busy. Will you go with me to the market? My husband does not want me walking alone this late in the afternoon, but I need to shop."

Adah fastened her leather sandals and wrapped the strap of her bag around her hand.

"You take that bag everywhere. You sleep with it too, don't you?"

"Yes." She shifted so it was opposite Tavi.

Tavi eyed the bag. "It must hold something of great value. What is in it? Is it heavy?"

"My clothes. I could leave those here." She pulled the tunics out and laid them on her bed. "Bits and pieces my imma gave me, a jar, and a letter from a friend. That is about it." *It was almost the truth.* "It does not sound like much, but it is all I own. Oh, and two little rocks. One from Mount Arbel and one from Mount Qasioun."

"You collect rocks?"

"Not usually. These two remind me of places we have passed that I liked."

Tavi's eyebrow rose slightly. Was it disbelief or scorn? "Oh. How...nice."

Definitely scorn.

"It is late to begin shopping. Are you looking for anything particular, Tavi?"

"A bracelet or ring and a cure for my sister, of course—Adah, look to your left. The hat on the Shenzhou man. It looks like it has wings."

Adah nudged her forward. "You are gawking. Stop it. Keep walking."

From across the way, Zahra waved and beckoned. "Adah, Tavi, come see what I found."

Dragging her feet, Adah followed as Tavi wove through the crowd to Zahra's side. Zahra pointed to a curved blade. "I know it is not for a woman's use, but, Adah, look at the craftsmanship of this knife. See the handle? It is ivory. See all the tiny animals carved on it? It reminds me of one my brother has."

"Beautiful," Adah murmured. "I have never seen anything like it." Is this how Femi would kill her?

Zahra hefted the knife, traced the curve of the blade. Tavi shuddered and backed away.

"I-I promised to stay with Tavi. Come with us, Zahra."

Zahra shook her head. "Maybe later I will catch up with you, but not right now, my friend."

Friend? Adah gritted her teeth at Zahra's audacity. How tempting to reveal all she knew and see the woman's face when she realized her plot had been discovered. But years of masking her emotions and holding secrets kept a civil smile in place. It was better to hold the information close than to reveal her knowledge. She nodded acceptance and searched for Tavi, who had wandered away.

Like a chicken, Tavi bobbled across to the opposite side of the crowded area, stopping, stretching upward, stepping first one way and then the other. "There has to be a physician somewhere." She pointed to the end of the market. "Over here. See the sign, the Eye of Horus? That's a symbol of healing and restoration. I think this man is a physician. He is selling something—maybe a cure." She grabbed Adah's sleeve and dragged her forward.

The vendor crooked his finger. "Do not be afraid. Come closer."

Adah pulled free. "Whatever he is selling, it is not good!" She gagged. "Tavi, do not stop here. It smells sour—not like cheese, like rot."

"But if it is medicine to help my sister..."

The vendor bowed to Tavi, ignoring Adah. "You seek healing. Are you sick?"

Tavi nodded then shook her head. "My sister. Nothing has..."

"Let's go. Now." Adah retreated a step, giving Tavi space to follow her.

The man pulled at the sparse hairs on his cheek. "Nothing else has worked, and you are desperate to help her. Yes, you seek a cure, a miracle, and have come to the right place."

"And it is all my..."

Adah poked her. "Stop talking." Didn't Tavi see how the man worked the information into his lure?

"All your fault, no. You could never hurt her. It is your deepest desire for your beloved sister, to be well. You will do whatever is necessary, not consider the time or the effort or the cost—"

Adah pulled Tavi's arm. "We are leaving, Tavi. He is probably selling pig blood."

"You are disgusting." Tavi shrugged from Adah's grasp. "And you do not understand a sister's love."

"I understand more than you know, and I know deceit when I see it. Look around. If this is such a powerful medicine, where are the others lined up to buy it? Why does the seller sit alone in the dirt with only a ripped shade to cover his head? Open your eyes."

The merchant spat, revealing his blackened teeth. Spittle clung to the uneven edge of his beard. "Tell me why this person beside you—certainly not a friend—wishes your sister to remain ill? Wait! I see clearly. She is jealous of the beauty of you and your family."

Tavi blushed and shook her head. "I am not... My sister is the beautiful one, or was until—"

"Until she became ill." He clutched his chest. "My dear woman, I understand your pain. I too have a cherished sister who suffered miserably, until I created this elixir. Now she is restored to perfect health—vows she feels younger and better than ever before. Give thanks, the gods have led you to the right place."

Adah rolled her eyes.

"I—I don't believe in gods. My people have one God."

"Whom she displeased? Ahh, that requires more of this rare elixir."

Adah saw him eye Tavi's silver bracelets.

"My sister did not displease the gods—I mean, God. She is good and kind."

Adah grabbed Tavi's elbow and yanked. "Now. Enough. I am leaving with or without you. No? Fine."

"Adah!" Nathan's voice was the most beautiful sound she'd ever heard. "What are you doing?"

"Tavi wants to buy from this merchant. I do not trust him."

Tavi pulled away from Adah. "Leave if you wish. I trust him. There is a caravan starting for Jerusalem in a few hours. I am sending this cure with them."

"Adah is right, Tavi, but it is of no matter. Your husband commands you to return. It is almost dark, and we may be leaving immediately."

"He will understand. I will just buy—"

Nathan grasped her arm and steered her away. "He said immediately."

"No! I don't know if a better cure really exists." Temper flaring, Tavi twisted, trying to loosen his grip. "Stop! Let me go."

Nathan turned Tavi to face him. "You return with dignity, or I will carry you over my shoulder. When the captain of the caravan issues a command—husband or not—it must be obeyed without a second of delay. He may be aware of a danger unknown to us—a raid, a spreading sickness, even a coming windstorm."

Tavi jerked free. "I am not afraid of a little wind."

"You should be. Out here, they are called 'skinning winds.' The winds are so violent, they tear the skin from your body."

Tavi blanched. Crossing her arms, she walked stiffly between Adah and Nathan through the town and across the camp to their tent. She entered without a word to either of them.

"Nathan, skinning winds? Really?"

"It is true, but they are more likely to blow farther to the east. Skinning winds skin you or suffocate you with their unimaginable force."

"Are we really leaving immediately?"

Her heart beat faster at his slow smile. She swallowed and then blushed, knowing he had realized she was flustered.

"As soon as possible but probably not tonight. Dror said to be ready since Nehemiah received a missive from the king." His smile disappeared. "Adah, be careful. I don't want anyone to harm you. That ring…"

"This ring is a gift from Omari. He entrusted it to me, and I want to honor his request. I plan to show it to Nehemiah tonight. Maybe he can read it."

"I think I might come listen to what he says about it. I will check on the mules and meet you at the campfire. Do not wander off, Adah. Stay in the tent until I come back."

Adah edged inside, the cloudy night making the tent dimmer than usual. Tavi sat with her back to the entrance, her shoulders shaking as she sobbed.

"Tavi, I am sorry. I have met men like him before. They put anything in a bottle and promise miracles. I know you are worried about your sister, and you are trying to find something that will help her. I was trying to be your friend, to keep you from being cheated. I know—"

"Nothing. You know nothing. You never lost a sister. You do not even have a sister."

"Yes, I have lost—"

Tavi's voice broke. "This may have been my one chance—my only chance—to send a cure in time, and you ruined it—you and your lover."

"Nathan is not—"

"Do not think you slipped out unnoticed the other night. I heard you talking to him."

"Yes, but…" Adah stopped. Tavi would hear nothing while she was this irrational.

"If my sister dies, it is your fault." Tavi slung the words with the force of David swinging his sling at Goliath.

"Tavi, please, I was trying to help."

"Leave me alone!"

Adah backed away, uncertain how to calm Tavi.

She looked at the tent door. Twilight's solitude beckoned. She sighed. Walking out now would bring another accusation. In a few minutes, she'd leave to meet Nathan and Nehemiah. Sitting with them in plain sight could not be criticized.

Crossing to her pallet, unable to block Tavi's sobs, she dug through her bag in search of a bit of comfort. She checked over her shoulder. Tavi lay curled on her bed, a pillow over her head.

Alert for the rustling that would warn her of Tavi's approach, she removed the map. Cradling Imma's gifts in her hands, she felt the prick of the bone needle that had come out of the bag with it.

If she closed her eyes, she could almost see Imma's head bent over a torn cloth, tediously mending what most would consider a worthless rag. Her imma considered it worth saving. Worth saving… Something about God tickled her mind like a sneeze twitching the inside of her nose or the tantalizing aroma of an almost forgotten delicacy.

She rummaged through the bag for Emili's letter. Where was it? Where—

"Adah! Adah!"

At Zahra's frantic call, she slipped the map into the folds of her waist sash and shoved the needle and other items into the bag.

Zahra raced into the tent, looking first in Tavi's direction and then in hers.

"Adah, thank goodness I found you." Zahra slapped her hand to her chest and noisily gasped for air. "Nathan needs you immediately. A crisis—something about a twitchy mule? I do not know. The man he sent to find you said to drop everything and come right away. He said the mule was hurt and Nathan needed you to help calm it. They are at the end of the wagon line."

Adah hesitated. Maybe it was simply her distrust of Zahra that made something feel wrong. But if Nathan needed her, she dared not risk ignoring his plea for help. She fastened her sandals and raced out of the tent. Weaving between tents and campfires, dodging those who ambled about the camp, she sped to where Nathan's wagon stood.

"Nathan?"

The silence hit hard.

She'd known it was not right. All of it. Zahra's glance in the wrong direction, her dramatic breathing. The mules would be hobbled with the other beasts, not here far from the main camp. Nathan wouldn't retract his warning that she was not to wander away. He'd not send for her to come out so late.

A whiff of cardamom. Femi was here. Her nostrils flared, lips parted to scream.

Femi's cold, bony hand covered her mouth, pressing hard against her teeth until she tasted blood. His arm crooked around her throat and tightened. Adah clawed his arm, fighting for breath.

God! Did He hear her silent scream? *God! Help!*

Awakened by something crawling across her face, Adah touched her bruised throat. Alive. She was alive. Femi was gone. She clambered to her feet and leaned against the wagon until her head cleared. With a deep breath, she pushed away but faltered.

Rocks crunched beneath heavy feet. Whoever approached did not try to hide. She forced herself to breathe, prepared to run. A man-sized shadow fell across her path and, despite herself, a hoarse sob escaped.

"Adah? Are you here?"

She slumped against the wagon, relief weakening her more than fear. Tears seeped from beneath her lids. Safe. Nathan was here. She was safe.

"Nathan." Her voice refused to work.

"I told you not to wander away. You know Femi is hunting you. Nehemiah is waiting for you, for us. What were you thinking?"

She shook her head vehemently, strained a whisper past the bruising. "I…you…Zahra…"

"Zahra? What does she—"

Clouds shifted, revealing the moon—and her disarray. Nathan started toward her, his arms outstretched. She saw him flinch, and fear flashed across his face.

"Femi." She held her hands around her neck. Would he understand?

"He choked you? Did he…"

How could she answer both questions? She shook her head no, hoped he understood.

"Can you walk?"

At her nod, he moved forward and circled an arm around her shoulders. He held her close and guided her back to the camp and her tent. Shaking violently, she wished he'd never let her go.

"Adah, I do not want to leave you, but Nehemiah must be immediately informed. Can you go inside and rest? Do you think Zahra had anything to do with this? I will return as soon as possible, and I intend to sleep outside your door tonight." He pressed his lips against her forehead and she leaned into him, not caring who saw them or whose rules they broke. He released her and she felt the loss.

No! Do not leave me. But the words did not emerge from her bruised throat. She started after Nathan, but he had already disappeared. Exhaustion threatened to see her crumple in the dirt in plain view of everyone.

God, help me. God understood. He'd been with her when Femi attacked.

With great reluctance, she pushed aside the tent door, stepped inside, and stopped short, dumbfounded. Strewn across Tavi's bed were the contents of her bag—needle, scarf, coin purse, comb, earrings, and Omari's jar of balm.

Tavi stared past Zahra at her. "She did it. I did not do this—"

"It is all over your bed, Tavi. Who else would do this? I would not. Adah and I are friends. You are the one who argued with her in the marketplace. Everyone heard about it."

"You did it, Zahra!" Outrage twisted Tavi's features. "You dumped it here."

"Adah, I had just returned from searching for the man Nathan had sent so I could ask if he needed more help. I walked in and tried to stop her but…" Zahra twisted toward Adah. She gasped and paled. "What happened to you?"

White-lipped, Adah moved brusquely to Tavi's bed. Jerkily, she gathered her things. Thank God she'd had the ring and map on her person. She halted. Had that been God's protection too?

Ignoring Tavi and Zahra, she wrapped her arms around the bag and curled on the bed with her back to them. She groaned at the scratch on the tent and the voice of Joezer, Nehemiah's servant. If her throat was not throbbing, she'd have demanded to be left alone. She sighed. If her throat did not hurt so much, he wouldn't be here.

"Our Nehemiah sent me. Forgive the intrusion, please. Most unusual—I have never, well…" He bobbed his head evidently agreeing with himself. "Our Nehemiah is most concerned about the attack on Adah. Most concerned. He ordered me—although I was glad to do this—to hasten with a honeyed drink for your injury."

How did Nehemiah tolerate such a nervous man? The image of Imma bent over the torn cloth, the worthless cloth, came to mind. Was Nehemiah slowly mending the man, or rather, had he seen past the raggedness to the wound, and like Nathan said, was using his gifts for others?

She sat up and managed a semblance of a smile for him.

"Our Nehemiah decided we will stay here several more days. You can rest, and he can find the culprit. He is a good man—of course, only God is good—but next to God, oh my, is that blasphemous? I did not mean to compare. Comparison leads to great woe."

She patted his hand and shook her head. The furrows of his brow softened.

"He is fond of you, our Nehemiah, as if you were his little sister. He is most upset. We all are." Joezer tapped the tips of his fingers together. "Our Nehemiah has stationed additional guards front and back of your tent. It will not happen again, no indeed, it will not. You and the others are to stay in this tent until the evil one is found." He shuddered. "It will not go well for him, no indeed. When you are able, you will talk to Nehemiah?"

She nodded and yawned. Something in the honeyed drink was making her drowsy.

Joezer bowed. "Is there another need?"

She shook her head.

"No? Then I will go." He bowed again and maybe again, but Adah closed her eyes, wanting only to escape.

CHAPTER TWENTY-ONE

I am here again, Adah, on our Nehemiah's orders." Joezer beamed at her the next morning. "This time it is with his request that you join him if you are able. Or maybe even if you are not." His brow wrinkled. "He did not say."

Adah hastened to allay his fear. "I am able." She smiled at his concern. "Just hoarse."

She followed Joezer to Nehemiah's tent, where Nathan waited inside. Both men scrutinized her until she lowered her head and blushed.

Nehemiah gestured for her to sit down. "Forgive me, Adah. I deeply regret what you have experienced. It is my failure as a leader that you were subjected to an attack, but I thank God you survived. It is my understanding that speaking is painful for you."

Adah dipped her head. "I can whisper."

"Can but should not until your throat heals." Nathan pointed his finger at Adah. "My imma once told me that."

"You do not know all of the story. I was looking in my bag for a letter. I think it has been stolen."

Nehemiah's eyebrow rose. "Help me puzzle out what happened. Zahra said someone—she was not sure who—told her Nathan sent for Adah. A problem with a mule. Nathan?"

"Untrue. Adah and I had agreed to meet at the campfire and ask you about the ring. I checked on my mules and went to the campfire but saw she was not there. You were speaking with someone else, so I went looking for her."

Nehemiah turned to Adah. "Adah, you went to Nathan's wagon? Yes? Was he there?"

She shook her head.

"You were attacked from behind?"

"And choked," Adah rasped.

"Did you see the attacker?"

She nodded.

"So you know who it was?"

Adah forced the word through the ache in her throat. "Femi."

Nehemiah frowned. "There is no one in the caravan by that name. Who is he? How do you know him? How do you know it was this Femi?"

It flooded back. Omari's eyes glazing over, blood seeping from Donkor's head, the protruding knife, the dust puffing from beneath Jonah's body when he fell. She shook her head—throat too swollen, heart too bruised—unable to speak, to explain.

Nathan reached for her hand. "Let me. I think I know most of the story."

He told it well. Nehemiah's lips tightened, and his eyes blazed with a fury she was glad was not directed at her.

When she could speak without pain, she'd tell them both how God had comforted her and made His presence known. The thought startled her. *That's* what she wanted to share? Not her fear or anger? Not the violation of her personal belongings?

The mysterious warmth, like a hug within her spirit, filled her, smoothing away the raggedness of distress. More. She wanted more of this—whatever it was. She wanted it to stay with her, never leave, to live in her so she could live in it. When she could talk, she'd describe it to Nehemiah. Maybe he knew what it was called, how to keep it.

"Adah, tomorrow, after you have rested, I will examine the ring. For now, stay close to the tent." Nehemiah's tone brooked no argument. "A guard will escort you to and from Nathan's wagon each day." He sighed. "Unfortunately, I can do nothing about the three of you sharing the tent, but I will have Zahra watched. You will speak of this to no one." His eyes twinkled. "I am confident you will not, since you can hardly speak at all."

Adah had a sudden urge to stick her tongue out at him. She didn't.

The next night, Nehemiah cupped his hand to accept the ring. He turned the ring over and held it close to his eyes, twisting it until the firelight illuminated the markings and warmed the gold to a fine sheen.

Haltingly, he read the inscribed words. "'God of light, I seek to return to You. Grant mercy to this nomad, lost child of the ark.'"

"I believe it indicates that the descendants of Ham also desire a return to Adonai's peace."

Nathan reached for the ring and held it to the light. "Why is it coveted?"

"It is quite old, perhaps more than a thousand years although it is not nearly as old as your map."

Adah jumped and removed the map from her sash. "Next?" she croaked.

Nehemiah smiled approval. "This is what is more important. I agree." He spread the thin leather on his knees and bent over it. "Ahh. These squiggly lines are a river. It must be the Euphrates—a large, very important river. It flows beside Dira ze urta." He shrugged. "A small town."

Nathan drew numbers in the dirt with a stick. "Two more weeks, maybe three?"

"Closer to two, I hope. We have just enough supplies to last us until the next town. Damascus was low on salt and grain."

The men shared a long look.

"What?" If they heard her question, they ignored it.

Nehemiah returned to poring over the map. He glanced up and smiled. "Adah, you said these holes in the leather were caused by your brother or an insect?"

Without waiting for her answer, Nehemiah continued. "Look up at the stars. There. See where I am pointing, the star at the tip?"

Confused, she shook her head. Of course she saw the stars, but which one at the tip of what?

Nathan drew a bear in the dirt. "Here, Adah. This is the Bear. Look there, where my finger is. See it?"

It didn't look like a bear to her, but she saw where he was pointing.

"At the end, two stars point to a little bear or a dog."

She studied Nathan's drawings, then the sky. That was a dog? Nathan was either not good at drawing or had never seen a dog.

"This star"—Nathan pointed to the tip of the dog's tail—"is Polaris. It does not move like the others."

Nehemiah cleared his throat. "Adah, Polaris is another of God's gifts. We navigate by it, true, but that is not its only purpose."

Adah saw Nathan frown, and then his face cleared. He nodded. "I had not thought of that."

She glowered at both of them. "What?"

Nehemiah chuckled. "Sorry, Adah. Our Abba God is like Polaris in that He is constant. No matter where we are, He can be found. He is our steadfast guide through life, our refuge."

Oh. She liked that. Adah stared at the star, then studied Nathan's drawing and the map. Frowning, she inspected them again.

"I see it too." Nehemiah's soft voice broke her concentration. "These holes on your map are not your little brother's markings nor an insect's boring. They replicate the star we call Polaris."

Chills raced up her arms. Nehemiah handed her the map. She held it up to the flames, and the tiny holes seemed to twinkle like stars.

"Adah, put the map away. Now."

Hearing the urgency in Nathan's voice, she lowered the map to her lap.

"Zahra is walking this way."

Adah pulled into herself, bringing her elbows to touch her side, tensing her shoulders. It was good that talking remained painful, or she'd need to clamp down on the soft flesh inside her mouth. She curled her lips inward as a precaution.

Zahra shuffled forward. She nodded at the men and knelt beside Adah. Did the Mizraite woman not feel aversion radiating toward her? This woman would allow her to be killed, had lied to her, had sent her into danger. Adah regarded her, allowing no expression to betray her thoughts. The corner of Zahra's eye twitched. She averted her gaze, sighed, and looked Adah full in the face.

"Adah, I am sorry this happened to you. I deeply regret my part in it." She glanced at Nathan. "Nathan did not send for you. I lied. I wanted to see what was so precious in your bag."

Scrutinizing her, Adah read genuine regret. Zahra omitted much of the story, but what she spoke seemed true. She nodded, accepting the apology.

"I saw you have a jar of balm. Rub it on your neck. It will help you heal. My abba had an obsidian jar exactly like yours that he treasured. It is excellent quality." Zahra stood. "I hope you will forgive me and we can be friends."

Friends? Adah felt her eyebrows shoot up to her hairline. Zahra could take it as delight or disbelief. She didn't care. If the woman didn't leave soon, she'd push past the swelling in her throat and, if she was never able to speak again, would be satisfied with the verbal laceration she'd inflict.

Zahra nodded to Nathan and Nehemiah. Her wide shoulders slightly hunched, she turned toward the wagons.

"Zahra." Nehemiah's soft voice carried a command.

She turned.

"It was brave of you to humble yourself before Adah."

Startled, she bobbed her head, straightened, and walked quickly away.

Adah glared at Nehemiah. He had praised Zahra?

Nehemiah sighed, compassion gentling his features. "That hurt you."

She stared determinedly into the fire.

"My precious Adah, you see what others miss. Do not let your anger blind you from seeing the hurt in those who hurt you. You do not know—may never know—Zahra's story. I do, and I promise you it is as harsh as yours, though very different."

"Tavi?" Even a whisper hurt.

"Our Tavi carries deep wounds and yearns for a trusted friend who will hear her without judging. I will say no more than this. Take it to our Abba God."

She frowned. Take anger and resentment to God? Hadn't she already done that? Did he mean again?

"Yes, Adah. Again and again."

She stared at him. How had he read her mind?

"It is what I must do each day, sometimes each hour." Nehemiah swiveled to face Nathan. "And you as well?"

Nathan leaned forward to rest his elbows on his knees. "It never stops."

Zahra waited three days before she deemed herself calm enough to approach her brother. Additional men still guarded the women's tent, but she and the other two women were no longer confined within. As twilight deepened from gray to purple, she made her way to Femi's wagon.

His small eyes regarded her with indifference.

"I saw her neck. You could have killed her, you fool."

"I did not, though."

"There is not really a reason to kill her. Let her live. We just need to find the map and my ring."

"My ring." Femi stepped closer, squeezed her arm. "Not in her bag?"

Zahra tried to pull away. "Hands off. No. It was not there."

"Lie to me, Zahra, and you will pay."

Brazenly, she thrust her face closer to his. "Would I be here talking to you if I had found it and planned to deceive you?"

He released her arm. "No."

She rubbed at the pain from his grip. "Femi, we have to work together like we did as children when Abba thwarted our wishes. That is how we always got our way, remember?"

"You and Donkor did. Not me."

"I thought we wanted the same things."

He jutted out his jaw. "No."

Zahra fisted her hands on her hips. "Why did you not tell us?"

"Donkor talked louder and faster."

"Oh." She reached out to touch his shoulder in an apology.

He dodged her outstretched arm. "Donkor is dead. Now, you listen to *me*."

"Femi, I am sorry."

"Go away, Zahra. I have work."

"As you will, but Femi, let Adah live for Abba's sake. Our abba must have cared for her. He gave her his precious obsidian and gold jar of expensive balm."

She left, moving away until he could not see her, then circled back. Femi hated work. Whatever he was planning would hurt someone—that, he seemed to enjoy.

Femi crawled beneath the wagon and then onto its bed. She heard him grunt. Saw bags of grain moved. Moonlight glinted on his dagger.

CHAPTER TWENTY-TWO

Two days after leaving Tadmur

Nathan was waiting for Adah outside her tent. "Nehemiah has decided I am to drive the supply wagon and the new driver will take my place—the older man. He thinks such a large wagon may be too tiring for him. Nehemiah noticed that the driver seems agitated."

Nathan inspected the ground and the sky and the back of his hands. "He said you could decide to ride with the old man or with me. I will have the same mules."

"You."

Nathan looked up and grinned.

"I like Twitch and Crook."

He threw back his head and laughed. "They like you too, but no more talking and no singing."

He slung her bag over his shoulder and led her to the larger wagon. Nathan circled the wagon, checking the wheels and the mules' reins. "Looks good." Signaling the captain of the guard, he mounted. "Ready?"

Dirt surrounded them. Dirt-beige land, dirt-grayed rocks, dirt-brown hills. A few straggling grasses braved the sun's blaze. Adah supposed there was beauty to be found in the dirt-toned bleakness, but as hard as she looked, it escaped her. Nothing here was on her map.

She elbowed Nathan to get his attention. "Talk." Her voice was hoarse, and she knew he'd shush her if she talked, and after so many years of being unable to speak freely, she didn't want to be shushed.

"Why? I have nothing to say." He dodged her elbow. "Hmm. When I travel a desert, I think of our people leaving Mizraim and living in this"—he gestured to the arid expanse—"not for a couple of weeks but for forty years."

Adah made a face.

"I think it taught them about Polaris. Keep your eyes where they should be—on God's direction—and not where you want them to be—on you."

Where did she want to be? Home? No, not with Imma gone. Jerusalem? Beautiful, mysterious Jerusalem? Hebron? Absurd. City of blood and grief—and Emili. She wanted to be in Hebron with Emili. Emili, who was safety, acceptance, kindness. Emili, who said she was the daughter she'd always wanted, who'd offered a home to her.

"Nathan."

"Stop talking."

Annoying man. She'd miss him terribly. "Where will…" She dashed away a tear. "Where will you go next?"

"Home. Hebron. It is the most joyful place I know."

Her eyes bulged. Joyful?

"Think, Adah. Every city has death and violence, even Jerusalem. Hebron offers hope to those falsely accused. Families come alongside their own during the dark days. They reunite, and when they are free to leave, their bonds are stronger. Even those who are guilty can have a second chance—and forgiveness. Everyone needs that."

Forgiveness?

That word again. Rejecting Nathan's comment, Adah turned to look at the endless desert flats. She knew a few people who did not deserve a second chance, and the list had grown with Zahra.

"You do not like the idea, huh? You ever need forgiveness?"

She shrugged. None of his business.

"God forgives."

"I am not God," she ground out.

"No doubt there." Nathan chuckled when she clutched her throat to stifle a laugh. "None of us are, but His law says, 'Be holy because I, the Lord Your God, am holy.'"

"You?"

"Oh, Adah, I am far from it."

Adah jiggled her hands, palms up, waiting. "Listening."

Nathan turned his head from her. For a long moment, she thought he would not speak.

"God has forgiven me as has she, but I am deeply shamed by how I wronged my imma. I blamed her for my abba's death. I thought if she'd been good enough and kind enough, maybe he would never have ventured beyond the gates, never been killed, never left me... outside. Different.

"This is hard to share, to remember." He exhaled a deep breath. "In my fight to be included, to be like the others, I did things, said things, that set me more apart—the one the other abbas warned their sons against."

Nathan angled his body to face her. "Adah, I did not deserve forgiveness or a second chance, but I was forgiven over and over and granted a third chance and a fifth chance and a seventh chance. How can I not forgive others?"

Tears moistened his eyes. One slid down his face. Adah leaned against him to brush it away with her thumb.

He shifted the reins and caught her hand. "I will never be holy, but I will never stop trying to become more God-like."

Adah tugged her hand from his to wipe her own tear.

"How?"

Nathan cleared his throat. "Imma said it is twofold. One is realizing we forgive because we have been forgiven. The other is that sometimes the one who hurt you does not much care about being forgiven, so if you keep hurting and being angry, you are just hurting yourself. Or they might care a lot, but until you forgive, you are both trapped."

Adah pointed to where the captain was signaling for the drivers to halt their teams.

"That is strange. It is too early to stop. I will just check the wheels again."

Adah stood and stretched and nearly fell at Nathan's vehement bellow. "No!" He spun and crawled beneath the wagon.

"What?"

He emerged red-faced with his jaw set and his fists clenched. He leaped over the edge of the wagon and slung bags of grain to one side. Panting, he held up a limp bag. "Half have been slit. Grain spilling out with every turn of the wheel." He ran a hand around the back of his neck. "Nehemiah needs to know. Stay put."

No question of defiance as her knees buckled. She sat with a thump.

Moments later, he returned with Nehemiah and the guard captain. "There are half a dozen empty bags. I estimate we have lost several days' provisions." He held up one of the empty bags. "This was intentional. The slit is straight, slashed with a well-honed blade."

Nehemiah swung away and stood, his fists clenched. At last, he bowed his head, took a deep breath, and turned back to Nathan.

"Nehemiah, at the next town, replace me. If I am not part of this caravan, maybe the vandalism will stop."

"And me." Adah croaked as loudly as possible, but if she was heard, it was unacknowledged.

"No." Nehemiah slashed upward with his hand. "Here!" The roar of his command summoned guards and the other drivers. "Line the wagon with blankets so no more grain is lost. Work in teams of two. Nathan, with me." He swung onto the wagon and began shifting the bags to one side.

A grizzled driver clapped Nathan's shoulder. "Do not blame yourself, boy. I should have caught on. My mules have been fighting to stop and eat instead of walking. Not to worry. We will make it through." He chuckled. "It will not be the first time food's been scarce, and it will not be the last."

But Adah heard the strain in his laugh, saw the others avoid Nathan's eyes even as they nodded. This was the reason Nehemiah and Nathan had been concerned about the driver's replacement at the beginning of the trip. His character was unknown to Nehemiah, as was the driver Zahra vouched for.

The damage controlled, the caravan moved forward.

Adah swallowed, her throat gravelly. "What happens now?"

"We ration. And pray for Elisha's miracle, except that instead of olive oil being multiplied, grain is multiplied."

"Does God still work that way?"

"I hope so. Or it is going to be a long week."

Adah's stomach rumbled as she frowned into her bowl. Elisha's miracle had not been repeated. The grain dwindled. The misery multiplied. She hoped whoever did this was suffering as much as she was. She'd often gone hungry, but nights with two irritable women and a grim Nathan by day made it worse.

At least not talking for most of a week had changed her voice from raspy to scratchy. Not that she talked to anyone but Crook and Twitch. Nathan seemed convinced the vandal and her attacker were the same person. Focused on scrutinizing everyone, he no longer shared stories or laughter. She missed him. Missed them. More than she wanted to admit.

Except for the apology by the campfire, neither Zahra nor Tavi had spoken to her nor, as far as she knew, to each other since the night Femi attacked her.

She was tired. Bone-deep tired. Tired of being on guard about the map and the ring and what she observed about her tentmates but would never say. Because of Femi, she had another reason to be guarded—staying alive. The outward bruising had faded, and she was no longer sore from struggling against him or falling to the ground. The inward bruising remained– tender scars invading her dreams, the feel of his hand hard against her mouth, the outrage as her strength fell to his.

Peace. Safety. Acceptance. In this moment, the reasons she'd undertaken this venture seemed far away—as distant as they had in Jerusalem.

Adah returned the bowl of her uneaten food to the tray and left the tent. She needed to see Nehemiah. She needed some answers.

Joezer, blessedly subdued for once, admitted her to Nehemiah's tent. Watching Nehemiah sign documents, she saw weariness hovering over him. Deepened lines, more strands of gray, his face thinner—this journey had aged him.

Looking up, he smiled a welcome and waved her to a seat. "Rejoice! Soon we will renew our supplies in Dira ze urta and approach the great Euphrates."

"Nehemiah, forgive me for coming unannounced. I need...I do not know what I need...but I am tired and afraid and confused."

He set down his pen and leaned forward. She loved how Nehemiah listened to everyone who spoke to him—as if the speaker was the only person who mattered in his world, as if for this moment, his entire purpose was to hear beyond the person's words and into the reason for their words—the hurt or fear or pride.

Adah cleared her throat. "You and usually Nathan and Emili—his imma—have a strength I do not understand."

He regarded her with the attentiveness she'd learned to expect from him yet sensed he was hearing something she did not hear.

"Adah, you know I was cupbearer to the king for longer than you have been alive. Do you understand what that means? A king's reign is always tenuous. His next breath uncertain. His life in constant danger. The easiest way to kill royalty is to poison the drink or food. Whenever he was thirsty, I tasted his drink before offering him the cup."

"You could have been poisoned instead of him."

"I risked my life for his. I faced death beside him. Each morning, I woke knowing it might be my last day."

"I could not bear to live that way."

Nehemiah chuckled softly. "But you do. We all do."

She blinked. He was right. Of all the deaths in the last few months, only Imma had known her breaths were numbered.

"How?" She squinted in concentration. "How do you live with death always looking over your shoulder?"

"It is called peace. Peace with the God of heaven who created me. I am safe with Him. I am content with Him. King David declared, 'My times are in Your Hands.' Whether I flourish or suffer, my life is in His keeping."

She chewed her thumbnail. "How do I get there?"

"We have spoken of this before, and though you took the first steps toward it, you will not like my answer."

Adah grinned. "I usually do not. Tell me anyway, please."

"Forgiveness."

"You are right. I still do not like it." Her eyes narrowed. "Someone stole a letter from my bag. I am supposed to forgive them, and you are to forgive the one who slit the bags of grain?"

"I am sorry about your letter, and yes, I will forgive the one who robbed us of supplies. When caught, he will be punished, and I will not allow him the privilege of driving the supply wagon. But forgiven? Yes."

"Because?"

"I refuse to let his wrongs limit me."

"His wrong limited our food supply."

"But not our response. This has reminded me of the importance of knowing who is in my charge. My response to him or her is to learn. Do you understand?"

Joezer barged into the tent. "I interrupt only because it is necessary. I think it is. Only you can tell me, my Nehemiah."

"Adah, I must attend to this. Tomorrow, when we have camped by the river, we can speak of this more." He inclined his head and turned to his servant. "Joezer, your judgment is impeccable. What is needed?"

Disappointed, Adah meandered to her tent. Entering, she crossed to her bed and sat, angling herself to contemplate the other two women. If forgiveness was so important, she'd forgive. She wanted the serenity Nehemiah held close. No, more than holding it close, he lived in serenity as if it were his skin, his very being.

She eyed the people around her, people with hidden wounds. Her anger only wounded them more. She would forgive even Femi—she swallowed, her throat still tender—and Zahra, who watched her from the corners of her slanted eyes, and Tavi, who was studiously avoiding her.

She'd forgive all of them—tomorrow when she was not so tired and her head did not ache.

CHAPTER TWENTY-THREE

Near Deir ez-Zor and the Euphrates

The next morning, Adah woke alone in the tent. Head throbbing, she dragged her tongue across her parched lips and pushed herself to sit up on her pallet. Once the room slowed its spinning, she reached for her satchel and dragged it closer. It was so heavy today. Was she that tired? She touched her face, felt its heat, the dry, blistered skin. Water. She needed water.

On the third try, she managed to stand—swaying—and stumbled toward the low table that held bread, cheese, and water. She averted her eyes from the food and grasped the last cup, but her hands trembled like Omari's, and the water soaked the front of her tunic.

Someone groaned. Her? The voice sounded familiar.

Shards of light shot into her eyes as the tent flap was thrown open. She staggered back with a gasp of pain and threw her arm across her eyes.

"Good, you are awake."

The voice was so loud. Why was this woman shouting at her?

"I was worried, since you are always up first, but you seemed so tired last night I thought you had decided to sleep longer. Adah?"

The loudness moved closer.

"Adah? Are you all right? Adah?"

"Imma?" Only she had ever softened Adah's name to a lullaby, but Imma never raised her voice. "Imma?"

"No, not your imma. It is me, Tavi. Adah, you are sick. Adah, can you hear me?"

"Imma?" Adah turned, seeking the dear face. "Where...? I cannot find you. Do not leave me again. I need you." Spreading her arms did not stop the room's tilt.

Adah dropped to her knees to keep from falling. "I have it. I know what it is. Come with me, Imma. I am going to look for it, looking hard. Do not leave me."

Someone's sobs pierced the silence.

"What are you looking for...dear girl?"

Adah frowned. Imma never called her "dear girl."

"What are you looking for?"

"Map." Adah moaned and clutched her head. It was too heavy for her neck to hold up, and talking made the pounding harder. She forced her mouth to form the words. "The place."

"What place?"

"Eden."

"What? Adah, stand up."

She was melting. Adah watched the tent floor draw closer until her eyelashes brushed the dusty fabric. She closed her eyes. The voice above her faded.

———

"Stop." Adah protested the incessant jarring. It continued. She was awake. Why was Nathan shaking her shoulder? "Stop it."

"Adah? Did you say something?"

The voice was not Nathan's. She opened her eyes and immediately squeezed them closed against the sun's glare. A lightweight cloth was placed on her eyes, and a gentle, perfumed hand patted her shoulder. Definitely not Nathan.

"I am sorry. The road turned, and I forgot your face would be in the sun. Oh, and I decided to forgive you."

Forgive her for what? The dry thickness of her tongue made it hard to speak. "Tavi?"

"Yes. Good. You know me."

A skin of water was pressed against her lips and removed too soon.

"Of course I know you." Such a foolish thing to say. Cross, Adah struggled to sit up. "Why am I in here? Where is Nathan?"

"You have been sick. Too sick to do anything but sleep. Here, drink more but slowly. You slept in my wagon for two days and then yesterday, the Sabbath, in our tent."

Adah blinked. Scratched the nape of her neck where sweat had dried and stiffened her hair. She licked her chapped lips and tried to remember.

Her head had ached unbearably, and she'd been so thirsty. Imma had been there. Adah shook her head at the impossibility and winced at the remnant of pain lurking between her eyes. She'd *dreamed* Imma said her name, dreamed Imma had not understood, had forgotten about the—

"Oh no! My bag! Where is my bag?" Jerkily she twisted and scanned the space beside her. She touched the floor and swiveled to examine the area where she'd lain. "Where is it?" Her voice shrilled. "Where?" She burst into tears.

Tavi reached for the bag and held it out to Adah. "Here."

Adah snatched it from Tavi's hands and cradled it against her chest. "I am sorry. It is important to me."

"I noticed."

Shaking, she dashed unwelcome tears from her cheeks. "I cannot lose it. It is all I have."

"These things were your imma's? All of them?"

Adah's heart skipped. "Why do you ask?"

"You mentioned her when you were so sick—cried out to her."

Adah looked away to hide the panic she feared would stain her face. What had she said? Something unusual, or Tavi would not be so curious.

"Many call for their imma when ill. Don't you?"

Tavi fidgeted with her bracelets. "You insisted you were looking for something. It sounded as if you knew where to go, knew the right direction. It seemed important to you, and you begged her to go with you."

"Oh?" She shrugged to hide the tension rattling through her. "Did I say what I was looking for?"

Her stomach knotted as once again she felt the drag of each movement, the effort of speech, the slow yielding of her mind to betrayal. Had she revealed her destination? Had she spoken of the map? Her secret might no longer be secret.

Adah refused to lean on Tavi's arm, though her wobbly legs begged for reprieve. The river seemed no closer than it had when she left the tent. She paused until her labored breathing calmed, then pressed on.

Wading into the cold water, she knelt and let the gentle lapping bear her weight until she shivered uncontrollably. Her wet clothes dragged against the water, requiring her last bit of energy to crawl onto the bank and collapse against her bag.

"So sleepy." Tavi dropped down beside her, yawned, and closed her eyes.

Sun-dappled shade above and the lull of waves teasing the banks coaxed her eyes closed. Tavi snored softly beside her.

Adah woke when Nathan shook her shoulder. Groggy, she sat up.

He put a finger to his lips. "Bring the map." Reaching his hand out, he pulled her to her feet. "I can carry you, again, if you would like."

A smile tickled her lips. She'd like that very much but she shook her head. "I will walk."

His look of disappointment did strange things to her stomach.

They walked along the river, past the camp, and stopped by a pile of stones. Nathan took her hand and squeezed it. "I hope what you are about to see does not overly excite you."

"I will survive. Show me."

"When I walked by here earlier a man was stacking stones."

"He did a fine job. Did you tell him so?"

"I asked what the pile of stones represented. He did not know." Nathan stopped and smiled at her. "He said, 'This Ebenezer existed long before I was born or my father or my father's father. It may have stood here from the beginning of time. Each generation of my family ensures that it remains standing.'"

Adah stared at Nathan. "Did he say anything else?

"'It is what we do.'"

She clapped her hands over her mouth.

"There is more. Look." Nathan pointed to the tiny flaming swords on a half-buried rock.

Adah knelt and traced it with her finger.

"Come on, Adah. Nehemiah wants to talk to me, and I need to see you safely back with Tavi."

He helped her to stand. She did not refuse his hand, and she did not mind when he held on to her longer than necessary.

The wide blue river flowed steadily, placidly running its course—a well-mannered river. A smile quirked the corner of her lips. This was the river on her map! Excitement squiggled inside her. Soon she would enter the Garden of Eden. Would it be filled with sunshine? Would she see the Tree of Life and sit beneath its shade? Each day brought her closer to knowing.

Brought her and the others closer.

She eyed Tavi. Still sleepy, unguarded. This was a good time to understand Tavi's guilt whenever her sister was mentioned.

"Why do you think it is your fault your sister is ill?" She waited. Unblinking.

Tavi blinked until her eyes filled with tears.

The shallow breath, the wilted shoulders, the eyes that tightened, spoke of raw anguish.

"Tell me."

"Dror, my husband, wished to marry a daughter of a priestly family from Jerusalem. I wanted him to be mine. Noya is so beautiful—everyone says so. I knew he would choose her."

"But he did not."

"He did not have a choice. He never saw her, only me."

Adah leaned forward. "I am listening."

"My cousin knew I desired Dror and said she would take care of it." Tavi covered her mouth and shook her head. "I thought she meant to distract her that day. I never guessed my cousin would give Noya something to make her sleep. She gave her too much, and now Noya will not wake up. My abba discovered the truth and told my cousin's parents. They moved far away." Tavi buried her face in her hands, sobs wracking her body until she retched. "Our family is torn apart, and it is my fault."

"No, Tavi, that is not true. None of it is your fault. I wish I could help."

The sobs stopped. Tavi peeked through her fingers and sniffled. "Really?"

Adah tensed at the abrupt change, her gaze fixed on Tavi.

"Take me with you—to the Garden and the Tree of Life."

Deathly still, Adah seethed, berating herself for attributing Tavi's dramatics to genuine emotion. She'd missed the signs, the show of friendship, the display of near hysteria in the market, the wrenching confession—tearless, she realized.

"How long have you known?"

"Since you told Nehemiah in Jerusalem."

Adah thought of the leaf falling from the balcony. Wordlessly, she stood, reached for her bag, and began walking back to camp.

Tavi tagged behind, dogging her heels. "You will take me? I can go with you, since I know you have the map? Are you upset that I went through your bag while you were sick?"

Adah whirled. "You! You must be the one who stole my letter from Emili. Give it to me immediately."

"No! I took nothing, only looked at the map and returned it to your bag. I am not a thief."

"You are a liar and a thief." Adah lengthened her stride. Despite her legs' weakness, she pushed herself to walk faster and faster until she outdistanced Tavi and her pleas.

Rage as she'd never known crammed her mind, pounded through her veins, obliterating thought or reason. She stormed past her tent, past the camp, past the hobbled beasts. The sun had begun its surrender before she slowed. The camp—a dark blur—huddled at a distance on the desert.

Tavi's secretiveness shook her. She prided herself on seeing people's hidden clues but Tavi had thoroughly deceived her. Beyond her damaged pride, Adah ached at again being treated as little more than a slave. Tavi's searching her bag was yet another intrusion, another act of someone who saw her as one to be used, as unworthy of respect. This bag she cradled held the few things she could call her own. They were her memory treasures and her hope for a better future.

Reluctantly, she slowed her pace, turned, and started the journey back. Calmer, she admitted to herself that Tavi's only wrongs had been sifting through her things and stealing Emili's letter. Perhaps Tavi did not mean to overhear the conversation with Nehemiah. She obviously would do anything to find a cure for her sister, and if she believed Adah knew where to find the cure, maybe her actions were not so terrible.

Adah's feet dragged, weary and weak from her days of illness. She clenched her teeth and forced herself to continue walking. Fury had driven her far from camp. Grit would see her back. One more step. One more. Again. Step. Breathe. One more step.

"God." Step. Breathe. "Help." Step. Breathe. Had the camp moved farther away? The last sunray faded to a shadow. Her knees buckled. Falling forward, she locked her elbows, landing on all fours. Dragged herself up. Balanced. Stepped.

The camp's fires were visible when she heard Nathan call her name. Mouth too dry to speak, arms too tired to wave, she stood still. He'd see her. How, she didn't know, but he would.

He did.

"Little fool. You do not have the sense you were born with, woman. What were you thinking?"

His chiding—music.

He held a skin of water to her lips.

"I will not return to that tent."

Nathan touched his finger to her lips. "Nehemiah has rearranged things so Dror and Tavi will share a tent. Only Zahra will be in the tent with you."

"He heard?"

"A servant saw you leave camp. When he finally thought to inform Nehemiah, Tavi was questioned and the arrangements made."

"Thank you."

"Adah, can you walk the rest of the way?"

"Yes." She drew in a ragged breath, thrust her chin out, and limped forward.

"Hmm." Nathan bent, unwound the bag from her grasp and slung it across one shoulder, then bent again. One arm circled her back, and the other slipped behind her knees.

"Put me down. I can walk."

He ignored her. Too worn to fight his strength, she sighed and rested her head in the warm curve of his shoulder. He felt like safety. He felt…right.

Zahra watched silently as broad-shouldered Nathan laid the sleeping Adah on her pallet. He lifted each foot to unlash her sandals, then grimaced.

Peering around him, she saw Adah's swollen, filthy feet. A basin of water stood by the tent's entrance. She carried it to Adah's pallet and knelt only to be met by Nathan's snarl.

"Do not touch her."

She recoiled and stiffened her shoulders. "I am not her enemy, Nathan. I wish her no harm. She is safe with me."

His gaze bored into hers and then widened a fraction in surprise. It surprised her too, this admission. True, she wanted—and would have—the ring and the map, but not tonight, not with Adah defenseless.

Tonight, Zahra ached with the longing for something else this peasant girl had. Her gaze drifted to Nathan. Adah held a treasure more valuable and rarer than either the ring or map. She had someone who looked at her as if she was worth ten rings and maps.

Zahra held out a cloth to clean Adah's feet. "I will inform Nehemiah of her safe return. She has become as a younger sister to him."

"Stay, Zahra." Nathan wiped a hand over his face. "It is better if you care for her. I will return when Nehemiah knows to recall those searching for her." He reached for Adah's bag. "This stays with me."

Zahra nodded, her estimation of Nathan increased. Her abba and her husband would have protected her in the same way. Though in truth, she'd not thought to search for the ring while Adah slept. Femi would be perturbed. She shrugged. He'd never know.

Zahra dipped the cloth in water. She smoothed Adah's hair back and washed the sweat and dust from her face and neck. She rinsed the cloth and lifted the edge of Adah's tunic to wipe where a few drops of water had trickled. Adah cried out and shoved Zahra's hand away. It must yet be tender, or the memory of Femi's hands was still fresh.

More gently she dabbed a smear at the base of Adah's throat. Adah moaned. The oil lamp flickered, gilding a circle around her throat. Zahra squinted in the dim light. A chain dipped between Adah's breasts. A gold chain. Zahra followed a faint line to where a small bulge was barely visible.

"Take it."

The sickly sweetness of Femi's perfume alerted her to his presence just before his sour breath burned her ear. He must have slipped into the tent under cover of Adah's moans. She'd forgotten his uncanny ability to move with a cheetah's speed and stealth.

It would be so easy to let Adah assume she'd lost the ring in her desert trek. No suspicion would fall on her. Zahra touched the chain warmed by Adah's skin. The ring was hers by right. Abba had promised it to her.

And wrongly gave it to Adah.

She slipped her hand behind Adah's neck. Take it, and the waiting would be over. Take it, and Femi would wrest it from her. Take it, and she would lose it forever.

"Take it."

She winced as Femi pinched the tender spot between her neck and throat.

"Take it."

Flinching from his touch, she cautiously pulled the sturdy chain from beneath Adah's tunic. It snagged on a loose thread.

Take it, and she became a liar like the one who'd violated her trust, stolen her innocence. Take it, and she became a thief. Take it, and she'd break her word to Nathan.

"No."

He shoved her aside and lunged for the chain draped around Adah's neck. Adah opened her eyes.

A billow of cool desert air drifted through the tent announcing Nathan's arrival. "Zahra? Who is this? What's happening?"

Femi clutched the chain. One finger at a time, he let it slip through his hand. She heard his teeth grinding together, the rough exhale of failure.

"My cousin. Nehemiah hired him when the other driver was found dead."

Nathan's eyes were slits, his hands, fists. "How convenient your cousin was available."

"I have spoken so often of Adah, he came to assure himself she would recover from her ordeal." Zahra slid her gaze to Adah, whose eyes had rolled back into her head. A length of the chain lay exposed. Slowly, as if only now noticing it, she tucked it beneath Adah's neckline.

"See, Fe…dor, she is resting. Tomorrow, I will tell her of your concern. It is best you leave now so she can rest undisturbed."

Zahra did not need to look at Femi to gauge his reaction. Waves of fury emanated from him. Had he been a dog, froth would have foamed through his snarl. Ragged, uncut nails raked her arm as he backed away and sidestepped Nathan.

The tent flap closed behind him. Without thinking, she released a long sigh of relief.

"Zahra?" Nathan's low voice would not be heard if Femi lingered outside the tent.

She avoided his eyes and shook her head, more shaken by her brother's fury than she wanted to admit, more confused by her reluctance to snatch the ring than she could understand.

Adah stirred and opened her eyes. A frown grazed her features. She looked at Nathan and Zahra and then past them as if searching for someone else.

"Is he here? I must have dreamed it." She struggled to sit up.

Nathan crouched beside her. "Who? Dreamed what, Adah?"

"That he was here, standing over me, reaching for my throat."

"Femi?"

She nodded and winced, as if the motion pained her.

Perspiration beaded Zahra's brow. "Only my cousin was here, Adah. He was concerned about you."

Nathan's jaw tensed. He cocked an eyebrow, his gaze pinning her against her lie.

"They look alike, my brother and cousin." Appalled at what she'd let slip, she eked out an awkward laugh. "Not that you know my brother, of course, but there's a strong family resemblance between all of us. Quite remarkable."

She reached for the discarded cloth, busying herself with washing Adah's hands finger by finger then moving to her dirt-encrusted ankles and feet. "It is shocking, seeing them side by side. If my cousin was not so much older, they could be twins." She bit her lip. Donkor's death and Femi's vengeance were not what she wanted Adah to remember.

She felt rather than saw Nathan scrutinizing her.

"I need fresh water, excuse me." Exiting the tent, she tossed the filthy water to one side. They were close to the placid river, so it was only a quick walk to refill the basin. She knelt on the bank and let the water swirl into the bowl.

A bony hand shoved her face into the river. The bowl flew from her hands as she clawed the sand, the water, the air. Her head was pulled back and plunged again into the river. Released, she gasped and coughed, spitting out the salty water. Her breathing steadied. She waited for Femi's threat hissing in her ear. Hearing nothing, she looked behind her and saw the basin he'd left filled with water. He'd said nothing. There was no need.

Though neither Nathan nor Adah commented on her appearance, she saw them share a long look.

"Adah, Zahra, I am sleeping at the entrance to this tent."

Adah didn't argue. Nor did Zahra.

CHAPTER TWENTY-FOUR

Two Days Later
Beside the Euphrates

Stacked mud houses protruded from the rocks like bored specta-
tors of the tranquil river, the water's blue silk startling in con-
trast to the ragged mountains around it.

Adah shielded her eyes with her hand. "So much sun and water,
but the green is as scarce as the hair on an old man's chin."

"Here, yes. Where the river begins far to the north, there is more
green than you can imagine."

Adah pulled her sleeve up to scratch a mosquito bite just as
Nathan turned toward her. He startled.

"What happened to your arm?"

She glanced down and covered the scars.

"It was a long time ago. I was fourteen."

"And now you are what? An old woman of fifteen?"

"Seventeen."

He whistled. "I was way off. Somehow, I thought you were
betrothed to Jonah when you were twelve."

Adah laughed without mirth. "I was eleven for several years.
Father never told my true age to Inbar or Omari. That's how I earned

these marks. I contradicted him in front of Inbar. He was so afraid Inbar wouldn't believe him and then not hire me, he dug his nails into my arm until the marks bled. The swelling and red streaks disappeared, the marks did not. He said it was to remind me I was a fool."

She pulled back her sleeve. "It does not—never did. It reminds me he was afraid to be challenged. But I am not sure why I had to be eleven for so long. I did not look that young even then."

"Essentially, until you are twelve years and one day, you are a minor and completely under your abba's control."

Adah nibbled her lip. "So much I did not know."

"You do not seem upset."

"What good would it do, Nathan? Was it you or Nehemiah—you two sound alike sometimes—who said forgiveness is so important?"

"You have already forgiven your abba for that?"

She lifted her hands and shrugged. "I will pile it in with the other ways he used me."

"Then you are ahead of me. I would be livid."

"Maybe by the time I find the Garden of Eden, I will be able to forgive everyone everything. Honestly, Nathan, I do not want to think about it. I want to imagine clusters of grapes as tall as I am and melons bigger than a mule's head and wonder what else grows in the Garden and how long it will take me to discover all of Eden's secrets." She pulled out the map. "I am not sure, what is the next marker?"

Nathan yawned.

"This bores you?"

"No. That is from sleeping, or rather, not sleeping on the ground outside your tent." He arched his back in a long stretch.

"Nehemiah has guards there. You do not need to sleep at the entrance."

"Too many things bother me, Adah, such as Tavi knowing about the map all this time. Now I wonder who else knows and is after the map—maybe a guard?" He scratched his chest. "And then you dreaming Femi was there."

"It was a dream." Unconvinced, she rubbed her temples. "It had to be a dream."

"Was it?"

"Nathan—the new driver—have you seen his hands?" At his look she angled her chin. "Trust me. Tonight, before it is dark, find a way to see his hands. Are they an old man's hands, gnarled with loose, wrinkled skin and the veins bulging, or are they a young man's hands?"

She studied Nathan's hands as he held the reins, debating on describing what he should look for. Nathan's hands were strong and callused. The smooth skin sun-browned with tiny dark hairs feathering his fingers, his nails trimmed short. She moistened her lips. "Like yours."

Nathan nodded. "Good idea. I would like to watch how agile he is getting in and out of the wagon and hitching the mules too. Nehemiah should know our suspicions."

"I am meeting Nehemiah tonight for another lesson on God's law. Come with me and tell him then. If anyone is watching us, it is less suspicious than a private meeting in his tent."

Nehemiah held his hands closer to the fire. "The remainder of our journey will be easier now. More fresh water and shade, less desert, although soon we may see snow. We should be able to meet almost every night if you would like, Adah."

"I have missed it." Even when she didn't like what he taught and found it difficult to make it part of her life, she wanted to know more about the God who spoke to her, the God who didn't mind her interruptions no matter the time and no matter how many others were also talking to Him.

"Welcome, Nathan. Join us." Nehemiah beckoned him closer. "Adah, a while back you mentioned strength—the strength you saw in Emili and that you see in Nathan and in me."

She ducked her head. He hadn't needed to mention Nathan, although it was true. Nathan had been strong enough to change and to ask his imma and God for forgiveness when he'd hurt them.

"This is the secret. The joy of the Lord is my strength."

She waited for him to continue. He didn't. Even Nathan's brow furrowed with confoundment, but then he nodded and smiled.

"Exactly, Nehemiah. I had not thought of it that way." Nathan looked as pleased as if he'd uncovered a stash of gold coins.

It irritated her when they shared a knowing look and she had no idea what they were thinking. She frowned, searching to connect the words. *Joy. Lord. Strength.* Desperate to understand, trying another way, she whispered similar words. *Happy. God. Power.* No, maybe— *Delight. Lord. Might.*

"Tell me." She did not ask, she demanded.

"Above all else, you must accept this is a choice."

She nodded impatiently, wishing he'd speak plainly. A choice of what?

"It is a decision you make each day in each situation, whether it pleases you or causes discomfort, even pain. You choose to turn to the Lord, and you choose to find joy even if you are feeling disheartened."

"So I decide to be happy no matter what. I make up my mind and that is that." She slid her gaze from his, disappointment shifting to irritation. She'd been doing this for years—deciding to think for herself, trusting her observations, holding tightly to dreams of safety and peace. What was the difference?

"It sounds that way, doesn't it? But, no, happiness and joy are different. Allow me to explain it further."

They looked up at the sound of rapidly approaching steps. Dror halted in front of Nehemiah. He removed his helmet, releasing the sweat collected behind it, and shivered as the cold wind touched his skin. He wiped his brow with the back of his hand and leaned close to Nehemiah.

"A wagon and its team are missing. May we speak privately? Nathan, please join us."

They left without another word or a backward glance at her and entered Nehemiah's tent. As the flap closed, two guards positioned themselves in front of it, their stance and weapons a warning to anyone who'd try to venture too close.

Adah wandered to the blurry edge of darkness and then a step beyond the flickering circle of the fire. As her eyes adjusted, she saw to the left the outline of the guards' tents, their pointed tops a row of teeth in the dimness. Closer, and to her right, was a copse of trees. Two people sheltered in its shadows—one tall and thin, one in billowing skirts.

—————————

"Zahra."

Zahra turned at the whispered call. "Tavi?"

Tavi emerged from a stand of tamarisk trees silhouetted in the violet twilight. "Over here. I need to talk to you." She set a lamp on the ground between them.

Zahra moved closer but did not join Tavi in its circle of light. "I am listening."

Tavi spoke rapidly, her hands clasped forward in petition. "I need you to help me. Adah knows where the Garden of Eden is. She has a map."

Zahra shrugged, feigning disinterest. "Then talk to her, not me." She turned on her heel.

"Zahra, stop." The desperation in Tavi's voice slowed Zahra's retreat. "She will not talk to me, or rather, I am not allowed to speak to her unless she speaks first. After the other day when I said something and she became so upset that she walked out of camp, Nehemiah and my husband forbade…" Her voice trailed off.

Zahra turned back to the forlorn figure. How sad to be told who you could and couldn't speak to. Mizraite women had so much more freedom, and even though her imma was Jewish, Abba had treated her with the respect of an esteemed Mizraite wife.

"What do you want, Tavi?"

"The map."

Zahra snorted. "As if such a thing exists. Even if I believed it was real or was worth taking and wanted it, Nathan sleeps at the entrance to our tent. Adah and her precious bag are guarded every minute by him and Nehemiah's guards. No one can touch her or her things without her permission."

"During the night, while she sleeps, slip it out of her bag. I will share its secrets with you."

Incredulous, Zahra stared at her. "Did you hear what I said?" She shook her head. "I will not risk myself for you, Tavi. Nathan and Nehemiah are protective of her. Only the gods know how she has charmed them, because I certainly do not."

"Please, Zahra. It is for my sister."

Zahra brushed away Tavi's plea and left the thick grove of trees. When it was the right time, she would leave with the ring and map—not share them. Not with Femi and definitely not with Tavi.

For a moment, Adah's heart sank, watching Tavi and Zahra converse at the edge of the grove. She'd been right about both of them, and yet, a seed of hope—of mere possibility—no bigger than the tiniest speck of sand had raised its head, had teased her with the promise of friendship—Tavi's chatter, Zahra's concern. She let hope drift through her fingers into a desert of lost hopes.

Seeing them together confirmed what she knew in her gut—not to trust either. They had shown who they were at their core.

She brushed her hands together, dusting away trust in either Tavi or Zahra. "I see you. I know who you are. You will never again step within the small circle of those I trust."

Father's words crackled through the smoke like wet fuel. *"Watch them. They cannot hide who they are inside."* What did people believe she was? Bold, courageous, determined, capable? Is that what others saw, or did they see brazen, foolhardy, impetuous—and with everyone guarding her—needy?

She turned her back to them. Since it was too early to seek her bed, she returned to the campfire. It was safe with the guards close by and the fire's light bright enough to prevent an unexpected attack and to deter the spiders and vipers. Safe.

For all her years and for as many days as they'd traveled, she had sought safety. She was still seeking safety. Still seeking peace. Still seeking to understand God so she'd be worthy to enter the Garden. Good heavens, she was still seeking markers to the Garden. Is that who she was, who she would always be—a seeker?

Adah rubbed her neck to thwart the spreading tension. She had hoped Nehemiah would have answers about the strength she saw in him, the strength she sought, but—joy? How was joy strength? Relentless determination, yes, but joy?

She was a strong woman who'd survived without joy. Honestly, she'd survived without any of the things she now sought—joy, peace, safety.

Nehemiah regarded her thoughtfully. "It disappointed you when I said that the joy of the Lord is strength. It seemed an odd answer, ludicrous, if you are honest, that you have questioned since we last spoke."

She'd forgotten he could discern her reactions as well as she discerned those of other people.

"You have been patient during the most recent challenge of this journey. Thank you. Now, let me explain more fully." Nehemiah raised his chin and pursed his lips. At last, he nodded. "Adah, the best way to explain is through the words of my imma. 'I revel in joy when I remember who I worship—the God of abundant goodness. I rest in joy, knowing beyond any doubt that God is working—for me, in me, despite me.'"

She leaned forward, soaking in his words, determined to understand.

"It is all connected, dear girl. Praising Him, striving to obey His commands, forgiving others—all these draw me closer to Him, and the more I see His goodness and follow where He leads, the more I experience His tender mercies. Joy in Him becomes a refuge. It becomes my strength."

"To me it is a shield." Nathan pointed to the shields of the guardsmen. "I do not carry one like that in my work as a driver, but He is a shield around me."

Adah eyed the scar by his eye. "Not a good one."

Nathan shrugged. "I have been wounded physically, true. I am thinking of how He has kept me safe in a relationship with Him whether I rebelled or obeyed."

"Adah, do you know the word *dichotomy*? No? Think of it as a contradiction that seems impossible. The more I depend on the Lord, the stronger I am."

She searched Nehemiah's features. Lines circled his eyes, with dark moons hanging beneath them. His face had thinned since they left Jerusalem, and his clothes hung loosely on his frame. The tracks between his brows had deepened.

His eyes...

His eyes shone as if nothing could dim that light from inside. No despair or bitterness lurked there. Only a river of trust that would not run dry.

"Adah, you and Nathan may have heard part of the story, but did I ever tell you how God brought me to Jerusalem?"

Without waiting for their reply, he closed his eyes and began. "I was in the king's service—had been for twenty years—an honor I hold dear. We were at the palace in Susa—he moved between Babylon and Susa depending on the season. My brother, Hanani, had just returned from a journey to Jerusalem, and I asked about our people left behind and the state of our beautiful city."

Tears ran down his cheeks. He opened his eyes, ignoring the drops dampening his face. "Adah, the joy of the Lord does not mean there is never sorrow. It means despite my sorrow, in my sorrow, He is my strength."

She blinked and said nothing.

"Hanani told me of the suffering of the survivors and the deplorable condition of our holy city, its broken walls and burned gates." Grief darkened his eyes. "Nathan, you saw the destruction. I remember seeing you. You worked alongside the priests in rebuilding the Gate of the Friend."

Nathan touched his heart. "An honor I cherish."

Amazed, Adah stared at Nathan. He'd helped rebuild Jerusalem and never mentioned it?

"I sat down and wept." Deep furrows marred Nehemiah's brow. "There would be no safety, no peace for my people until the walls were rebuilt. Adah, I wept for days and fasted and prayed. I praised God—"

She quirked an eyebrow. This was too much. "You praised God for news that made you weep?"

He responded slowly, as if to a child. "I praised God for His power and might. I thanked Him for His faithfulness. I confessed my sins and the sins of my family and of our people. Only then did I ask for His favor. Remember, I was cupbearer to the king."

She nodded. He'd said that before. He'd said he risked his life every day.

Nehemiah's gaze pierced Adah. "I was so afraid."

"You?"

"Very much. But I trusted God to lead me. The king asked why I looked so sad—it was a singular occurrence—and I told him. Without hesitation, he granted permission for me to travel to Jerusalem with a guard and supplies to rebuild." He winked. "And an extravagant tent for the journey."

"Which you shared that first night with me and…"

"Zahra and Tavi." He spoke the words she would not, their names dry and dusty in her mouth.

"It has been a difficult journey for you, Adah, and I fear it is not over. I look at you and see the strength of a survivor like those in Jerusalem. Like our city, your walls have been besieged with the theft of trust, your doors burned by those with no honor. You yearn for safety and peace. That is why you seek Eden."

Adah listened, mesmerized. He knew. He saw her.

"There is one way."

She stiffened, guessing his next words—dreading what he believed was truth.

"Forgiveness frees you. Joy in the Lord strengthens you. Peace, Adah, is in right relationship with your Creator."

They sat in silence, the embers begging for longer life until Nathan added wood and they leaped with enthusiasm.

"Adah?" Nathan's touch was feather soft.

She shook her head. It was too much. Too foreign. Too hard. Nehemiah's "one way" was too dangerous.

It demanded she stand at the edge of all she knew and risk everything for all she did not know, for all she craved. What if she was unable to forgive? What if joy in the Lord wasn't enough? What if, when God looked closer, she was unworthy of any type of relationship?

"What if" was not only a child's game.

"Adah, lift your head. Look at me." Nehemiah spoke as one who expected immediate obedience.

She looked up.

"At the beginning of our journey, I told you that what you sought is hidden in plain sight, remember?"

She nodded, as confused now as she had been then.

"You must seek the joy of the Lord as your strength. It begins with forgiveness."

Again? She resisted rolling her eyes. He'd said this a thousand times and could say it another thousand until her hair turned gray. There must be another way. If she could find Eden, she could find peace without forgiving.

"Moses said it clearly. 'Now what I am commanding you today is not too difficult for you or beyond your reach. I set before you life and death. Choose life…love the Lord your God, listen to His voice, and hold fast to Him, for the Lord is your life.' Adah, that is the source of peace, the truth that few wish to pursue."

She looked past him, not wanting to see the conviction in his eyes, not wanting him to detect the resistance in hers. He said she had the strength of a survivor. Maybe that was enough, and this elusive search for joy and peace and safety was a child's dream.

CHAPTER TWENTY-FIVE

Near Babylon

Adah, sing. Something is bothering the mules. Maybe your singing will calm them."

Nathan struggled to keep the mules moving along the road. Finally, he jumped from the wagon to grab their harnesses and lead them forward.

Adah turned to look behind them. "It seems like the other drivers are having the same trouble. Maybe they smell rain."

"No clouds."

"It is raining somewhere. There is a rainbow."

Nathan looked where she pointed. "Get off the wagon. Now."

After pointing skyward and shouting to the other drivers, he began to unhitch the mules. Leading them a short distance away, he hobbled them and then raced to where she stood by the wagon.

"Nathan?"

"That is not a rainbow. It is a rainbow cloud, an earth-shake warning. The mules know it is coming. That is why they have been so hard to handle." He snatched her hand and ran. "Here." He pushed her down where the ground dipped. "Lie still."

The ground stirred—a bump, gentle as when baby Jace had rolled next to her in his sleep. Nothing else happened. She raised her head from the safety of their furrow as the earth rose to meet her, jarring her until her head hit the ground. She bit her tongue and tasted blood.

The earth shakes stilled. Nathan helped her to stand before leaving to attend to the mules.

Apparently assessing the damage, Nehemiah strode past, Joezer close behind. Without pausing he called out. "Adah, are you able to help the injured?

"Yes."

"Follow me, please."

She trailed behind Nehemiah and Joezer. A few wagons had been damaged. One driver had not dismounted in time to release his mules before the frightened beasts capsized the wagon. The man lay sprawled beside the road, surrounded by those who'd come to help.

Adah looked, and looked again. Zahra knelt at his head, talking to him as his injuries were being examined. Never would she have imagined Zahra wiping away blood from a head wound.

Causing a head wound, yes. Tending it, no.

Judging from the crooked angle of the man's leg, it would need to be set. Adah crouched beside Zahra. It would take several people to hold him still. She placed her hands beside Zahra's on the man's shoulders.

Zahra didn't know why she wasn't surprised. Adah working beside her seemed natural. Something she'd seen sisters do—aware of the other's need, responding without hesitation. Odd, because this woman, while not an enemy, was neither friend nor sister.

They worked together to calm the man and hold him still. Words were unnecessary, as if they'd done this before. She knew Adah's thoughts. It seemed Adah knew hers.

The man writhed when his leg was jarred. She leaned closer and whispered comfort in his ear as Adah began to hum a child's song. He calmed. They shared a knowing glance but not a smile.

What if... She stopped. "If"—a word of unfathomable possibilities. But it was a waste of time. Not since the time of their ancestors Ham and Shem had there been accord between their peoples. There could be no reconciliation.

Adah braced herself against Zahra's shoulder. Another man gripped the invalid's arms. It was over quickly, the man mercifully fainting.

She rose and walked away. If Omari had lived and reconciled with his daughter, she and Zahra would be family. They'd have worked together, eaten together, laughed together. They might have become close friends. The loss of what could never be saddened her. She paused and looked over her shoulder. Zahra stood, watching her leave. Was she wondering the same thing—if in another time they might have been friends or lived as sisters?

Adah shook her head. Now they'd never be friends. Zahra had dropped her mask, shown who she was—a woman not to be trusted. It shouldn't hurt.

When she returned to the wagon, Adah shifted the bag at her feet. She tucked her headdress tighter and rubbed her hands together for warmth before placing them over her cold nose. She stretched, bent to scratch her ankle, and looked over her shoulder.

"You are as restless as the mules. What is wrong with you today?"

She angled herself on the wagon seat to face Nathan. "This strength you and Nehemiah talk about."

"You jump right into a subject, don't you, Adah?"

"I do not understand it. Can you explain it to me?"

Nathan gripped the reins more firmly. "These mules need to settle or we will be fighting them rest of the day. Come on, boys."

She tapped his arm. "I asked you a question."

"I heard it. I think you understand it just fine. You do not like the answer."

"Why would you say that?" Her head still ached and, cross at his perception, she snapped the question.

"Adah, like Nehemiah said, you have had to be a strong woman to survive." He canted his head and smiled sheepishly at her. "I like that about you. But now all that strength is getting in your way."

Unsure how to respond—was that a compliment or a criticism?—she crossed her arms and stared straight ahead at the plodding mules.

"See the mules? Twitch stops every few steps. Crook's pulling to the left. Makes for a hard ride."

Adah sighed. He was going to share another of his lessons whether she wanted to hear it or not.

"You are like one of those mules."

She shot a sideways glance at him. Now she was a mule?

"These boys are strong. When they do what they know to do—follow my lead—they are a good team, provide a smooth ride, take us where we want to go. When they do not obey me, they tire each other and us. Adah, I think you're smarter than a mule—"

"Thank you."

"That is not what I meant…I…never mind. I think you do not want to let our strong God be in control of your strength. You are fighting Him like Twitch and Crook are fighting me. Whatever happened in your past, is…past. Are you going to let God heal you, or keep fighting Him?"

Fighting God? Despite being irritated with Nathan, she knew that was dangerous.

"I am just not sure—"

Nathan drew the wagon to a halt. "I am going to walk with Twitch and Crook before I say something I regret to you."

"Such as?"

He sucked in air through his teeth then clamped his lips together. In one agile move, he vaulted over the wagon's edge to the ground.

Stunned at his frustration with her, Adah gaped at his back, her heart sinking. All she'd done was ask a simple question for clarification. His reaction was uncalled for. Piqued, she scowled at his head bobbing beside Crook.

The steady rhythm of the moving wagon calmed her, slowly cooled her ire. He was correct, she admitted to herself. She did understand what he and Nehemiah kept saying. He was right that she didn't like it, although she'd been trying to forgive and trying to be joyful. It didn't work for everyone, she assured herself, and knew she was speaking a lie.

Above the clop of the mules, she heard Nathan talking. He was probably praying for her, and if he was that annoyed with her, maybe she should be praying too. She wrapped her mantle closer—a flimsy shield against uncertainty.

It had been a while since she reached out to God, but Emili had said He was always waiting for her to turn to Him. Had Emili spoken of that in the stolen letter? She cleared her throat and swallowed.

"God, I wonder if I'm talking to You because You are my last hope. Does that make it wrong, or did You cause it to be that way?" She plucked a loose string from her sleeve.

"I do not understand You, and I do not understand Your patience or my hesitation. You have been Abba to me. Still, I doubt. You have kept me safe. Yet I distrust. You have answered me, guided me, and I turn away."

She tilted her head back and closed her eyes against the sun's cold glare. "If I am being honest, I am afraid You will tire of me and withdraw Your presence and I will be more alone than ever. I am afraid that if I struggle to forgive, You will become impatient. I am afraid You will agree with those who have said I am a thorn and worthless. And God, I *hate* being afraid, but You scare me."

Hot tears crept from beneath her closed lids. "God, see me. See that I want the joy and the peace." She pressed the heels of her hand against her eyes. "Make me willing to trust You, to believe what You say."

The wagon stopped. Adah opened her eyes. Nathan stood watching her. She quirked a smile at him. "You are right. I understand and do not like it—no, that is not true. I am afraid to trust, and I hate being afraid. So how do I stop the fear and start the trust?"

Nathan leaned against the wagon. "That is the easiest and hardest part." He shaded his eyes against the sun's low rays. "I will tell you tonight."

Adah scooted closer to the fire. She wrapped her arms around her legs and rested her chin on her knees, snuggling into the warmth of the thick cloak Jonah's uncle had provided. Nehemiah and Nathan did not seem bothered by the cold or the flakes of snow. She stuck her tongue out to catch what looked like tiny stars falling from the sky.

Snow had been rare in her little not-quite-a-village. She'd loved the marvelous way it turned drab into sparkling and hid the ugliness of their squalor. It never stayed on the ground long enough to please her. Melting, it left the world muddy and dreary.

Nathan added more wood to the fire. "Warm enough? Ready to talk?"

The tiny flakes had caught in his lashes and beard, turning them white and him into an old man, but his eyes shone bright and soft. She could look into those eyes for a long time. Yes, she was warm enough.

"Adah, I shared your question with Nehemiah." He looked uncertainly at her. "The three of us have been talking through things together. I hope it was all right."

She nodded. "As long as I can learn once and for all how to have what the two of you have that I do not. I have heard 'forgive' a thousand, ten thousand times. I have heard 'joy' until I almost hate the word. I need to hear how to trust so that I can choose the other two."

The fire danced and sang in the crackling cold.

"I want to be like those flames—dancing and singing with nothing holding me back—living in trust, not in fear. Tell me how. Please. Nathan said it was easy." She dismissed Nathan's warning. If it was easy, it could not also be hard.

Nehemiah smiled, the lines around his eyes folding into deep crinkles. "You make my heart glad, Adah. This is what you must do to trust the Lord. It is a simple, one-word answer."

She leaned forward, eager to hear it the first time he said it.

"Remember."

"Remember...what?"

"Remember the times He has been faithful, has heard you, has rescued you, guided you, warned, comforted, answered, forgiven, restored. Remember He is your Creator. He loves you. He chose you. He knows your name, your past, and your future."

Nathan touched her arm. "My imma said when she is worried and cannot sleep, she 'remembers' until once again she is able to choose trust. Then she leaves her concerns with Him, reassured He cares for her."

Adah looked at the fire then back at Nathan. "Remembering will free me? That sounds so easy. What is the hard part?"

Nathan threw a stick in the fire. "Choosing to remember."

"Nathan is correct, Adah. When troubles come—and they will—most of us panic. We think we have to face our difficulties alone. We turn inward instead of to the Lord."

"Even you?"

Nehemiah dragged a hand over his face, freeing his beard of the snowflakes that had clung to it. "Even me. I had a godly imma who taught me and my brothers how to obey the Lord, how to love Him, how to rejoice in Him. As cupbearer to the king, I never, ever, forsook that training. Yet, when word came of Jerusalem's brokenness, and though I prayed to God and trusted Him to lead me, I was afraid when facing the king. For a moment, I let myself forget God's faithfulness, that He keeps His promises."

"If someone like you forgets to remember…" She scrunched her nose at the oddness of that thought. "How can I remember *not* to forget?"

Before Nehemiah could answer, she shook her head. "This sounds like when you said I must decide to turn to the Lord and decide to find joy. Now I am supposed to decide to remember."

Nathan shrugged. "I told you it was hard."

Nehemiah held up his hand. "Adah, we explained it to you backward. If you first choose to remember His faithfulness, the other choices will be easier, more natural. However, the choices are still yours to make."

A gust of wind swirled the snow upward and sideways until once again the flakes fell to the ground. Adah looked past Nehemiah. She could not go back to who she'd been any more than the snow could return to the heavy sky or the river wind backward along its banks to its beginning.

"I will…" A hazy fear snaked in blurring what seconds ago seemed simple and clear.

She avoided looking at either of the two men. "I will choose to think about it."

Nehemiah nodded. "A wise decision, dear girl. What you determine will impact all of your life. Think. Pray. When you decide to trust the Lord—and I believe you will—do so without reservation. Commit yourself wholeheartedly to Him."

She ventured a glance at Nehemiah. No condemnation tightened his eyes or mouth. Neither revealed impatience nor disappointment. Seeing no shadows of anger, she felt another barrier crumble within.

A hard-edged wind sliced through her mantle. Shivering, she stood. "I am too cold to think now, but I will, I promise."

"Tomorrow, we will meet in the warmth of my tent. I did not expect it to become so cold so quickly. Forgive my lack of planning. Nathan, it is too cold for you to sleep outside Adah's tent. See her inside, and I will station another guard for tonight."

Nathan stood. With a quick nod to Nehemiah, he and Adah trudged into the wind to her tent.

CHAPTER TWENTY-SIX

One Week Later
Outside of Babylon

Realization hit raw and cold. Adah sat up, embracing her awareness in the dim morning light. Unlike the longing to return to the Garden of Eden, she did not want to return to what had been the forces in her life. She wanted to move forward into the promise of joy and peace. *God, I understand.*

She dressed hurriedly, pulling on another layer of clothing. She'd find Nathan or Nehemiah and tell them she was ready to make a choice.

Cold air swept into the tent. Thinking the wind had blown the ties loose, she shivered but did not look up.

"Adah."

Tavi stood inside the entrance, clasping and unclasping her hands. "I am not supposed to be here. Nehemiah and Dror will be angry with me, but I need to talk to you." She gestured at Zahra's empty bed. "May I sit down?"

Talk now? When she wanted to announce her choice and begin a new life unhampered by fear? Had Tavi finally decided to confess her theft and return Emili's letter? Nothing else Tavi thought or said would interest her. Adah shrugged one shoulder.

Tavi smoothed Zahra's precisely folded bedding. Her eyes flitted from one side of the tent to the other. She wound a finger inside a bracelet and smiled up timidly, revealing overlapping teeth behind the cracked, chapped lips.

Adah groaned. Reaching into her bag for Omari's balm, she held it out. "This might help your lips."

Tavi's eyes lit up. "Thank you. I prayed you would understand."

Understand her lips were chapped? Tavi prayed about that?

"I knew you would forgive me for looking in your bag and that we could still be friends. I will not know anyone except you when we arrive in Susa, and you will be there for a year or until the king allows Nehemiah to return to Jerusalem."

Adah looked at her questioningly.

"We will be in Susa in another week. I thought we should settle things before we arrive."

"Settle what?"

"How we will spend the next year together. We need to live close to each other so we can visit every day. You explain to Nehemiah, and I will explain to Dror. When they realize we are in agreement, they will acquiesce to our wishes."

Our wishes? Adah blinked. Tavi looked so pleased with herself. Tavi understood nothing, but she was about to be set straight.

Adah gathered her ammunition stone by stone as if once again collecting pebbles by the stream for Jonah's slingshot. Tavi would not be standing when she finished. Never again would the woman dare speak to her, let alone beg to travel with her to the Garden of Eden.

Seemingly oblivious to the turmoil churning inside of Adah, Tavi fingered her stack of bracelets. "I knew you would understand if I explained why I searched your bag. I wanted to see the map so I could find the Tree of Life and send my sister the cure."

Too angry to speak, Adah pointed to the tent's flap, her hand trembling with fury. Understand? She understood that if Tavi wanted to do something, nothing stopped her. Stealing another woman's suitor, going through another's things, seeing a map. God only knew what else.

God.

Still shaking, she lowered her arm before Tavi looked up again. Moments ago, she'd decided to live a new way, and already she'd failed. Not in her words or actions but in her thoughts.

Adah released her lovely ammunition. The accusations, the sting of betrayal, the scorn she felt for the weak-minded woman. It lay scattered at her feet, begging her to retrieve it and sling it stone by stone until Tavi was utterly convinced her inner ugliness was more hideous than the discord of her features.

For a moment, Adah ached to release her own anger by destroying Tavi. Tavi looked up. Seeing Adah's face, Tavi showed the confusion and dismay that replaced the hope that earlier had lit her face. Before Adah's eyes, Tavi shriveled. Her shoulders curved inward, and her eyes drooped. She stood and shuffled to the door.

"I will not bother you again. I guess what my imma said is true. I am as unlikeable inside as I am ugly on the outside." The tent flap closed behind her.

Adah's stomach wrenched. A knife to her gut could not have hit harder, hurt more. *Dear God, what have I done?*

There was no answer.

Adah ran to the entrance. "Tavi? I am sorry. Come back. Where are you?"

Tavi was not in sight.

A guard pointed to her. "Your tent is next to be dismantled."

Adah nodded and ducked back inside. She'd find Tavi later today and listen to her with every skill God had given her. She'd ask Nathan more about forgiving. She'd pray and ask God to help her. Methodically, she folded her bedding. She wrapped her cloak close. Gathered her bag.

If she hurried, maybe she'd have time to speak to Tavi before the wagons began rolling. Outside, she hurried toward the front of the line, only to be intercepted by a guard.

"Five days to Susa. Starting early and stopping late. Time for this trip to end." He grinned past the fatigue etched on his face. "My wife is waiting for me in Susa. We are moving out. Head to your wagon."

She didn't argue. It had been made clear that the guards' orders were to be obeyed. She turned and trudged to where Nathan waited, talking to the mules as if they understood his every word. Twitch lifted his head and snorted. Crook bumped against him then nudged Nathan.

"A few long days and late nights, my friends. I am counting on you," Nathan told the mules as they waited for his command.

Adah climbed aboard. "The guard said five days until Susa?"

"If we push hard and have no troubles. At most, six days, but everyone is eager to be done."

Adah hunched over in the cold, burdened from the encounter with Tavi. She'd wounded someone already wronged—that hidden wound Nehemiah referred to so long ago. She'd gone backward instead of forward in her search for peace and joy.

Adah looked over her shoulder as the desert slowly swallowed the walls of Babylon. She wished they could have entered its towering gates, but Joezer had confided that the message from the king urged Nehemiah to "continue with all speed" to his palace in Susa.

Maybe as they were returning to Jerusalem, they'd go inside and she could get close enough to touch the blue Ishtar Gate and the shining jewel-like bricks. Nehemiah said there were sixty lions, each slightly different, on both sides of the processional way.

Bundled in her mantle, she practiced "remembering" until her eyelids drooped, lulled by the cozy warmth and the wagon's steady rocking. She woke to find her head on Nathan's shoulder, his arm around her and a smile on his face.

Abruptly, she pulled away and sat up. "Sorry."

"I am not."

They rode in silence. Adah watched the mules' breath puff in the cold air and tried to think of something to say instead of what needed to be said.

At last she sighed. "I failed again."

"Want to tell me?"

"With Tavi. She came to the tent. Asked me to forgive her. I could not." At his look, she sighed. "Very well. I chose not to forgive her. Worse, I judged her."

"Need another secret?"

"There are more? Yes. I need a lot of help."

"Forgiving can happen in stages."

"More decisions?" Did she sound as forlorn as she felt?

"Afraid so. First, choose mercy or revenge."

"I usually ignore—turn away. Is that mercy?"

Nathan thought for a bit. "No. It is quiet revenge."

"Yes, I suppose it is. What else am I doing wrong?"

Nathan twisted to face her. "Is that what you think Nehemiah and I are saying?" He rubbed the back of his neck. "Adah, you are an amazing person. You fight to understand. You are determined to understand this before you weave it into your life, not just give nods of agreement and change nothing. This sounds crazy, but Nehemiah and I are trying to honor you with undiluted truth."

Those were not tears in her eyes. It was the stinging cold that made them water.

"Then what is the next truth you want to honor me with?"

He chuckled. "You choose to resent or—here come your favorite words—choose to forgive. When you realize you are as fallible as everyone else, it is easier to wish them well in spite of how they have dishonored you. You can even pray for them."

"Do you pray for the people who hurt you?"

He ran a hand over his beard. "I was hoping you would not think to ask. Yes. It is still a challenge every time something reminds me of it."

"The scar…"

He shot a look at her. "How did you know?"

"Whenever you touch it, your face darkens and your lips move. I guessed you were praying."

"I struggle with it still." Nathan expelled a long breath that puffed out his cheeks. "I believe Imma told you how my abba struggled with being confined in Hebron. The high priest had ruled in his favor, but the priest was younger than most, and the law states Abba could leave safely only when the high priest who acquitted him died." He stopped her with a raised hand. "Do not ask why it works that way. I am not sure."

"Your abba left the safety of Hebron."

"He had escaped many other times and always returned. That last time should have been no different." Nathan's jaw worked. "He and another man—Daven—had quarreled. Imma doesn't know why they quarreled, only that Daven had been drinking heavily. Daven left the city—he was not there as a refugee. He found Abba's accuser and told him how Abba slipped in and out of the city in plain sight."

"Revenge."

"It was years before the truth was revealed. A friend somehow learned of it and came running to tell me. I guess he thought I would be glad to know it was not Abba's blunder that caused his death. When he told me, I could hardly breathe. I called him a liar. I broke his nose, and he blackened my eye. Daven was the abba of my best friend."

"Oh, Nathan."

"Daven had taken me fishing and hunting and stood with me when I read the scroll in the synagogue. But he did not care about me. He was trying to assuage his guilt."

"Did you tell him you knew?"

"I confronted him with my eye swollen shut. For a long time, he blocked my blows to his face, but I was a strong youth, and eventually he shoved me away, hard. I fell against a rock. Hence the scar." He sighed. "At least Imma never knew of Daven's betrayal, but that's what turned me away from God. That was when I began to avoid going to synagogue, when I became so angry with God—as if He had been the one to betray me—that I could not bear to stand and hear His truth."

"I don't know what to say."

"There is nothing to say, Adah. When we began to believe our way was better than God's way and acted on it and the Garden of Eden was closed to us, we became a world where people hurt people. I told you that story so you would realize that I know what I am talking about when I say you must choose to forgive and choose to find joy in the Lord. It is not easy, but it is right."

"The hidden wounds."

"Nehemiah has his own wounds. We all do. Daven, Femi, Tavi, Zahra, even your abba."

Adah turned away, uneasy at the thought.

CHAPTER TWENTY-SEVEN

One Week Later
Outside of Susa

Zahra moved noiselessly through the tent. Once outside, she shivered in the cold morning air and wrapped her arms around herself deep within her cloak. Head down, avoiding eye contact with anyone who might be roaming through the camp this early, she picked her way to Femi's wagon.

He'd be sleeping on his back, hand by his side, gripping a knife, if she knew her brother. He, who hated body hair more than any Mizraite she knew, had been forced to let it grow as part of his disguise. A coarse strand lay against his forehead. She hadn't known his hair curled.

Her stomach twisted. She hadn't known this brother at all. She and Donkor were like-minded, though Donkor had been quick-witted and quick-tempered and she was a methodical thinker. Femi... A sliver of regret pierced her. Femi had been a shadow of them—physically faster but slower to understand.

Zahra stood at his feet—the safest place. She'd seen his reflexes, seen his knife-holding hand arc and slash before he was awake enough to open his eyes. She whispered his name.

He grunted and opened one eye a mere slit. "Go away."

His grunt left no doubt of the displeasure of an older brother having his little sister disturb his sleep. He'd probably never forgiven her or Donkor for the tricks they'd played on him while he slept.

"Femi, we have to talk. Sit up." She nudged his foot. Unsure if he was safer awake or asleep, if he was sitting, she'd be better able to gauge his reactions. "Femi, are you listening? We are almost out of time. Tell me everything you remember about Adah. Where she lived, how she dressed, if she had friends, everything. When did you see her the first time?"

Propped on his elbows, Femi yawned. "Lived near Beit She'an. She looked like she wanted to escape after Abba bought her. Donkor and I came around the corner, and she realized she'd never make it past us."

Femi rambled on, but one word filled Zahra's mind until she could hear nothing else.

Bought. If Adah was a slave who belonged to Abba, then now she belonged to them.

"Femi. Think hard. Are you certain he bought her? I thought Abba married her or adopted her, since he gave her the ring."

"Hair is dirty and uncivilized." He scratched the back of his neck. "He bought her. Donkor and I were at the edge of their hovel. We saw Abba give a small bag of coins in exchange for her. Her abba said they were married. They were not. There was no priest like the Jews do. No jewelry like we do. No agreement or willingness like we have. She begged her abba not to make her come with us. She said she would disappear and never return if he would relent."

Zahra waited for Femi to realize what he'd said. He scratched his oily hair, rubbed a hand over the scrub on his face, rinsed his mouth with water, and spat it out. He frowned and canted his head.

"Zahra, Donkor is dead. You left us." His eyes bored into hers. "I inherit all. I inherit Adah. Abba bought her. She belongs to me. Her ring belongs to me."

Zahra scolded herself. *At times, Zahra, you are as slow as Femi.*

A sneer fixed itself on Femi's face. "Go to your tent and order my slave to attend me."

Behind her, Zahra heard the camp waking—men called morning greetings, beasts stomped their feet demanding food. Darkness had eased into grayness. Even Femi would not be rash enough to harm her when he might be seen and questioned about his actions.

She stood as if quick to comply with his command. A safe distance from his long-armed reach, she retorted, "Tell her yourself." His growl followed her. Poor Adah. She faced misery for the rest of her life. There was one thing she could do to make amends for Adah's fate at the hands of her family.

───

Zahra brushed aside the tent flap and stood at its entrance. Adah glanced up then looked again at guilt on Zahra's face.

Zahra took a breath and released it. "Tavi did not take your letter. I did. I thought it was the map and that I could persuade my brother to give me the ring if he had the treasure map. A few days ago, I saw you with the map, so this must be your letter. Here." She thrust the parchment at Adah and left.

Adah smoothed the crumpled letter. Tavi had not stolen it. Adah cringed, thinking of the hurled accusations and the anger she had harbored. Would Tavi allow her to apologize? Would she accept an apology? Could they become true friends?

Adah pressed the letter against her chest. She'd ask Nehemiah to read Emili's words—maybe twice, so she could memorize them and think of them when she was lonely. Then she would find Tavi and ask for forgiveness.

Tomorrow, when they entered the gates of Susa, Nehemiah would return to service with the king. Their group would disband. Tavi would meet her new family. Zahra would… Adah had no idea what the woman would do.

She hoped Nathan would help her search for the Garden. They'd seen all the markers except the flaming swords at the Garden itself. They had to be close.

This was the time to bid farewell to Nehemiah and thank him for allowing her to travel with the caravan. It might be a year before she saw him again—when they returned to Jerusalem.

Guards announced her. Joezer beckoned her to enter the tent. It still caught her by surprise, the thickness of the rugs, the luxury of the fabric walls.

Nehemiah's smile was strained. "The Lord has brought us this far. Give thanks unto Him. You remain determined to seek the Garden? I have not persuaded you otherwise?"

Her smile wavered. Abandon her search when the finding was so close? Did he not realize how important this was to her?

"I am determined."

"My prayers will never leave you, Adah. Now, how may I help you today?"

"I have a letter from Emili, Nathan's imma. Would you read it to me?" She placed her bag in the tent corner and pulled the crinkled parchment from inside.

Nehemiah accepted the letter and scrutinized the seal. He frowned. "Adah, are you certain—"

"Halt!"

Wood cracked against wood as if guards had crossed their spears, locking out an intruder. A grunt. The barrier tested? She heard a scuffle and then a shout.

"Nehemiah. Show yourself!"

Joezer blanched and scurried to a corner as the tent flap was torn open.

"Forgive the intrusion. This creature attacked one of my men." Dror planted himself in front of Femi and fisted his hand to hit the prisoner.

Nehemiah raised his hand, his voice blade-sharp. "Dror. Stop."

A snarling Femi railed at the guards who held him. "Release me. Move aside! He has what is mine."

Adah crept backward until, pressed against the tent's wall, she could go no farther. Femi's rage-hot eyes raked over her.

Nehemiah stepped forward. "Control yourself, and you will be released."

Femi writhed and bucked against the muscled guards, who stood without budging—his attempts to free himself requiring no more of their effort than swatting a gnat.

Nathan bolted through the entrance and scanned the room. "Nehemiah, Adah, are you hurt?"

Behind him, Tavi fluttered in. "Dror?"

"You should not be here, Wife."

"Dror, I was worried about you." At her husband's scowl, Tavi retreated to the tent's corner where Joezer was cowering.

On their heels, Zahra stormed in, speaking to Femi in Mizraite.

Femi swung his head to look at Zahra. For a moment, nothing happened, and then something in his sister's face calmed him. When Femi's breathing slowed and evened, Nehemiah gestured to the guards to release him. Femi brushed off their hands as in synchronized formation they took two measured steps back.

Nathan hurried across the room to stand beside Adah. He squeezed her shoulder. "God is with us, Adah."

Returning to the seat behind his desk, Nehemiah sat and folded his hands on the documents covering it. "You wish to speak with me? What is your name?"

"Femi."

"You bear a marked resemblance to a driver I hired who happened by when my driver was murdered."

Femi sneered. His eyes narrowed to slits. "She is mine. She belongs to me."

"She?" Nehemiah spread his hands as if unsure of Femi's referral.

Femi pointed his long, meaty finger at Adah.

"No." Instinctively, she shrank away. *Dear God, please, no. Not Femi.* Would she never stop paying for her father's greed? Never be safe?

God is with us. Clinging to Nathan's words, she caught herself. She did not need to be invisible to survive. She stepped forward, chin up, defiant. "I belong to no one."

Femi smirked. In spite of herself, she braced for his reaction.

"I witnessed you sold as a slave to Omari, my abba. I am his sole survivor. I inherit all his belongings." Femi's head swiveled toward his sister. He fixed her with his gloat. "Including the ring."

Zahra narrowed her eyes at him. "It is mine."

Adah darted a look at Nehemiah to gauge his reaction, but a document appeared to have distracted him. He peered at it as if mesmerized. Puzzled, she shook her head to clear her mind.

The Nehemiah she knew would not have forgotten her. Was he so intrigued with his royal duties that he ignored the precariousness of her freedom? He'd brought her safely to Susa and fulfilled his commitment. They'd become friends. He was her teacher. Surely he'd not so easily dismiss her.

Femi lunged across the room. Before Nathan or the guards could move, he seized Adah and shoved her to the ground, grabbing her hair and jerking her to one side so that his knife rested against her throat.

It was odd, what one saw, twisted bizarrely with a knife cold against warm skin. Tavi, huddled in the corner, unobtrusively arranged her voluminous skirts and shawls over Adah's unguarded bag. Zahra, edging closer to her brother. Dror and the other guards, watching Femi as a snake obsesses over a mouse. Nathan's gaze riveted to hers. His lips moved. She guessed he was praying. Nehemiah appeared unaware of the drama, caught up in what he was perusing.

She was alone. Alone. A word with two faces—the pure joy of no one expecting anything from her and the cold terror of being insufficient on her own.

This time, alone was frigid. Dark. A precipice of terror, the plummet inevitable, the depth fathomless.

No one could rescue her from Femi. Despite her bold words, bitter though it was, he had spoken truth. Omari bought her. Femi owned her.

She offered a shallow smile to Zahra, thinking of the friendship that might once have been possible. She blinked at Tavi, wishing she could apologize and thanking her for hiding the bag—better Tavi have it than Femi.

Lastly, she looked at Nathan and opened her heart, letting every thought show in her eyes, willing him to know she understood he was powerless and that she...loved him.

Dror and the other guards spread to a half circle. As one, they shifted their weight to the balls of their feet. The shush of steel as it slid from scabbards filled the room.

Kneeling before Femi, at his mercy, Adah felt his grip tighten and his breath quicken as his anger teetered into desperate fury. She was his, to kill or to command, and if the guards charged him, she did not doubt his choice.

God. You are my only hope. Realization swept through her as powerful as when the earth shook and rumbled.

He had always been her only hope. It wasn't the map that held hope, or the secrets of the Garden, or learning to read, or journeying to Susa. It was God. All this time, Nathan and Nehemiah possessed the true map, had tried to show her how to follow it, how to find the Garden, how to reenter Eden.

Nothing else matters except You. Not past cruelties nor the blade at her throat. Not Tavi's lies nor Zahra's pretenses. The awareness pierced her every shield. Nothing was important except seeking Him. Was it too late? She shuddered, and Femi's knife slipped against the sweat of her throat.

Forgive me, Lord God. She had been so stubbornly blind, so determined to find peace where and how she wanted it to be, to name safety in her own selfish way. *Forgive me for hesitating to trust You, for doubting Your goodness.*

A holy hush swelled before the sacredness, filling her with the fire she'd first been drawn to—His peace, warmth on a cold clear night. Recognition became understanding. She was seen and known, chosen and loved,

His peace, His presence, His love—oh, more than she ever imagined. She did not have to be worthy, only accept He knew her name, waited to help her, to lead her with His love.

God—her city of refuge. The beauty of it silenced her.

Femi's knife shifted, the edge twisting sideways.

In the face of death, her lips curved upward. *I am not yours, Femi. I am His.*

Nehemiah spoke into the deathly stillness. "Femi, if it is as you say, and Adah is your property, then under the law, I cannot contest your right to take her. Guards, stand down."

Nathan choked out a protest. Nehemiah quieted him with a glance. Femi's tension eased. He slid the blade from her throat, his other hand still gripping her hair.

"Femi, I have given you my word." Nehemiah's stern authority rang clear. "Release her. Adah, stand up. I have a question for you. Come here."

Adah stood. Head held high, she crossed on wobbly legs to where Nehemiah had risen to stand behind his desk. Let him hand her over to Femi, let Nathan disappear from her life, let Tavi take the map, and let Zahra have the ring.

She held inside what could never be taken away. No, she'd never see the Garden of Eden. She did not need to. Peace was not a place. Peace was being right with Him.

She looked into Nehemiah's eyes. They twinkled. Twinkled? She knew this man. He would follow the letter of the law, but he'd not find pleasure in consigning her to Femi's ownership.

"Adah, do you recognize this parchment?"

She nodded, confused. Of course she did. It was the one from Emili she'd asked him to read to her.

"Did someone hand this to you?"

"Zahra just returned the letter to me. It was in my bag when I arrived at Aaron's house. Nathan's imma gave it to me."

Nathan shook his head. "My imma does not read or write."

"Zahra, would you look at this?"

Zahra avoided Femi as she moved to stand beside Adah. "It is my abba's writing."

"Zahra, do you read?"

She shook her head. "No, but Femi does."

"Femi read this. Aloud, please."

Femi scowled. He brought it close to his face.

"'I purchased the girl, Adah, to comfort me in the sorrows of my old age. She has dealt well with me. Now behold, I have made her a freewoman in the land of Pharaoh.'"

Femi wadded the letter and flung it away. "This is a lie!" He swung toward Adah. Nathan blocked his movement, pushing the women behind him even as the guards charged forward to grip Femi's arms.

After reassuring himself that Adah and Zahra were unharmed, Nehemiah positioned himself in front of Femi. He clasped his hands behind his back and stood close, speaking in low tones that Adah strained to hear.

"Femi, I understand this has been a difficult time in your life, a time of grief. Your abba is dead, your twin killed. I imagine you are angry and bitter. When we arrive in Susa, do you plan to remain there, or return to your abba's holdings in Mizraim?"

Femi sneered, his face the color of anger.

"I offer you my assistance as a royal close to the king's ear. In exchange, I would need your honesty—even if it involves confessing choices you have made that you might regret."

"I regret nothing."

"As you wish. Think hard, because your future—your life— hangs in the balance."

Femi stretched his long neck forward. Almost nose to nose with Nehemiah, he spat.

Nehemiah stopped the guards with an upward flick of his hand. Deliberately, he wiped his face clean. "Femi, you are charged with assaulting a servant of the king, with sabotage of the king's goods, with the murder of a driver in the king's pay. I would have helped you as much as possible, but you have made another poor decision. I no longer offer you assistance."

Dror hustled out with the guards as they removed Femi from the tent.

Tavi stood and shook out her skirts, leaving the bag behind. Without a backward glance, she started to leave.

"Tavi, wait." Adah left the safety of Nathan's arms. She hurried across the room and knelt beside her bag. Rummaging inside, she unfolded the silk-wrapped map and removed Imma's gifts.

"Forgive me for accusing you of stealing and for my unkindness to you. Here, Tavi, take the map." She smiled at Tavi's startled look. "I want you to have it. Edon was once a true place." She shrugged. "Maybe it still exists, and, if so, I hope you find it as well as the cure you are searching for. But Tavi, you cannot enter Eden, the place of healing and peace and unspeakable beauty, until you forgive— yourself, your cousin, even your sister for her beauty."

Adah turned to face Zahra and removed the necklace from around her neck. "Zahra, it is yours by right. I should not have kept it from you." She stood on tiptoe and slipped it around Zahra's neck. "Your abba loved you. Missed you. Whatever he did to break rela- tionship, I hope you will forgive him. It will bring you what I think you are searching for too."

She turned to Nehemiah. "For just a moment, I wondered… Forgive me for doubting your friendship."

He opened his arms, welcoming her into his embrace, and kissed the top of her head.

Nathan waited to one side, watching her. Blushing, she moved to stand before him. "Your imma invited me to return to Hebron and live with her like her daughter. When you travel back, I want to return with you—if you think she meant it—and if she would let me bring Jace to live with her too."

"No. I do not think that would work."

"Oh." Rebuffed, she stiffened and stepped back, her smile fading.

"That would make you like my sister."

Nathan swiveled to face Nehemiah. "I meant to ask you earlier. Her abba is not here, and you are like family to her."

Nehemiah covered his smile with his hand. He cleared his throat. "Ask me about what, my friend?"

Nathan exhaled. "You know."

Adah frowned at Nathan's retort.

Nehemiah smiled blandly. "Do I?"

"I meant to ask your blessing and permission."

Nehemiah placed his hand on Nathan's shoulder. "You have both, but it is her choice."

Adah picked up her bag and started to leave. "Nathan, I am sorry. I will find a different caravan and return with them. I can remain in Jerusalem. I do not want to be a bother."

"You bother me a lot, Adah."

Behind her, Nehemiah began to laugh. "You are making it worse, Son."

Nathan held out his hand. "Adah, wait. Please. I do not want you to be *like* a daughter to Imma. I want you to *be* her daughter." He reached for her hands. "If you want to be. Will you return to Hebron as my wife?"

"Oh!"

Adah clasped both hands over her mouth. Her eyes filled with tears. Today held as much joy as the Garden of Eden. She was at peace with Tavi and Zahra. She knew the presence of her dear Adonai. And forevermore she'd be with her beloved Nathan.

FROM THE AUTHOR

Dear Reader,

Garden of Secrets: Adah's Story is the story of Adah's faith journey. It is also the story of my most recent faith journey. Unlike Adah, I grew up knowing the stories and believing God loved me. And yet, at times, I struggle with faith as much as she does—even in writing this story.

So many unexpected and difficult parts of "life" intruded into this writing time that I began to question how God would manage to provide what I needed to complete the story.

Friends, I was scared!

At my lowest point, a friend told me "Your writing is sanctified." This gave me the strength to remember His faithfulness, to remember the opportunity of writing is a gift from Him, and to remember His plan is perfect.

Whatever is done as unto the Lord is sanctified. I pray that in the faith journey of your work, you too will choose to *remember*.

Gratefully,
Texie Susan Gregory

THE WALL THAT FAITH BUILT: NEHEMIAH AND HIS VISION IN STONE

By Reverend Jane Willan, MS, MDiv

One of the places Adah visits in *Garden of Secrets* is Jerusalem, where she passed through the gates and the city's rebuilt walls.

In 586 BC, Jerusalem stood on the precipice of history. The cultural and spiritual identity of the Jewish people was about to change forever. Nebuchadnezzar II laid siege to the city, destroying the sacred temple and reducing its magnificent encircling wall to rubble. This catastrophic event marked the beginning of the Babylonian Exile, a period of deep sorrow and upheaval that set the Jewish community on a path marked by suffering and displacement.

The destruction of Jerusalem's sacred buildings and vitality spelled disaster for its inhabitants. Particularly devastating was the loss of the city wall, which had both offered practical protection and symbolized the divine safeguarding of God. The wall, built in the days of King Solomon, had been over twelve feet high and several feet thick, constructed of massive limestone slabs.

Other ancient cities, like Babylon, Athens, and Jericho, were also surrounded by immense walls. Babylon's wall was renowned for its immense size and strength. Athens used its city wall for defense and to safeguard its democratic way of life. Jericho, one of the oldest known walled cities, used its wall for protection and to control trade routes. These walls were not only physical barriers but also symbols of each city's identity, strength, and resilience in the face of challenges.

The destruction of Jerusalem's wall held immense significance for the Jewish people, extending well beyond the loss of physical security or regional identity. Its destruction symbolized a deep rupture in their sense of divine safeguarding. The wall embodied God's unwavering protection for His people. The Psalms often portray God as a fortress or shield, which is strongly echoed in the symbolic meaning of the city's wall.

With the siege of the city, thousands of Jews were taken captive and exiled to Babylon. Some people, however, stayed in Jerusalem despite brutal conditions. They endured the hardships of a conquered city and the loss of much that they cherished. Particularly distressing was their state of vulnerability, living in a city stripped of its protective wall.

Enter Nehemiah. In the heart of Susa, the bustling capital of the Persian Empire, Nehemiah dreamed of reviving his hometown—a fallen Jerusalem. He was the cupbearer to King Artaxerxes. The role of a cupbearer in ancient royal courts was both prestigious and essential. The cupbearer brought drinks to the king and tasted them first for any signs of poison. If the cupbearer suffered no ill effects, he gave the cup to the king.

The cupbearer, a trusted member of the royal court, had close access to the king, serving as both a confidant and adviser. Due to its prestige, only the most esteemed court members were chosen for the role. Nehemiah's role as a royal cupbearer, with its associated honor and access to high-ranking officials, ideally positioned him to assist the Jewish people.

Depressed by the news of Jerusalem's dilapidated state, Nehemiah decided to approach King Artaxerxes. First, he prayed for success and then asked the king for permission to go to Jerusalem and rebuild its wall. Nehemiah's request was a significant risk, as approaching the king and making personal requests could be dangerous. However, the king eagerly responded, granting Nehemiah permission to depart for Jerusalem, providing him with resources, such as timber, and issuing letters to ensure safe passage and provision for rebuilding.

Although royal support was crucial, Nehemiah knew he needed more than the king's backing. He needed the help of the people of Jerusalem. And they responded enthusiastically, with over a thousand workers pitching in. Interestingly, these individuals were not just laborers but came from all occupations and social statuses: priests, goldsmiths, perfumers, merchants, women, and children. Each individual or group contributed to a section of the wall. Their involvement reflected a collective spirit, where every person played a role in the monumental restoration.

The project faced significant challenges, including ridicule and threats from neighboring regions, whose leaders sought to discourage and intimidate Nehemiah and his team. Sanballat, a Samaritan governor, and Tobiah, an Ammonite official, opposed Nehemiah's efforts to rebuild Jerusalem's walls for political, economic, and religious reasons. Their opposition stemmed from a potential shift in regional power dynamics. A fortified Jerusalem would strengthen the Jewish community, diminishing their own influence. Further, a rebuilt Jerusalem could control key trade routes, impacting neighboring territories' economies. The longstanding religious and ethnic tensions between these groups further fueled their resistance. Powerful people wanted the Jewish people to stop building the wall around Jerusalem.

Nehemiah and his resolute workers refused to back down. They persevered, often with a tool in one hand and a weapon in the other, demonstrating a blend of diligence and readiness to defend their cause.

The new wall stretched for two and a half miles and stood more than twelve feet high. Designed to be imposing and protective, the wall was constructed from large limestone blocks eight feet thick. It was as immense and strong as the wall built by Solomon.

Amazingly, they completed the monumental task in only fifty-two days. The speed of the construction was nothing short of miraculous, a testament to the collective willpower and faith of the people. The newly erected wall not only provided physical security, but also symbolized a rejuvenated spirit and identity for the inhabitants of Jerusalem.

In the unfolding chapter of Jerusalem's past, Nehemiah's rebuilding of its wall marks a defining moment, highlighting a time of renewal and resilience. Under his unwavering leadership and driven by collective faith, the once-insurmountable barriers transformed into stepping stones of communal triumph. This achievement did more than just rebuild the wall. It reforged Jerusalem's identity and strength, brick by spiritual brick. And so, as the last stone was set, Jerusalem did not just have a new wall—it had a renewed soul.

The Bible says that faith can move mountains, but as Nehemiah showed us, it can also move stones.

TEXIE SUSAN GREGORY

Every night when Texie Susan was a little girl, her mother, with an expressive voice and face, brought life to a Bible story. The stories became so familiar that sometimes the people seemed like distant relatives—Grandfather Abraham, Uncle Paul, Cousin Esther.

After discovering Elizabeth Speare's book *The Bronze Bow,* she realized people other than those she "knew" had lived and loved and laughed during Bible times. Astonishing!

Thus began her quest to write the stories of both the unknown and the well-known people of biblical times.

Studying why people act and respond the way they do fascinates her. She has a master's degree in school counseling as well as in religious education.

North Carolina-born-and-bred Texie Susan is an empty nester along with her husband, loving life in Michigan, next door to their two amazing grandchildren and said grandchildren's wonderful parents.

Nonfiction Author

REVEREND JANE WILLAN, MS, MDiv

Reverend Jane Willan writes contemporary women's fiction, mystery novels, church newsletters, and a weekly sermon.

Jane loves to set her novels amid church life. She believes that ecclesiology, liturgy, and church lady drama make for twisty plots and quirky characters. When not working at the church or creating new adventures for her characters, Jane relaxes at her favorite local bookstore, enjoying coffee and a variety of carbohydrates with frosting. Otherwise, you might catch her binge-watching a streaming series or hiking through the Connecticut woods with her husband and rescue dog, Ollie.

Jane earned a Bachelor of Arts degree from Hiram College, majoring in Religion and History, a Master of Science degree from Boston University, and a Master of Divinity from Vanderbilt University.

*Read on for a sneak peek of another exciting story
in the Mysteries & Wonders of the Bible series!*

AMONG THE GIANTS:
Achsah's Story
BY JENELLE HOVDE

Outside of Hebron

The taunts of foolish boys followed twelve-year-old Achsah as she marched toward the well. Clouds of powdery dirt swirled beneath her new sandals and belted tunic, coating her toes with dust. In her urgency, her long braid danced behind her, slapping her back as she rushed up the hill. Beside her, Rebekah, her niece and closest friend the same age, struggled to keep pace.

"Wait!" Rebekah called out, her high voice breathy from the long walk. "I am not as fast as you. It is only Haim. He means no harm."

Achsah slowed for but a moment, but her skin crawled as she clutched her water jar to her chest. Haim always meant harm, but arguing would ultimately prove useless. Of course, she would never retreat to the safety of her courtyard. Not with *Abba* as one of the greatest generals in all of Israel. But despite her bravado, a tremor had rippled through her when she passed a gathering crowd of six young men at the edge of Hebron, including the lean but ever-growing Haim, who now towered over her.

"I am not afraid of Haim. I am merely tired of his squawking," she retorted as she kept her gaze trained on the stone well, despite the urge to see if the boys had followed her. The well waited, quiet at this early-morning hour. Which meant she had only Rebekah to count on, should trouble arise. Next time, she would take her older servant, Bel. Bel would know what to do.

Brash laughter rippled in the breeze, sending a smattering of prickles across Achsah's skin. The weather felt hot and dry, thanks to the changing season, while the sun shone bright within a cloudless sky. All around her, the densely overgrown hills, covered with thick pine, oak, and mighty terebinth trees, provided plenty of hiding places for the mischievous youths. The land, too rocky for sheep, had been burned to clear the brush and layered into undulating terraces of grain and barley, lentils and millet.

Surely the boys ought to be in those very fields, working side by side with their fathers instead of loitering around the well, spying on girls.

"Achsah!" one youth, as tall as her abba, cupped a hand by his mouth to shout. She darted a quick look at him before catching herself. She refused to stare at him and give him the satisfaction of knowing that he had, indeed, rattled her. Taking a deep breath to steady her nerves, she set her clay jar on the dusty ground. Oh yes, she recognized the owner of that deepening timbre.

"I think he wants your attention," Rebekah whispered loudly as she glanced over her shoulder.

Haim, at sixteen years of age, was proving to be a thorn in Achsah's side.

"Let him try," she said through her gritted teeth as she snatched the rope that dipped into the watery depths. "I am too busy today to bother with the lot of them."

After several yanks, the water bucket appeared, sloshing precious liquid over the sides. As carefully as she could, she set the bucket on the thick stone lip. She was reaching for her jar when Rebekah gasped as a long muscular arm reached out and slapped the water bucket back into the well.

The wooden bucket clunked against the walls, the sound hollow and taunting until, at last, a splash reverberated deep below. Achsah whirled to see Haim's grinning face flashing a mouthful of crooked teeth. Somehow, he had crept up behind her with nary a sound. Why hadn't Rebekah warned her?

"You really ought to offer me water." He crossed his arms across his chest. "After all, you are a girl, and I am a man. A very thirsty man."

Brown curls, greasy and far too long, clung to his perspiring forehead. And the breeze brought a hint of stale odor that made her nose wrinkle.

She leaned forward, furious that despite her recent growth spurt, she barely reached his chin. That pesky fact didn't stop the roil of rage from kindling inside of her. "No."

"Oh, leave her be, Haim," another boy called out. Lanky and thin, with a shock of auburn hair, he trailed after Haim just about everywhere. "She is the daughter of Caleb, and you do not want to make her abba mad. Trust me."

"Be quiet, Dov," Haim growled. The young men had predictably followed Haim's example, as they had done a year ago. She understood some of it, after growing up in a military home—the way they pressed in to follow the strongest leader, like a pack of wolves in need of an alpha. The boys stood, almost as if indecisive, unsure whether to stay and see what might happen next or hurry to the fields before someone spotted them.

She squared her shoulders and kept her face impassive. But all her resolve to appear as fierce as her father only brought laughter. Haim jabbed her shoulder, his finger sure to leave a bruise. "You need not put on such airs around me. I do not care what the other villagers say about your abba. He is old. An old useless dog who does what he is told. One day, no one will listen to him, or Joshua."

Her father's name, Caleb, truly meant faithful servant or dog. But she had never viewed the name as a slur. Instead, for years, men had whispered about his battle exploits with awe. Battler of giants, they said. The right hand of Joshua and Yahweh. The man with a sword in his hand and never a plow.

Hearing Haim's derision proved too painful to bear. Worse, his family remained an enemy of hers, ever since the twelve spies sent by Moses returned with nothing but tales of woe regarding the promised land.

Scorn dripped from her voice like vinegar. "And *your* grandfather's name ought to be coward. He spread lies about the enemies, leaving Joshua and my abba alone to bear Yahweh's command. Why don't you scurry back to the wilderness, since you think it is safer?"

To prove she didn't find Haim a threat, she yanked on the rope and hauled up the bucket with a mighty heave, despite her age.

Laughter, much louder, tainted with barbs aimed at Haim, filled the morning air.

Rebekah stood by, her eyes wide and her mouth rounded. But no help came from Achsah's niece and closest friend.

As soon as Achsah placed the bucket on the lip of the well, Haim leaned over and knocked it into the shadowy depths again, where a sound echoed. *Thunk. Thunk. Thunk.*

Like the beating of her heart about to leap out of her chest.

Silence ensued. She felt the weight of the young men's stares and the weight of expectation regarding what a young daughter of a famed military leader might do. If they expected her to cry big salty tears, they would be sorely mistaken. Instead, fire crept into her cheeks when she saw Haim's smug grin as he folded his arms across his chest.

Before anyone could stop her, she rushed him, planted the flat of her palms against his chest, and shoved with all her might. He stumbled backward, flailing, and might have landed in the well if he hadn't caught the stone edge just in time.

The chuckling turned to shrieks of laughter as Haim jumped to his feet, his cheeks a mottled color.

"How dare you!" He clenched his fists at his side, as if to strike her. "You think you are so special because of your abba and Joshua? We have had enough of your airs, with your nose pointed to the sky. When Joshua dies, we will finally be free of Caleb."

She braced herself, shifting on the balls of her feet while the youths pressed closer, ready to duck as her abba had once taught her. Rebekah released a timid shriek.

"Stop!" a harsh voice cried out. The crowd parted, revealing a young man who was glowering at everyone. With black hair and the beginning of a beard darkening a square jaw and lean cheeks, he swung his molten gaze at Haim.

With a shiver of relief, she recognized Othniel, a family friend who spent most of his days at her home. Now seventeen years of age, he had spent countless evenings with her brothers and abba rather than with his family. She had grown used to his silent company.

In fact, she had heard him utter hardly any words at all in the years she had known him. Today proved to be quite astonishing. Othniel shouldered through the young men until, at last, he faced Haim. Wearing a rough-spun tunic, although a bow replete with arrows remained slung over one shoulder, he appeared that he would be prepared for any threat as he worked the fields.

"Haven't you children work to do? The men have already begun harvesting," he demanded, jabbing his thumb toward the terraced hills. "Why are you pestering the young girls?" Othniel's chiding had the intended effect. The now sheepish boys turned away from the well, leaving only Haim. After a strained pause, Haim blew out a harsh breath and brushed past her, his face drawn in sullen lines, leaving her, Othniel, and Rebekah behind.

Othniel glanced at Achsah, his expression unreadable for one long moment. Without another word, he followed Haim down the hill, toward the wealth of barley crops waving in the distance.

Exhaling, she watched him descend as clouds of dirt swirled beneath his sandals. She had expected him to chide her, just as her brothers enjoyed doing, but Othniel had returned to silence.

"Achsah, why must you provoke Haim so?" Rebekah protested as she tucked a stray lock of brown hair behind her ear. Her gaze followed the young men fleeing toward the rippling fields.

Achsah pulled on the rope, her hands shaking so badly that she could hardly pour the water into the jar. Somehow, she managed, even though cool water sloshed onto her wrists and her olive-hued tunic.

"I am not provoking him. I do not even look at him most days. He brought me the fight, and I finished it for him."

Rebekah bit her bottom lip while she waited for her turn. "Thank goodness for Othniel's arrival. At least cooler heads prevailed. Did you see Dov with Haim? How tall he has grown this past summer."

Dov, the pasty-faced youth who loomed like a pole? He barely said much of value either, offering only the limpest of challenges to Haim's terrible behavior. Did Rebekah truly like someone as weak as Dov?

Achsah shot a glance at her niece, who carefully poured the water into her jar. Othniel's timing proved impeccable. He stayed close to her family, though she couldn't quite determine why—except for Othniel's great regard for her abba. A pity Haim didn't carry the same respect. Instead, he seemed eager to battle with her at every chance. But then, Haim's abba and grandfather had fought against her abba's desire to claim the Promised Land. Old family resentments ran deep, especially because Abba had been allotted some of the choicest property in the area surrounding Hebron.

"Haim cannot be trusted. He hates our family and makes it clearer with each passing day. All because my abba shamed those spies for their cowardly refusal to enter the Promised Land, and still continues to shame them," she said, although it was doubtful Rebekah would listen.

Rebekah hoisted the jar to her chest. "Perhaps. But my abba says Haim's family is not completely to blame. After all, we have had nothing but war these past years. War with the tribes of the giants and the Canaanites and the Jebusites and the Philistines and the Ammonites. Anyone whose name ends with *ite*. We have been at war with everyone!"

Achsah hoisted her water jar and pressed her lips tightly together. By now the sun shone brightly, chasing away the faint pink dawn. In the distance, women came in small groups to draw water before the heat of the day. Rebekah's opinions shouldn't surprise her. Her niece was just echoing what her abba—Achsah's older brother, Iru—complained about to everyone who would listen. So many Israelites protested further war these days.

"We have done our share," Iru often grumbled when visiting Abba's home. "Let the others fight if need be."

No wonder Rebekah hadn't come to Achsah's defense. Only the silent Othniel provided help. A sigh escaped Achsah as she glanced over her shoulder while descending the powdery slope. To her surprise, Othniel stood in the distance, his gaze in her direction.

She shifted the water jar to her left arm and raised her right hand to wave at him, but she was too far away to catch his expression. Regardless, after a pause, he raised his hand. Almost reluctantly, to her way of thinking.

"Othniel remains a favorite of Grandfather, and he is not even family." Rebekah tugged on Achsah's sleeve. "My abba says Othniel wishes he could be adopted into the family. I hope Grandfather will do no such thing. We cannot afford to divide our land any further."

As her friend led her away, Achsah frowned. Did Othniel linger at the family table because he had designs on Abba's vast holdings?

It wouldn't be the first time someone fawned all over the mighty general, hoping to secure some sort of favor.

"I also heard that Othniel is poor, with an abba who died in the wars. So, whatever you do, Achsah, do not look at him and give him any foolish ideas."

"I am not giving anyone ideas," Achsah retorted, clutching her water jar close to her chest. Still, at the bend in the road, she turned her head ever so slightly to let her gaze wander to the fields where the men headed, disappointed when she saw that Othniel was gone.

If you enjoyed Mysteries & Wonders of the Bible, check out our other Guideposts biblical fiction series! Visit https://www.shopguideposts.org/fiction-books/ biblical-fiction.html for more information.

EXTRAORDINARY WOMEN OF THE BIBLE

There are many women in Scripture who do extraordinary things. Women whose lives and actions were pivotal in shaping their world as well as the world we know today. In each volume of Guideposts' Extraordinary Women of the Bible series, you'll meet these well-known women and learn their deepest thoughts, fears, joys, and secrets. Read their stories and discover the unexplored truths in their journeys of faith as they follow the paths God laid out for them.

Highly Favored: Mary's Story
Sins as Scarlet: Rahab's Story
A Harvest of Grace: Ruth and Naomi's Story
At His Feet: Mary Magdalene's Story
Tender Mercies: Elizabeth's Story
Woman of Redemption: Bathsheba's Story
Jewel of Persia: Esther's Story
A Heart Restored: Michal's Story

Beauty's Surrender: Sarah's Story

The Woman Warrior: Deborah's Story

The God Who Sees: Hagar's Story

The First Daughter: Eve's Story

The Ones Jesus Loved: Mary and Martha's Story

The Beginning of Wisdom: Bilqis's Story

The Shadow's Song: Mahlah and No'ah's Story

Days of Awe: Euodia and Syntyche's Story

Beloved Bride: Rachel's Story

A Promise Fulfilled: Hannah's Story

ORDINARY WOMEN OF THE BIBLE

From generation to generation and every walk of life, God seeks out women to do His will. Scripture offers us but fleeting, tantalizing glimpses into the lives of a number of everyday women in Bible times—many of whom are not even named in its pages. In each volume of Guideposts' Ordinary Women of the Bible series, you'll meet one of these unsung, ordinary women face to face, and see how God used her to change the course of history.

A Mother's Sacrifice: Jochebed's Story
The Healer's Touch: Tikva's Story
The Ark Builder's Wife: Zarah's Story
An Unlikely Witness: Joanna's Story
The Last Drop of Oil: Adaliah's Story
A Perilous Journey: Phoebe's Story
Pursued by a King: Abigail's Story
An Eternal Love: Tabitha's Story
Rich Beyond Measure: Zlata's Story
The Life Giver: Shiphrah's Story
No Stone Cast: Eliyanah's Story
Her Source of Strength: Raya's Story
Missionary of Hope: Priscilla's Story

Befitting Royalty: Lydia's Story
The Prophet's Songbird: Atarah's Story
Daughter of Light: Charilene's Story
The Reluctant Rival: Leah's Story
The Elder Sister: Miriam's Story
Where He Leads Me: Zipporah's Story
The Dream Weaver's Bride: Asenath's Story
Alone at the Well: Photine's Story
Raised for a Purpose: Talia's Story
Mother of Kings: Zemirah's Story
The Dearly Beloved: Apphia's Story

SECRETS FROM GRANDMA'S ATTIC

Life is recorded not only in decades or years, but in events and memories that form the fabric of our being. Follow Tracy Doyle, Amy Allen, and Robin Davisson, the granddaughters of the recently deceased centenarian, Pearl Allen, as they explore the treasures found in the attic of Grandma Pearl's Victorian home, nestled near the banks of the Mississippi in Canton, Missouri. Not only do Pearl's descendants uncover a long-buried mystery at every attic exploration, they also discover their grandmother's legacy of deep, abiding faith, which has shaped and guided their family through the years. These uncovered Secrets from Grandma's Attic reveal stories of faith, redemption, and second chances that capture your heart long after you turn the last page.

History Lost and Found
The Art of Deception
Testament to a Patriot
Buttoned Up

Pearl of Great Price
Hidden Riches
Movers and Shakers
The Eye of the Cat
Refined by Fire
The Prince and the Popper
Something Shady
Duel Threat
A Royal Tea
The Heart of a Hero
Fractured Beauty
A Shadowy Past
In Its Time
Nothing Gold Can Stay
The Cameo Clue
Veiled Intentions
Turn Back the Dial
A Marathon of Kindness
A Thief in the Night
Coming Home

SAVANNAH SECRETS

Welcome to Savannah, Georgia, a picture perfect Southern city known for its manicured parks, moss-covered oaks, and antebellum architecture. Walk down one of the cobblestone streets, and you'll come upon Magnolia Investigations. It is here where two friends have joined forces to unravel some of Savannah's deepest secrets. Tag along as clues are exposed, red herrings discarded, and thrilling surprises revealed. Find inspiration in the special bond between Meredith Bellefontaine and Julia Foley. Cheer the friends on as they listen to their hearts and rely on their faith to solve each new case that comes their way.

The Hidden Gate
A Fallen Petal
Double Trouble
Whispering Bells
Where Time Stood Still
The Weight of Years
Willful Transgressions
Season's Meetings
Southern Fried Secrets
The Greatest of These

Patterns of Deception
The Waving Girl
Beneath a Dragon Moon
Garden Variety Crimes
Meant for Good
A Bone to Pick
Honeybees & Legacies
True Grits
Sapphire Secret
Jingle Bell Heist
Buried Secrets
A Puzzle of Pearls
Facing the Facts
Resurrecting Trouble
Forever and a Day

A NOTE FROM THE EDITORS

We hope you enjoyed another exciting volume in the Mysteries & Wonders of the Bible series, published by Guideposts. For over seventy-five years, Guideposts, a nonprofit organization, has been driven by a vision of a world filled with hope. We aspire to be the voice of a trusted friend, a friend who makes you feel more hopeful and connected.

By making a purchase from Guideposts, you join our community in touching millions of lives, inspiring them to believe that all things are possible through faith, hope, and prayer. Your continued support allows us to provide uplifting resources to those in need. Whether through our communities, websites, apps, or publications, we inspire our audiences, bring them together, and comfort, uplift, entertain, and guide them. Visit us at guideposts.org to learn more.

We would love to hear from you. Write us at Guideposts, P.O. Box 5815, Harlan, Iowa 51593 or call us at (800) 932-2145. Did you love *Garden of Secrets: Adah's Story*? Leave a review for this product on guideposts.org/shop. Your feedback helps others in our community find relevant products.

Find inspiration, find faith, find Guideposts.

Shop our best sellers and favorites at
guideposts.org/shop
Or scan the QR code to go directly to our Shop

Find more inspiring stories in these best-loved Guideposts fiction series!

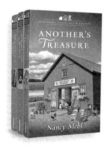

Mysteries of Lancaster County

Follow the Classen sisters as they unravel clues and uncover hidden secrets in Mysteries of Lancaster County. As you get to know these women and their friends, you'll see how God brings each of them together for a fresh start in life.

Secrets of Wayfarers Inn

Retired schoolteachers find themselves owners of an old warehouse-turned-inn that is filled with hidden passages, buried secrets, and stunning surprises that will set them on a course to puzzling mysteries from the Underground Railroad.

Tearoom Mysteries Series

Mix one stately Victorian home, a charming lakeside town in Maine, and two adventurous cousins with a passion for tea and hospitality. Add a large scoop of intriguing mystery, and sprinkle generously with faith, family, and friends, and you have the recipe for *Tearoom Mysteries*.

Ordinary Women of the Bible

Richly imagined stories—based on facts from the Bible—have all the plot twists and suspense of a great mystery, while bringing you fascinating insights on what it was like to be a woman living in the ancient world.

To learn more about these books, visit Guideposts.org/Shop

Printed in the United States
by Baker & Taylor Publisher Services